Intaglio: Dragons All The Way Down

Also by Danika Stone:

Intaglio: The Snake and the Coins

Tathagata

Ctrl Z

Intaglio: Dragons All The Way Down

by Danika Stone

Copyright, Legal Notice and Disclaimer:

Stone, D. (2012). *Intaglio: Dragons all the way down.* North Charleston, NC: Create Space Books.

©www.danikastone.com
Published by Dancing Dog Productions
978-1480239975

Cover Illustration Design by K. Goble

Original Image: Hendrik Kobell 1775, The Shipwreck. Painting.

This book is dedicated to my two favourite DLs in the world.

: : : : : : : : : :

To D: for inspiring and assisting in the creation of this novel.

To Deena: for being a 'super golden' friend, and the best sort of editor.

: : : : : : : : : :

You are BOTH the reason this happened.

Love Sonnet 92, Pablo Neruda

92
My love, should I die and you don't,
let us give grief no more ground:
my love, should you die and I don't,
there is no piece of land like this on which we've lived.

Dust in the wheat, sand in the desert sands,
time, errant water, the wandering wind
carried us away like a navigator seed.
In such times, we may well not have met.

The meadow in which we did meet,
oh tiny infinity, we give back.
But this love, Love, has had no end,

and so, as it had no birth,
it has no death. It is like a long river
that changes only its shores and its banks.

(Translation by Terence Clarke)

Chapter 1: Unexpected Advice

In the aftermath of the explosive New Year's fight that had nearly destroyed their relationship, things between Ava and Cole had settled into a new balance. The altered equilibrium had its own challenges, but their time together held a promise of more… things once static, now pushed into motion. Sometimes, Ava believed it was because of her father's acceptance of their relationship. Oliver asked about Cole and Chim in the same breath now. Other times, she believed it was because they'd survived a fuck-up where both of them had been involved. The recovery from the turmoil that seemed almost too good to believe. On rare occasions, Ava mused if it was because they were planning their first trip back to Cole's parents after the first visit's trial by fire. No matter the reason, things had shifted, the two of them drifting into new territory; one where the foundation was built on stone rather than sand.

They were settled together now. No questions asked.

Today was the day before the Spring semester began and the four of them – Cole, Chim, Suzanne and Ava – were downtown in the street-side shops frequented by the university crowd. Ava needed some new clothes before classes began. She'd destroyed her last good pair of jeans in the New Year's Eve painting session and needed a business outfit as well. The Director of the National Gallery had invited her to attend a visioning meeting later that Spring. The graffiti show scheduled for the following summer was quickly moving into the realm of reality.

Ava had nothing appropriate to wear.

Suzanne offered to go with Ava while Cole and Chim wandered off together to check out the hardware store. As every art student knew, there was always opportunity to pick up cheap art supplies there. Ava was glad Chim had suggested it. There had been a stiffness between Marcus and Cole since the events of New Year's. Ava knew Chim tended to be overly protective of her... and while she loved that aspect of his character most times, it bothered her to see her oldest friend holding out on Cole. The two men left the store arguing over the inherent value of art versus art as an agent of change, laughter audible long after the door banged shut.

Two hours later, Ava and Suzanne were in one of the larger consignment shops, looking for Ava's meeting-wear. The Director had assured her everything was set, but she still needed to attend the meeting and present her portfolio. The entire Board and the show's curator would be there; high heels and a dress seemed like a small fee to pay for being taken seriously. While Ava and Suzanne pulled dresses off the rack, someone called out to her from the men's section.

"Oh, for god's sake," Suzanne groaned. "It's Kip Fucking Chambers."

Ava turned in surprise. Suzanne had a very Chim expression on her face right now; her nostrils were flared, lips pursed. She looked like a pit bull about to attack.

"Be nice, Suzanne," Ava hissed. "He's alright. Just being friendly."

Suzanne's hand snaked out, wrapping painfully around her wrist. Ava's eyes widened.

"Don't be stupid," she warned, "anyone who looks at you the way that guy looks at you is NOT trying to be your friend."

Ava tugged her hand away, turning back as Kip neared. She was suddenly aware of all the unconscious details suggesting Suzanne was right. Kip was smiling, for one, but his eyes were on Ava alone. There was something about the way he ignored everything else around him, moving around people and objects as if caught in an undertow that had Ava's nervousness re-emerging.

"No..." Ava said slowly, shifting guiltily. "He's just like that. Kip's used to getting his own way. He's famous."

She wondered if her words sounded as lame to Suzanne as they did to her. The answer came half a second later as her friend spun on her.

"Are you trying to fuck things up with Cole on purpose?!" she snapped.

Ava stepped back in shock.

"N-no," she answered shakily, lifting her chin. "I'm not." Then again, more forcefully. "Honestly, Sue, I'm NOT!"

Suzanne sneered.

"Glad to hear it... because Cole deserves better than that."

She had no time to respond as Kip arrived. Suzanne muttered something that sounded like *'asshole'* before pasting on a fake smile and sticking out her hand.

"Why, Mr. Chambers," she drawled. "To what do we owe the honour of your company?"

Ava elbowed her but Kip just laughed. He reached out, shaking Suzanne's hand quickly before positioning himself nearer to Ava than needed.

"Nothing special. Just saw you guys, and uh... thought I'd come over and say hi."

Suzanne made a rude noise in the back of her throat, and Ava took a step away from Kip. Without seeming to notice, he mirrored her movement. Apprehension rose under Ava's skin.

This *wasn't* helping the situation.

"So what're you guys up to today?" Kip asked, shoving his hands in his pockets and grinning.

"Shopping, as you can see." Suzanne said dryly. She looked like she was about to throw a punch or a Molotov cocktail under a bus.

"Yes, shopping," Ava added, falsely bright. "I have a meeting and needed to pick up some clothes. So how about you?" she asked, her words tumbling faster and faster. "You here shopping with Raya? This store seems very... her."

Ava glanced over to Suzanne. *That's right, Suzanne, Kip has a girlfriend – ha! Score one point...'*

"No... no..." he muttered, dropping his eyes in embarrassment, "Raya headed back to her place on the Coast a few days early. I have a show coming up in Japan this summer, and I'll be moving on after that, although I'll be coming back in the summer, of course, for the film."

"And you didn't go with Raya?" Suzanne taunted. "That's interesting." Ava glared at her.

Kip laughed, boyishly ducking his chin.

"Raya and me, we kind of do our own thing. She wanted to visit her folks. I thought I'd party a bit here." His voice dropped slightly. "Hang out with friends."

His eyes were on Ava again: scrutinizing her. The whole conversation was making her increasingly edgy.

"Cool... that uh... that sounds fun," Ava answered, aware of how trite it sounded. "Well, when you see Raya, thank her for the cheque. It was really generous to hold up her side of the agreement."

"Sorry, thank her for what?" Kip asked.

"The cheque," Ava answered. When he didn't respond, she added, "you know, given that I hadn't actually done any of the work for the film."

Kip's expression shifted like dark clouds coming in from the horizon.

"You're not gonna be part of the film at all now?" he asked curtly.

Suzanne stepped between the two of them, interrupting the conversation with her physical presence. She was a full head shorter than Kip Chambers, but she more than made up for it with attitude. He retreated back a step.

"No," Suzanne snarled. "Ava's not on the film anymore. Your girlfriend, Raya, paid her off. Ava's done."

Chambers looked perplexed by the news. He looked over at Ava for confirmation. She shrugged.

"It's fine. She was really generous in paying me out," she explained. "To be honest, I don't mind. I'll be busy this summer anyhow."

Kip stared out the front windows for a long moment, as if considering her words. The darkness of his expression seemed poised to turn into something else, but when he turned back, he seemed to be in control. He smiled tightly at Suzanne before shifting his attention entirely to Ava. His voice was low, apprehensive.

"Look... I'm sure you've already thought of all this, Ava, but uh... make sure you send an official invoice to Raya, with the exact amount on that cheque. It'll take a couple days for the bank to process it and unless she has your invoice in hand, she might um... put a hold on the money and—"

"Screw you over," Suzanne ground out. "Well, you two are quite the pair, aren't you?" She was seething, her hands in fists.

"Suzanne!" Ava yelped, face aghast. Kip's hand went to Ava's arm, and she shrugged it off irritably. "Please," she pleaded, "don't start!"

"God, Ava, I don't even understand you sometimes," Suzanne said through clenched teeth. She turned on the man next to her. "So tell me, Kip Chambers... is your girlfriend always this much of a bitch?"

The blood drained from Ava's face. Horrified, her mouth opened, but nothing came out.

"Raya's got her moments," Kip growled, "but I really don't like your tone. She is an excellent agent and she has done an amazing job in promoting my career in the last—"

"Well that's all fine and dandy," Suzanne hissed. "But she's got a huge fucking problem with Ava here, and that makes Raya my problem."

Kip's mouth twisted in disgust, but he didn't respond. No one spoke. Ava had a sudden, desperate wish that she could just spontaneously combust, right here in Aisle C. It struck her that unless Cole barged in from the street, drunk and looking for a fight, there was no fucking way this scene could get any worse.

"Look," Kip finally said. "I don't think Ry' means to be like that. She's protective of me... and when she sees someone with talent, she gets defensive. I think with Ava here, she's just a little bit... "

He paused. Both Suzanne and Ava stared at him, waiting for him to acknowledge what they all knew. The thing which made Cole hate this man as much as he did.

"Jealous?" It was Ava who answered for all of them. Kip caught her eyes as she said it.

"Yeah." His voice was sincere.

Suzanne swore under her breath, jaw clenched.

"Ava," Kip said, reaching out again, "I really hope this doesn't affect our—"

She tore her arm away.

"Just stop!" she snapped angrily, "I don't want you touching me! Alright?!"

In two steps she was back next to Suzanne, whose arms were crossed on her chest, smirking. Ava held back the urge to slap her, too, just for being right!

"Sorry," Kip muttered, shoving his hands into his pockets again. The protectiveness that Ava felt for him began to rise.

"It's fine," Ava grumbled. "It's me, okay? Not you," she mumbled, guilt warring with annoyance. "So yeah... thanks for the headed-up on Raya's invoice."

"No problem," Kip said quietly. He wanted to say something else, she could tell, but Suzanne's presence at her side held him back.

"Look, Qaletaqa, I don't mean this to sound harsh," Ava continued, feeling Suzanne's gaze flicker over to her at the sound of Kip's full name. "But I think it's probably better if we just don't... don't talk any more. All right? It's just too weird for me."

Kip stepped back forward. His face was anguished, hands raised imploringly.

"But my dream, Ava... It had to mean somethi—"

"No it *doesn't*," she interrupted. "Not to me, anyhow."

"But when I'm around you," he insisted, "I just can't help but wonder if things had been different... if we could've figured it out. Me 'n you, you know?"

Suzanne snorted, and Ava glared at her in frustration. She could tell that her friend was just barely holding back from laying into Chambers here and now. She had the same look on her face that she'd had right before she and Chim had marched on City Hall last summer.

Suzanne was absolutely livid.

"Kip, I just..." Ava frowned. "I can't do this with you, okay?"

"Alright," he said quietly. "But if you ever need anything... or if you want to talk... ever... I, uh... I'll be away in Japan, for a while, then on the Coast. But you can always call me... okay, Ava? Anytime."

She nodded, extending her hand.

"It was good meeting you, Kip," she said. "I wish you all the best."

He nodded, taking her palm in his own. There was a sense of familiarity to the gesture; settling them as friends and nothing else. No snap of connection, just warmth.

It felt good.

"You too, Booker."

Chapter 2: Tuesday Morning

Ava was dreaming again, but this time she *knew* where she was.

She floated above the green field, her mind adrift on the wind. Her attention flowed and eddied in this place, moving from the sun-bright leaves down to the shadowy trees that followed the curve of the river. From there she moved to the bobbing seagrass that covered the sandy slopes, finally trickling out to the misty ocean beyond.

Ava smiled. Asleep, her lips in dreaming shadows did too.

'I'm free…'

Below her, resting, two figures remained. One was Cole. *'My Thomas…'* She could see the breadth of his shoulders, the curve of his jaw. The other was her, blue-lipped and broken. It didn't scare her to see herself lying still and silent in the bed of grass. She knew she was already dead (that she'd hovered near death since the winged carving had come down atop her during the storm). Ava waited there, watching them together, her soul content. Cole leaned forward, clutching her hand.

"I love you, Ava," he sobbed. "I have always loved you... I always will."

She knew she was mere moments before pulling up and away with a rush of release, her body over the landscape, just long enough to recognize all that it was. A new start for Cole: a beginning.

She followed his gestures, memorizing his face. Needing it to find her way back, the way she'd done before. Though back to where, she wasn't exactly sure. She only knew that he was the key. Where he was, she needed to be, too.

"No... please, no..." Cole gasped. "Don't leave me."

The wind rose, flicking a stray tendril of Cole's still-wet hair around his eyes. It intrigued Ava, the differences between the Cole she knew and this one. His hair was longer, the wind pushing it into his eyes, making him grimace and blink. She found herself soothed by that all-too-human gesture, the way his face wavered and changed.

Without warning, Cole lifted his head, catching sight of someone or something walking up the beach.

'Oh! That's new...' Ava realized, unsettled by the change.

There was a small figure, growing larger with each step. Ava's attention focused in on it. *'Her...'* A pale woman, her sodden hair hastily plaited. She was another survivor of the shipwreck. Her face was bruised and battered, the bottom of her skirt hanging in rags.

"Hullo...?" the woman called as she neared. "D'you need some help there?"

Cole sat up, wiping his face, seemingly confused.

Ava was torn in two directions. She could feel herself dissolving, her being returning to the millions of vibrations that formed all things. She fought the pull this time, needing to see who this was. Below her, Cole climbed unsteadily to his feet.

"Can I bring you some help?" the woman called again. "Can she be moved? I could get some'un to help you."

Cole shook his head, laying Ava's hand against her chest with tremulous fingers.

"There's no point," he answered brokenly. "She's already gone."

Ava was fading to nothingness even as he spoke. She struggled against it like a fish on a line, her departure slower than the last times. For the first time ever, she clearly saw Cole's reaction to her death, his inconsolable grief. His whole body quaked with the impossible truth that she was gone. Under the yellow-leaved trees, the sound of rushing wind – like rain – was rising. Ava's attention began to recoil just as the woman stepped out from the blue shadows of the woods. She was fair-haired and young, her concerned eyes resting on Cole's downturned face.

'My god!' Ava's mind announced. *'It's Hanna Thomas!'*

With a rush, she was pulled backwards and up, the figures below and her own body, broken like driftwood, fading into three small dots until only the snake and the coins were visible.

The wayward peace she'd once known was tinged with grief. A feeling of loss soaked through her thoughts as her vision expanded in an ever-widening arc of green. For the first time, she wanted to stay.

: : : : : : : : : :

The phone wouldn't stop ringing.

: : : : : : : : : :

Ava was late for class. She'd slept through her alarm, only waking when Cole had called her cell phone. He was in the printmaking studio waiting for her. Pulling on her jeans, layering one long-sleeved, one short-sleeved shirt, then donning her leather jacket, she headed out the door, swearing. She'd been up until midnight finishing her latest essay for Wilkins' class. The two Art foundations classes had become the bane of Ava's existence.

She jogged down the stairs, backpack in hand. It was laden with books for her afternoon classes and it banged hard against her shin as she ran. Ava swore again, hoisting it to her shoulder, and pushed open the front door with her hip, stepping out into the snow. There was a new prof teaching the first of her two foundations courses: Art of the Ancient World. It wasn't that Ava hated the woman, per say, it was that Professor Aichens – with her carefully articulation, insistence on thoroughness and her propensity to repeat herself endlessly – drove Ava nuts.

Cole teased her about it, of course. He'd taken this course in his first year of university (as most fourth year Art students had). He'd volunteered to proof all of her essays if she was willing to trade favours in return. Ava blushed, remembering. That aspect almost made the writing worth it, but she had to force herself to attend each day. Only imminent graduation (or failure) kept her there.

Reaching her vehicle, Ava fumbled for her keys. She found them under crumpled receipts and a half-empty bottle of water at the bottom of her pack, swearing until she got them in the lock. The door squealed open and Ava tossed her supplies onto the far seat before climbing in. Frost had settled deep into the vehicle. She rubbed her hands against the cold, not having time to wait out the chill.

With another blast of swearing, she started the engine, hunching her shoulders and heading back outside to scrape the windows. Minutes later, she clambered inside while the buzzing engine slowly dropped to a steady purr. The truck was old and irascible... and being twenty minutes late to class was better than having the beast die altogether halfway there. She did not want to walk in this weather.

Wilkins was teaching her second art history class this semester, which made it ten times worse than the first. It was Art since 1945, and Ava regularly kept late hours to keep up with the readings. There seemed to be as much written about the art, and what the dialogue meant, as the paintings themselves. Clement Greenburg had been the first of many. It drove her crazy, the convoluted doubletalk of artist and medium and historian. Though she loved the process of creation and the images themselves, she found it difficult to put her thoughts into words. She knew the dark history behind her own artwork, but Wilkins' focus on discussion made the class a struggle to manage. It was even harder to dissect about someone else's process with alacrity.

She thought of the completed essay sitting in its folder, printed and ready to submit. The process to complete that essay had been a hell of a lot easier than the first. After a week of late nights in the library, Cole had taken pity on Ava and brought her his carefully-written notes from the previous year. (He'd offered more than once, but she'd always refused.) Seeing them that evening, after hours of writing a paragraph and then deleting it in frustration, she'd burst into tears of relief. It'd turned out that a translation from Wilkins' inflated rhetoric into simple language was exactly what she had needed.

Cole's descriptions made sense.

Since that day, Ava had been making her own observations alongside Cole's; her purple pen appeared like a second language overtop his black script, taking notes for the first time ever in Wilkins' class. The phrases and scribbles and sketches swirled like clouds meshing with Cole's meticulous notations, leaving a multi-layered rendering of ideas, more detailed than the original.

Her second essay received Wilkins' highest praise: *"I hadn't thought of it that way."* She hoped this latest essay would do as well.

Feeling the first bloom of heat from the truck's heater, Ava popped it into gear. She headed onto the icy road, aiming for student parking near the Arts Wing where the Printing studio was located. She and Cole had only one class together, and it bugged her that this was the class she had to be late for. Of all her courses, printmaking was the one she enjoyed the most. It was a two-dimensional medium, but Ava had been surprised to discover how meticulous the process was, compared to painting.

Ava made it to the campus without incident, heading into the heated parking garage and swiping her pass at the gate. A space in the parking garage was one of her splurges, though with the age of the Beast, it was almost a necessity in the winter. She was late but not too bad, as the prof tended to give sketching and collaboration time for the first bit of class. Crossing her fingers that today would be no different, Ava pulled her bag off the seat and sprinted toward the building. Her lungs burned with cold, skin tingling within seconds.

The first few days of the semester, the class focused on mono-printing: spreading ink across the plate with the brayer, then wiping away the lighter areas with fingers and rags. It was a form of printing designed to capture that tenuous moment of creation. Ava loved it; Cole endured. By the end of the week, they'd started to branch into other aspects of printing. Today their first long-term project began. The phone in Ava's bag rang and she ignored it, running faster.

'When I said five minutes, Cole,' she thought in exasperation, *'I didn't mean it literally.'*

She headed up the back entrance, hoping someone was outside the fire exit taking a mid-morning smoke break. Rounding the corner, she got the first warm whiff of tobacco and grinned. She'd guessed right.

"Hold the door," she bellowed.

The woman up ahead pulled the door back open with a chuckle. In seconds, Ava was inside, making good time to the printing studio. Down at the end of the hallway, she saw their prof – a small, slightly-built woman with short, grey hair – stepping into the classroom. Ava loved Giulia and her informal approach (first names being a requirement with her). Ava gingerly walked into the large printmaking studio, hoping she hadn't drawn any attention to herself. She stepped up to Cole and eased her bag to the floor, sitting next to him. His hand gently squeezed 'hello' on her shoulder just as Giulia called everyone to put away their sketchbooks.

"Thanks for the call," Ava whispered, smiling as Cole's hand ran down her arm to capture her fingers under the table. "I totally slept through the alarm…" she added. "Dead to the world."

Cole chuckled.

"Have I been keeping you up too late?" he teased.

Ava smirked.

"Both you and Clem."

Chapter 3: The Multiple Print Project

Artist and printmaker Professor Giulia Cezzano stood at the high printing table, a variety of zinc plates and wood blocks along with their respective prints laid out in front of her. Cole tried to focus on the instructor's words, but Ava was beside him, and his concentration dragged away to her instead. Her breathing was slowing after her panicked run to class, and the sound reminded him of her fading pants after they'd made love. Letting go of her hand, he slid his fingers to her back, rubbing absent circles, his own breathing quickening at her nearness.

"Feels good," Ava murmured, leaning into his hand.

Cole chuckled. Praise like that wasn't going to help his concentration at all.

At the front of the class, Giulia began pointing out the various prints, talking and gesturing happily to the equipment around her.

"Since the start of the course, we've been working primarily with mono-printing and relief prints," she said, pulling out a carved wooden block and running her fingers across the surface. "For the next unit, we'll be starting to work with intaglio..."

Giulia laid out woodblocks while she talked, then picked up a heavy silver plate and a print of the image made from it, passing them around the table. The image looked like a pencil sketch of a little girl at a piano. The cuts were incised with precision, the simplicity of the image refined down to an individual line.

"...this one here," Giulia said, "is my daughter, Lucia. It's dry point, which means I've used a needle to cut a line into the zinc plate. When ink is applied, it fills the lines, and then it can be printed to reveal them. Rembrandt did many of these prints. They're the most like drawing of any of the printing approaches, and you can create some really interesting effects with the technique. It's a very immediate art form..."

Ava pushed into the movement of Cole's fingers. Feeling a knot of muscle that had formed a ridge in Ava's lower back, Cole switched to his thumb and the knuckle of his forefinger, kneading instead of rubbing. She moaned quietly under his ministrations and he grinned, digging his fingers harder into the band of muscles.

Another plate came by as the students passed them around. Ava gave it a cursory once-over before handing it back to Cole. It was a rendering of a river-bottom flower, the detailed shading of the image created in crosshatches.

"...and the second print that I handed out," Giulia explained, "is an etching. In yesterday's class, I showed you how to apply resin to a plate and use the acid baths to reveal the lines you've scribed into it. Well, today we get to start playing with that. The print of the yarrow was created by etching. That's yet another way that you can work with a plate... another form of intaglio..."

Next to Cole, Ava turned, her voice pitched low.

"Keep going," she whispered, "harder... lower..."

Cole's body jumped to attention at the sound of her voice. Ava knew exactly what those words made think about. He grinned, thumb pushing harder into her muscles, heading down her spine.

"...The last print I want to show you," Giulia continued, "is one that's created by burnishing with oil. It's a technique called mezzotint, and it's similar to dry point in that you roughen or damage the surface..."

Giulia lifted a small T-shaped tool, handing it to a nearby student. The tool had a serrated surface on the curved base like a meat texturizer. As Ava reached forward to take it, the low waist of her jeans flared open. Cole dropped his fingers inside. Ava squeaked in shock, swivelling back around, tool in hand. Her cheeks flooded with colour, her chest rising and falling in rapid pants. Again the memories of her under him flashed to mind and Cole smirked.

"Sorry... was that not low enough?" he asked, falsely innocent (secretly glad that they were sitting at the back, his hands hidden from view.) Ava giggled, sitting up once more in a semblance of studious interest. Cole's fingers ran back and forth along the lacy edge of her panties, and he watched her struggle not to squirm.

"...for mezzotint, you stipple the entire surface of the plate with the mezzotint rocker to create burrs in the plate's surface," Giulia said, her grey head bobbing. "It's a lot harder than you'd think. I suspect a few of you'll be complaining about tired arms by the end of class..."

Cole dropped his fingers lower, brushing the curve of Ava's ass.

"Cole!" she hissed. It was a warning, her voice breathless.

"Yes...?" he answered, laughter at the corners of the word. His fingers paused for a moment.

"Don't," she commanded, voice wavering.

Cole chuckled, his fingers picking up the movement once more, teasing along the line where the fabric met the soft skin of her back.

"Ava, I'm trying to listen to the directions here," he said with an exaggerated sigh. She scowled at him, then jerked as his fingers dropped lower.

"Cole...." she warned again, and a jolt of excitement lodged in his groin. It was very much like the noise she made when she was begging him for more. He was glad the table was blocking his lap from view, and even happier that Giulia was continuing her discussion of the project at the front. Right now, the prof was holding a variety of new tools aloft.

"...and once you have a solid black plate, you use a scraper and a burin with oil to burnish in the lighter areas of the image. Essentially you're filling it in with light rather than dark in this case..."

Cole leaned closer, his mouth directly next to Ava's ear. To anyone watching, it'd appear he was whispering some thought on the discussion.

"I want to fuck you, Ava Brooks," Cole whispered, lips brushing the shell of her ear. "Right here. Right now."

"Cole," Ava whispered. "Please..." She flushed from her chest up to her ears and Cole had the inappropriate urge to kiss her in front of everyone.

"Please what?" he asked darkly. "I like it when you beg."

"Don't!" Ava growled, catching his fingers, preventing him from moving.

He raised his eyebrow, trying to pull his hand back, but she held it tight. Up at the front, the professor sighed, calling to them.

"Cole and Ava," she said dryly, "could I get your attention? I want to make sure that everyone understands this next project."

With an embarrassed cough, Cole pulled his hand out of Ava's grip.

"Sorry, Giulia," he said, dropping his voice bashfully, "I was asking Ava about her project for the Student Show. Sorry, should've waited until break."

Giulia smiled indulgently.

"I'm sure we're all looking forward to the Student Show, but let's focus on this for now."

He nodded, and class continued. Ava waggled her eyebrows in admonishment, clearly trying to hold in her laughter. Giulia was now pointing out the series of plates before her.

"For this long-term project, you'll be working on ten different prints," she explained. "You will have to create each of the ten prints by altering a single plate..."

There was a murmur of concern as the project's parameters suddenly crystallized. A single image was hard enough, but with ten images being created on a single plate, the challenge became exponentially more difficult.

"... you need to obscure the image each time – either by etching in, or altering the design, or using a mezzotint rocker on the surface. I'd suggest starting simple at first... perhaps just dry point, because the more completely you use the plate, the harder it is to obscure it next time. Keep in mind you need to totally change your design, and the deeper you dig into the plate, the more difficult it is to alter it. I'm going to warn you," Giulia said, lifting the dry point needle in the air. "Don't cut too deep in your first prints."

"But what if we do dig too deep?" a girl in the front asked. "What happens then?"

Giulia reached out to the side, pulling up a print stained with inky shadows, but within its depths, the faint outlines of something else. An echo of what it had been still visible in the second plate.

"Cut too deep," she said, "and your image will keep coming back again and again, no matter how many times you rework it."

Chapter 4: Mediation

Cole sat in the cozy depths of the armchair, his eyes unfocused. He was supposed to be talking, but instead he was counting the minutes until his penance was over. Today was the first meeting with the counsellor, the one that both he and his father had agreed to see. Nina had been the one to suggest Marta Langden, the same therapist that Frank and Nina had seen years ago, and Nina swore that she had single-handedly prevented their divorce, assisting them through months of marital problems in the wake of Angela Thomas's suicide. That revelation was one Cole hadn't been expecting, but it made the suggestion to go for counselling with his father much easier. Being here, and talking about it, however, were two different things altogether.

Cole hated it.

The woman was in her early forties, with warm caramel skin, long dark hair, and a youthful demeanour. She had broad lips, and a wide grin, but most striking were her dark eyes; they sparkled with good humour. Cole liked her on sight, found her comforting in a way he couldn't explain. She'd suggested that for the first session, Cole and Frank simply talk. With this advice, both of them had fallen back into their old patterns. Frank grumbled on about life as he remembered it.

'How the fuck would he know?' Cole's mind hissed, *'he wasn't there anyhow...'*

Marta nodded and prompted Frank to continue, attempting to lure Cole into the conversation. He gave monosyllabic answers, letting his father's words wash over him like the tide. His responses grew further and further apart until they drowned him.

Now he sat in silence.

Cole's body was here, but he was floating somewhere and sometime else... wishing himself back to Ava. Thinking about the student show that opened this Friday at the University Gallery.

Reliving his hopes that Ava would like the statue he had created of her. Joking with Chim in the hardware store again, teasing him about his love of woodworking equipment (though Marcus had failed his only sculpture class). Fighting Kip Chambers in the alley...

Anywhere but here.

"...and it was a hard life," his father rambled, "I mean, I was working on my career, but Angela was a fine mother. Yes, she always kept good care of the kids. Had them well-dressed and fed all on her own. Mind you, most women stayed home in those days. She loved Hanna and Cole more than anything. Could never fault her on that..."

Cole's eyes drifted to the window. The last week had been warmer on the coast and the humidity and wind had completely dispersed the snow. He missed the white crispness of it. (A clean sheet hiding dingy bedclothes.) The day outside the window was a dull, muddy brown, the slate grey sky hinting at bad weather. For a moment, Cole wished he was out there on the ocean in a boat, moving across the water.

Free.

"Now, Cole," Marta said, pulling his attention back, "do you have any memories of your mother you wanted to share? Anything about the time when your father was away?"

He blinked, remembering her standing at the kitchen window, knuckles pressed against her mouth, trying to hold in sobs. He blinked again, and she was gone.

"Nope."

Marta nodded. Frank took it as his cue to continue.

"Angela and I had our issues, of course," Frank grumbled, "but she was a good mother. Hanna thought the world of her..."

his voice thickened. "Always thoughtful of how Angela felt... of her emotions. She was a good child. So caring..."

Cole's eyes drifted to the window again. The clouds had a purple hue, reminding him of a bruise across the sky. Not a good time to be boating... perhaps just trawling along the cliff's edge instead. Blending into the clouds and colours. Dissolving.

"How would you describe your times together as a family?" the therapist prompted.

"We weren't happy, but we weren't really unhappy either. We had different ideas about marriage. Angela was younger somehow... more naive. I was on a career path. I had things to do, places to be..."

Cole sighed, letting his eyelids half-close as his father's voice wrapped the room in shadowy tones, the words building walls between the two of them.

"...I remember a lot of family vacations together... and the kids playing in the ocean, once we moved here. It was good to have a home base. Angela really made it hers. Hanna loved the water." Frank laughed, remembering. "God, she was like a fish. We had some really good times there: barbeques on the beach and lobster roasts... lots of good memories. Hanna always used to say..."

Cole watched as the ghost of his older sister wandered into the mediation room. She was grinning at him, her sun-streaked hair tumbling over her shoulders, nose sunburnt pink and peeling. She was so real he could almost reach out and touch her. Cole imagined her perched on the edge of their father's chair, listening to his words, legs swinging. His sister would be teasing him if she was alive (as she always did), correcting the stories in the way that only Hanna had ever been allowed.

She'd been the favoured child... *the happy one.*

In the background, Cole's father began another tale of his eldest child, the words were nothing but the dull pound of the surf. Meaningless and disconnected. A snippet from a Mari Evans poem, half-forgotten, shimmered across Cole's consciousness like sunlight catching on water.

'...Where have you gone / with your confident / walk with / your crooked smile... / why did you leave me / when you took your / laughter / and departed / are you aware that / with you / went the sun / all light / and what few stars / there were?'

Across from him, Hanna winked.

Cole's expression wavered, remembering Hanna's light next to his darkness. His thoughts pulled him further and further back through time, a net cast out into deep water.

"Cole...?"

The counsellor's voice interrupted his musings. His head bobbed up like a sinker on a line.

"And how about you," Marta said, "how would you describe your family, Cole?"

He took several slow breaths, trying to focus on her question, his chest aching with the words he could not say.

"Cole," his father growled in admonition. Under the pain, a flicker of anger ignited.

"We *weren't* a family," Cole sneered, turning back to the window.

Frank made a disgusted clucking sound. Cole knew that if they'd been at home without a mediator, that statement would have already started a fight. Marta leaned forward, the long waves of her hair dropping like a curtain between her and Frank. She smiled gently.

"Could you explain that to me, Cole?" she asked.

He narrowed his eyes, pushing himself up and away from this place. Out, out over the churning water, out to the horizon where the clouds were turning black. He was heading into oblivion. Skimming over the sea, moving so far and so fast that none of this seemed real.

Far away from here.

"No."

Beside him, his father cleared his throat and began speaking again.

"You know, I think that things were just fine until Angela's death, but with that, it really started to get bad for Cole and me. I mean, we just didn't ever have a lot in common... Hanna went into the military like I had – a family tradition, you know – but Cole had no interest in that. Made no bones about saying it either. We had different ideas of what was worthwhile, what was important. Now Hanna, though... she had an ease with people... a way about her. A skill that would've served her well in life. If she'd lived, that is..."

Cole's eyelids fluttered as he saw the first flicker of lightning on the horizon, and he was gone.

: : : : : : : : : :

The room's deep chairs and benign, hotel-room style paintings, had completely faded in Cole's mind, replaced by Hanna Thomas.

It was a summer afternoon, and Cole's sister was laughing and happy, the way she'd looked when she'd graduated from high school. The two of them were at the cove two or three clicks beyond their parents' house, cliff jumping. Thirteen-year-old Cole was in the water below, watching as Hanna walked to the edge of the cliff face, high above him, grinning down. Her voice echoed down as she called out defiantly. Cole's sister, as always, was fearless. (Tempting fate.) In this memory, he floated face-up in the water, watching with his heart in his throat as Hanna threw herself from the precipice.

Her body formed a jackknife halfway down, stretching out like an arrow as she plunged into the inky depths.

Next to Cole's chair in this other place Frank Thomas stood up to leave. Cole stumbled to follow, sitting upright.

"Wait just a moment, Cole," Marta said, pulling him from the memory before Hanna resurfaced. "I need to talk to you for a little longer."

He blinked himself back into the therapist's office. His father stood, putting a square fist out to shake Marta's hand, assuring her that he looked forward to the next session. She gave him a pleasant goodbye, waiting with patient solemnity. Cole reached to pick up his coat.

"Hold on," Marta repeated, hand lifting as if she expected him to bolt.

At the door, his father turned back, his face dark and brooding like the day beyond.

"It's okay," Cole said, "Ava's coming by to pick me up anyhow, just in case..."

He left the rest unspoken.

"Thanks again, Frank," Marta said brightly, waiting for him to go.

As he headed for the front foyer, the therapist peeked out the doorway, calling out to the secretary at the desk.

"Just hold my next appointment for five minutes, all right?"

Pulling the door closed behind her, she gestured to the chair. Cole anxiously sat back down. There was a long, uncomfortable moment when she didn't speak, just watched him. She took a heavy breath, as if measuring and weighing something.

"This isn't going to work," she said.

Cole's eyes widened, his heart starting to pound. He was trying here. He wanted to get past his issues... for Ava and for himself. Wanted to—

"Cole, if you want to resolve things with your father, then you'll actually need to participate. I can't..." she frowned, leaning back, her fingers running over the seam on the chair's arm rest, "I can't do this for you. I can't make you better. The work is yours, and I'm not sure you're at a place that you can do it yet."

Cole felt himself sinking. It was like being dragged beneath the water's surface and drowning, the rocks closer than they appeared.

"I don't..." Cole managed to say, "I don't know how to try."

Marta nodded, sitting back up.

"I can help you with that part... but only if you want to. So I need to know," she said, hands opening before her, "is this something you want to do? Is this worthwhile for you?"

Cole swallowed, feeling Oliver's words in the room with them.

"Y-yeah, I do."

Marta nodded.

"Alright then," she said calmly. "The first thing we need to do is start meeting together."

Cole frowned in confusion.

"Sorry… what?"

"We need to talk – just you and me – about your feelings. About whatever it is that makes it so difficult for you to talk to him here," she said, gesturing to the now-closed door, "and then when your father is here, you need to be willing to share that with him. So what do you think?"

For a moment Cole flashed back to swimming in the cove with Hanna The moments of dread after she'd gone under, the fear that she'd never come back up again and Cole would be left alone. Waiting, terrified... and then the shaky relief when her laughing face broke surface once more.

Here in Marta's office, he had the same feeling.

"I can do that."

Chapter 5: Bedtime Stories

Ava waited in her truck, her eyes on the monochrome street. The light changed as afternoon slowly wore away. Earlier, there'd been a distinct lack of sharpness, just dulled layers of grey, like a murky watercolour painting with too much ink wash. Now bands of light slanted down as the sun moved toward the horizon. Bright yellows eked out of the drab day, hints of O'Keefe's bluish shadows in the alleyways and under cars. Ava smiled to herself, eyes half-shut, capturing it all for later.

'Cole should be here soon...'

A woman in a black coat pulled the building's door open and disappeared.

Another five minutes passed.

The door opened a second time and Frank Thomas strode out, face tipped into his collar. It was cold out, the wind coming gusty and brisk off the ocean as a winter storm brewed in the distance. Cole's father looked tired, more careworn than he had since the first weekend Ava visited. Her shoulders tensed as she followed his progress. He was heading to his vehicle, a grey SUV parked a few spots down from her own.

Seizing the opportunity, Ava rolled down the window, leaning out.

"Hey there, Sarge!" she called, grinning as he jerked up in surprise. The first hint of a smile pushed up one side of his mouth as he saw who it was. He changed direction, wandering over.

"Afternoon, Ava," Frank said, pausing by the window, his arm against the side of the vehicle. "What'd you and Nina get up to today?"

"She tried to teach me to make crepes," Ava scoffed. "Not sure that she knew quite how lacking I am in the kitchen."

"She always needs an assistant," Frank offered.

"She did NOT get an assistant though, she got me," Ava giggled. Frank's smile broadened. "We had to open all the doors to get the smoke out. The fire alarm beeped for a good ten minutes!"

His low chuckle joined hers and for a moment everything felt easy and right. Ava smiled to herself. *'See...? This is going to work.'*

"So how'd the meeting with you and Cole go?" she asked. With her words, a curtain fell across Frank's face, cold control replacing his laughter.

"Mmph..."

"Not good?" she prompted.

He grumbled again, lifting his hand from the truck, and taking a step back. *Pulling away.*

"You know," Ava rushed to explain, "the first session's the hardest." Frank's eyes widened in surprise. "At least that's how I remember it."

He cleared his throat, standing silently. He glanced back to the building, then back to her.

"I'm glad you're here to pick him up today," Frank answered, the lines on his face deepening. "I don't know if this will work, Ava. Cole's just not..." He shook his head. "It's like he's not interested."

"It'll take time," Ava said quietly. "Cole's here. That's huge. Try to keep that in mind." Her voice dropped. "And of course it's hard to begin with. I'm sure you and Nina found the same thing."

He pulled his glasses off and cleaned them on his shirt.

"Maybe," he said tiredly, putting the glasses back on. He reached out, rapping his knuckles once on the side of her truck. "Alright then, Ava, I'm gonna head home. Thanks for coming by for Cole." He stepped up to the curb, then turned back. "Nina's right, you know."

Ava tipped her head, confused.

"About what?"

"You're good for Cole."

Heat rose up her neck to her cheeks.

"Um… thank you, sir."

Frank laughed at the formality.

"Why do I think when you say 'sir'," he said, raising a bushy eyebrow, "you actually mean something totally different."

Ava winked.

"Because you're a wise man."

: : : : : : : : : :

Ava was fiddling with the radio, smiling in bemusement, when Cole came out of the office. He climbed in the truck, ashen-faced and unspeaking.

"Hey," she said. "How'd it go today?"

He made a choking sound, letting his face fall into his hands, body curling down. Ava slid past the gear shift, fitting herself next to him on the bench seat. She put her hand against his back, rubbing lightly.

"That good, huh?"

Cole laughed bitterly. Ava wrapped her arms around him, her chin settling on his shoulder. Beyond the pitted windows of her truck, the afternoon sun slanted across the buildings, lighting them with the golden tones and deep shadows of an Edward Hopper painting. She waited, but he sat motionless, face in hands.

"I hated going at first," Ava said quietly. "I didn't have a choice about going... wasn't making an effort, like you are..."

She closed her eyes, remembering this other version of herself, her rage coming out against everyone and anything. It was strange remembering herself this way. It reminded her just how lucky she was to have had her father with her.

"I had to go to counselling as part of my probation," she admitted, her hand circling gently against his shoulders and arms, her face next to his ear. "It certainly wasn't something that I wanted to do, and I fought it tooth and nail. You think you were a rotten teen? I made my dad's life a living hell."

For some reason, it was the last statement that broke the melancholy mood. Cole choked back a laugh, glancing at her.

"I don't believe you."

Ava punched his thigh twice, indignant.

"You're damn right, I did. Total fucking badass."

"Uh-huh?" Cole said, chuckling again. This time she grinned, leaning back in, brushing her cheek against his shoulder.

"Cole Thomas, I've got street cred you can't even dream of having." He snorted, and Ava continued. "The first session was really hard," she said, tightening her arms around him. "Really fucking awful."

She felt Cole shifting so that he could move his arms around her too. She smiled against him as he pulled her into a hug. The two of them were side-by-side, the light on the buildings becoming burnished, blue shadows lengthening. Cole's hands, clung to her like he was in too-deep water and she was a raft.

"Must've been hard," he said. His face was hidden from view against her ear. His voice was thick and close to tears.

"Yeah, it was," she admitted, her fingers running down his back, feeling the tension ebb away. "But it had to be, because if you don't get the hard stuff out, then you can't move past it. That's the whole point."

He nuzzled her hair, lips brushing her neck.

"Was it worth it?" he asked.

There was more than that to the question... layers of self-doubt and fear, and she knew it. Ava pulled back after he said it, her hand running down the side of his face, comforting him.

"You, Cole, are *absolutely* worth it," she said, answering the question he hadn't asked.

He nodded, leaned in to kiss her with sudden passion. When they finally broke apart, she could see that some of the worry was gone, the despair faded to resignation.

"Thank you," he said, "for coming to get me."

She giggled.

"You're not the only one who can break someone out of jail, you know."

: : : : : : : : : :

The storm blew in that night, leaving the lights flickering angrily for ten minutes before finally going out, plunging the house into darkness. Cole suggested he and Ava drive back to the city, but Nina refused. She was full of reckless excitement. Marta

Langden had been her suggestion and Nina seemed determined to use the first meeting to force Cole and Frank together.

"Family was the whole point of you two coming out," she argued. "Power outage or not, I want my family time, and I'm getting it."

Nina was adamant and no one was willing to argue. Cole and Ava were staying the night, no questions asked.

Under her instruction, the group gathered in the den next to the stone fireplace, surrounded by the warm glow of candles set around the room. There was stilted silence between Frank and Cole, so Nina told stories about her childhood and her many years as a journalist. She was happy and lighthearted; the atmosphere was easy as heavy drops of rain snapped against the windowpanes. Her words eventually slowed and then stopped, the roaring rain filling the room with dull static.

The lightning was blinding when it hit, and for an hour, flashes came in quick succession, leaving bright after-shapes that slowly faded from view. Torrents of rain fell in heavy sheets, leaving the room reverberating with a buzzing sound that crackled in its sheer intensity. The four of them were together, secluded by the noise. Wrapped in the vibration of it.

Nina and Frank sat on one couch. She was tucked under his shoulder, watching receding flashes of lightning on the water while he stroked her arm. Frank's gaze was soft and hazy, his attention lost in the distant storm, a pensive look painting his brow.

Cole and Ava sat across from them, nestled together on the second couch. Ava lay partially-reclined across Cole's lap, his fingers combing her hair. During the heaviest part of the squall, she asked him about living here as a child... about what it was like to see these storms.

His words were muffled from Frank and Nina. He recounted the memories in a hushed tone, starting with his childhood fears of lightning and the angry ocean storms... later switching to happier tales of learning to sail with his grandparents, and then finally... inevitably.... to Hanna. By this time, the sound of the rain had faded, hiding but no longer obscuring his words. Ava lay in his arms, the two of them focused solely on each other. For the first time in many years inside this room, Cole's laughter was genuine and happy. He told her one story after the other, reliving the details of his sister's life and their years together, ending finally with cliff-diving that long-ago summer.

"God, Ava, you just should've seen her. No fear, though she should've known better!" Cole chuckled, but there was truth in his words. "If Dad had known, he would've killed us, but Hanna was determined to do it... wanted to say that she had." Cole laughed. "I think it actually had more to do with her showing off for all her friends than anything else, but damn if Hanna wasn't single-minded about the idea."

Cole was grinning ruefully. Their eyes were on one another, everyone else forgotten.

"I was down at the bottom of the cliff," he continued, "floating in the water, waiting for her to jump. There are rocks there – like I said, Dad had warned us... threatened us really..." Cole shook his head, "...but we were there anyhow. Two stupid kids pulling the dumbest stunt we could've pulled. I remember Hanna jumping off the cliff and me just waiting there terrified. So scared shitless you can't imagine. But she asked me not to tell him, and so I didn't. I thought she could..." His voice broke. "Thought she could do anything."

Ava put a hand against his cheek, smiling sadly.

"She sounds like a pretty amazing sister."

Cole nodded. There was a slight lull, the rain fading until it was only a steady hum in the air.

"She really was," he said mournfully. "You can't imagine what Hanna was like. Everyone loved her, and she just did everything full tilt. Present in the moment." Cole paused, his expression soft. "I've never known anyone so… so… *alive* like that…"

From on the other couch, Frank Thomas cleared his throat, the sound pulling everyone's eyes to him.

"I have," he said quietly. "I see that same quality in you, Cole."

Chapter 6: The Student Show

Ava wore a form-fitting dress from a consignment shop and a new pair of high heels. She'd done her eyes with winged liner and her hair in a retro Marcel wave. The ensemble left her feeling adult and sophisticated. Even her father did a double take as she walked out of her bedroom. He was coming to the show tonight, though Frank and Nina wouldn't be attending until later in the semester, as Frank had come down with the flu.

Chim and Suzanne were at the university gallery when Ava and her father arrived. Oliver walked up to Marcus, and Ava did a slow circle, wondering where Cole might be. As she finished the turn, she got her answer. He was watching her from the side of the room. Ava smirked as she took in his apparel: he was dressed in faded blue jeans, a wrinkled black t-shirt, and a motorcycle jacket. He walked across the room, eyes never leaving hers.

"Really dressed up tonight, Cole," she said, raising an eyebrow as he reached her side. "Classy..."

He laughed, taking her arm and pulling her closer.

"There's no point, baby," he answered. "I don't clean up half as nice as you do and besides," he said, dropping his eyes down her body in that way that made her heart pound, "I kind of like the idea that you're slumming it by being here with me."

She giggled and he draped his arm over her shoulder.

"You look amazing," he whispered as they wove their way through the crowd. "Almost makes me wonder if you'd look better in or out of that dress. You think I might find out later?"

Ava led them over to Chim and Suzanne and her father.

"Only one way to find out," she said lightly. "You've got to test your theory."

The gallery was a series of rooms, each one packed with people. With parents and students along with the invited guests from the art community, it was hard to move. Chim's large piece, featuring a repeating portrait of Nelson Mandela overlaid with carefully rendered commercial images – a dust-buster, an ab-roller and a Big Mac, to name just a few – dominated the wall near the front entrance. Ava grinned as they approached; there was a growing group gathered around the image. Two unfamiliar suited men were there. One was scribbling notes into a small coil-bound book, the other muttering into his cell phone. They were clearly not parents or students or teachers.

'Art dealers looking for the talent,' her mind announced. *'Marcus Baldwin is definitely going somewhere as an artist.'*

Ava put her arm around Cole's waist. Her father was talking to Suzanne about her own artwork, which involved creating containers to house random household objects. There was a velvet-lined, form-fitted box enclosing a hair dryer; sitting next to it, a silk-covered sphere for holding a bar of soap. The mundane contained within the extravagant. Oliver found it fascinating.

Ava leaned into Cole, her lips brushing the curve of his ear.

"I want to see your sculpture of me," she said, smiling. "I never did see it finished."

Cole nodded, leading her to the back of the gallery.

"It's back this way…"

: : : : : : : : : :

Cole had helped the curators position the piece back in December, and he'd seen it again tonight when he'd first arrived. Ava's painting The Snake and the Coins was nearby, and there was something inexplicable about the painting which seemed recognizable, like it was meant to be a companion piece to his sculpture of the woman.

He'd stood in front of her painting for a long time. It still bothered him, though he honestly couldn't explain why. The image was a blend of gold and blue and green, painted in swirls and speckles, thickly impasto in some areas, faint washes in other. In a purely aesthetic sense, it was absolutely beautiful. The word 'ethereal' came to mind when Cole looked at it, but there was another part of his reaction that left his hands in fists, heart pounding.

The image was like a photograph he thought he should be well-acquainted with, but which was obscured in some way. He stared at it when he'd first arrived, unsure why the colours in particular held such anguish... it was like a glimpse of a half-remembered dream, something he was sure he would recall if he just gave himself time enough. It was there on the tip of his tongue, even now.

Up ahead Professor Wilkins stood, a glass of wine in hand. He nodded to Cole and Ava as they stepped around him, finally reaching the small alcove where Cole's artwork had been placed. Cole knew the shape of the statue better than he knew his own hands, so he watched Ava's face for her reaction. People – the red-haired guy from Cole's studio class, Giulia Cezzano and a friend of Ava's – moved past them like currents of water, and suddenly they were in front of it.

Ava's expression rippled in shock, and she pulled back, face aghast, her hand tearing away from Cole.

It wasn't exactly her, of course. The trouble with carving the arms prevented it... but when Ava had suggested just carving what the stone wanted to be, things had become much easier. Now Cole wondered if that had been a terrible mistake.

His sculpture was a nude woman standing upright, leaning forward. Like Henry Moore's work, it was suggestive and simple, rather than explicitly rendered. The woman's face – wearing Ava's features – stared forward, her legs tangled together, her torso thrust forward. That's where the similarity ended. The figure had no arms. Instead, two wings emerged from her shoulders, pulling back and away, poised in flight. It looked like a roughly sculpted image of a primitive deity or, perhaps, Cole thought wistfully, like the figurehead of an old ship.

"No!" Ava gasped, taking a shaky step backward, ankle twisting. She spun, pushing away from Cole and walking almost headlong into Chim and Suzanne.

"Ava, you okay...?" Marcus asked, looking to Cole for an answer.

Beside Chim, Ava's father stepped forward, his own face concerned. Her growing panic was tangible.

"No," she cried, knocking into people in her rush to get away. "No, I'm not okay! I need to go, Chim. I need to GO!"

Cole followed, making it to her side as she struggled through the throng of people.

"Ava?"

She didn't answer, just shoved past a laughing couple, stumbling again. Cole put his hand on her elbow, but he didn't hold her back. Her reaction – almost exactly her reaction when she'd seen the Francis Bacon painting in class that day – terrified him. Instead, he moved along with her, trying to get people out of her way as she lunged for the door like a trapped bird in a too-small cage.

"What's going on?"

"Cole," she sobbed, "I can't... I just... I need to get out..."

Her chest heaved with panicked gasps, her body trembling. Cole kept pace with her as she sprinted down the hallway toward the exit door, heels clattering. His hand on her arm steadied her as they ran. Behind them, the gallery doors opened, a murmur of voice rising like the surf and then falling once more. Behind them, Cole heard Oliver calling, but they didn't slow down.

Ava was determined to get out, and Cole wasn't letting her go alone.

She slammed her hand against the exit release and stumbled onto the icy steps. Cole caught her elbow and righted her against the bracing cold. Ava leaned forward, heaving in ragged pants as if she was about to vomit. Cole slipped off his jacket, draping it over her shoulders before worriedly easing her down beside him. There was something very wrong.

'This time I caused it...'

Next to him, Ava chattered almost inaudibly under her breath, tears running down her cheeks.

"...and it came down on me," she hissed, voice panicked, "the angel... it came down across my back. Dragged me down into the water... couldn't breathe... couldn't escape it..."

Cole frowned, catching bits and pieces of her words, his arms wrapping tight around her as she continued.

"Ava, it's okay," he whispered, wishing that he'd never created the sculpture, that he'd bashed it to pieces the day his anger was out of control.

"It's a warning," she cried, face crumpling. "Don't you see it, Cole?" She turned to him, her hands going to his chest, fisting in his lapels. "I can't get away from it. It doesn't matter what I want! It's the same as that painting... the Bacon one. It's the angel of death. It's a warning for me!"

The hair on the back of Cole's scalp crawled, adrenaline surging to match Ava's terror. Suddenly the almost-memory Cole felt from her painting seemed to press against his awareness, wanting out. He recognized it now... There was something to do with death. Something he knew but didn't want to remember.

'Something I dreamed...'

Behind him, the door squealed open. Oliver stepped out, his face cut deep with worry.

"What the hell's going on?"

On the step, Ava continued mumbling.

"...seen in before... remember that... I was in the water... and the angel was there..."

"I don't know," Cole admitted. "She just saw the sculpture I made and... and..."

"What sculpture?" he asked, dropping next to Ava.

"The statue... the woman with wings, not arms," Cole admitted.

"The statue of Nike?" Oliver asked, "I saw that one."

Cole nodded. Ava huddled on the step, voice slowly disappearing.

"This happened to Ava once before with—"

"The Bacon painting," Oliver answered for him. "Yes, she told me about that."

Oliver put his arm around her back next to Cole's, the two men on either side of her as her panic slowly waned. A few minutes later, she was breathing hard, her sobs buffeted by their nearness.

"It's okay, Kiddo," Oliver muttered. "You're not alone. I'm here." He glanced up, meeting Cole's eyes over the top of her bowed head. "Cole's here too."

She sniffled loudly, glancing up at her father, then turning to Cole. Her eyes were red-rimmed, her lashes wetly spiked.

"Uh... sorry," she rasped, rubbing her face and leaving a smear of eyeliner across her temple. "I don't know why... I just..." She took a shaky breath, rubbing her face again.

"It's okay," Cole answered, voice anguished. "I'm sorry, Ava. I never knew."

She nodded, icy fingers reaching out to take Cole's hand. Oliver leaned in to place a kiss on her forehead. When he pulled back, he gave her a sad smile.

"I think it's time the three of us had some tea."

Chapter 7: Three Chipped Cups

They sat in the kitchen of Ava and Oliver's apartment, a steaming kettle, sitting on the counter. Three cups of tea were laid before them on the table. Oliver's process was always the same: one quarter teaspoon of Darjeeling loose tea topped with boiling water. It had to be drunk black... no cream or honey to muddy his reading. The cups he used were thrift store specials, with the requisite curved-base bottom to let him read up through the passage of time. The cup was turned clockwise three times for the first cup, the next year stretching up the sides of the vessel to the rim. The cup was then tapped out onto a napkin, three turns more, the next cup holding the hints of the year after and beyond.

Ripples reaching backward from the future...

There were only three teacups in total – all of them chipped – though there were four saucers on the shelf. They had a pattern of green and russet leaves. They were vaguely Japanese in design, the porcelain fine enough that light passed through the narrowed edge of the rim. They were remnants of an old woman's treasure-trove, likely from a wedding trousseau predating the first World War, now damaged and worn through endless use. The veins on their aged surface were a web of grey against the pale blush of forgotten youth.

Oliver pushed a steaming cup toward Cole, his face gentle and persuasive. Ava knew this routine, but Cole felt like he'd stumbled into some arcane Templar practise, his sense of ease disappearing the moment the cups were pulled from the shelf.

"Drink up," Ava's father said, head tipping to the side as his daughter's often did.

It unnerved Cole, the similarity between their two faces – one young, one mature – tonight more than ever. But he didn't want to be the one to fracture this strange calm after Ava's panic, so he picked up his cup and drank. The hot liquid scalded his mouth and burned his throat on the way down, leaving him tasting ashes and nothing else. Oliver prattled on about the warm weather, and his hope for more snow. He was only here until the end of February, when the orchestra's next tour was starting, and he wanted to enjoy the winter before living in the perpetual half-light of late night performances and hotel existence. Cole nodded and drank again, waiting nervously as the three of them slowly emptied their cups of tea, his body pulsing in anticipation.

'This isn't real,' a voice inside him hissed, fingers trembling on the handle of the cup. *'It's not possible.'*

Beside him, Ava blew on her tea leaves; they lifted and swayed under the surface like seaweed. Her face was scrubbed clean of makeup, curls dishevelled and loose, making her look all the younger for the elegant dress she still wore. Cole blinked and the dress looked grey rather than black, but then perhaps it was just the light in the kitchen. She was beautiful tonight. He longed to hold her and make this thing – whatever had happened! – okay again, but he was afraid he would scare her off. Ava had been abnormally quiet since the gallery, keeping her gaze averted. She'd been shaken by tonight's events, and he had been, too.

'This won't work,' the voice inside him chided. He stared down at the black leaves swirling under the amber liquid. *'It can't work.'*

They sipped and Oliver talked. Outside the sound of the traffic dulled as the hour grew late. It was almost a surprise when Cole found his teacup empty. He looked up to find Oliver watching him, a paper napkin in hand.

"Place this on your saucer," he advised. Cole did as asked, and Ava's father motioned to the cup. "Now set the empty cup upside down on the napkin. Let it drain, but don't touch it. I'll be right back."

He stood up from the table, wandering into the living room. With unsteady hands, Cole turned the cup upside down as Ava did the same. Oliver's cup was wiped clean, the leaves in a wadded napkin to the side.

"Why not your Dad's?" Cole asked, pointing to it.

Ava answered without looking up.

"Because it's bad luck to read your own future," she said, staring at the underside of her cup. "Dad will read other people's tea leaves, but never his own… It scares him."

Cole nodded, swallowing hard. It scared him too! Behind them in the living room, Oliver shrugged on his grey coat as he stepped toward the stereo, turning on a vinyl record. The speakers snapped and popped before an old big bad tune began to play, hollow with the passage of time. It was a scratchy, faded live recording from many years ago. There was something about it that set Cole's teeth on edge, as if too many other things were going on in this room. Oliver grabbed a crumpled package of cigarettes from the side table, jogging down to the foyer and heading outside.

"Back in a minute," he called as the door closed behind him.

There was only the sound of the disembodied music from the other room. Cole stared through the kitchen doorway, weighing the desire to leave against the need to stay. *'Ava needs me…'* He turned back, surprised to catch her staring at him. She gave him a weak smile.

"What he sees, Cole, it's only an option," she said, answering his unspoken fears. "Anything can be changed. You should know that before he starts. It's not a certainty or a sentence. It's a… a… hint of what could be. Remember that."

Cole nodded, trying to appear calm even though his body was jittery with unexpected nerves.

'I don't believe any of this,' a voice inside him whined, *'It's not real.'*

Ava reached out, bridging the space between them. The moment their hands touched, he felt more settled.

'I'll stay for her...'

Around them, the music played on, rollicking trumpets and a woman's breathy voice, heavy bass undertones wrapping them in sounds from another time. Cole shifted uneasily while next to him, Ava hummed along to the music. He waited for Oliver to return, his fingers tangled in hers.

'It's a parlour trick,' he thought, *'like palm-reading, or tarot cards, or horoscopes... Lucky guesses and gullible people. Nothing else..."*

Cole was still running through an endless number of ways that this thing he didn't believe in wouldn't work when Oliver came back, the warm cigarette smoke lingering in his clothes like incense in a church. Ava shuffled her chair closer to Cole's, dropping her gaze to the upside-down cup. Her father rolled his long sleeves up, as if ready to start some yard work. Seeing him approach, Cole pulled his cup and saucer back toward him, unwilling to be the first to go.

"Don't touch it!" Oliver said sharply, his tone surprisingly unlike the man Cole knew. "Just leave it where it is."

Cole nodded, putting his hands in his lap. His body was growing tenser with each passing second; the music and Ava's reaction and the whole fucked-up scenario were fighting with everything he knew to be true.

'Things don't work like this,' his mind observed. *'It doesn't make sense...'*

Oliver watched him, his blue eyes dark like deep waters. He seemed heavier than usual; his light good humour was gone. There was no more chatter about the weather or his tour or random quotes, just pensive seriousness.

"Are you okay with this?" he asked. "You can leave if you want to, Cole. No one's making you stay here."

Ava lifted her eyes, face drawn.

"Cole?"

"No, no, it's fine," he mumbled. "Really... I want to do this." His voice shook, but he wanted it to be true.

Oliver reached out for Ava's cup a moment later, his attention falling onto her.

"Make a wish," he said, taking her hands in his. "Then turn the cup clockwise three times."

Ava closed her eyes, her face becoming serious and focused. After a few seconds, she turned the cup once... twice... and a third time.

The breath caught in Cole's throat leaving him gaping like a fish out of water.

'Not REAL!'

"When I read tea leaves," her father explained, "it's like getting a shadow of something from the future. Nothing's ever set. It's only ripples of what can be. You know what that means, right?"

"You always have a choice about it," Cole answered tightly.

"Exactly," the older man said with a nod, then turned back to Ava. "Alright," he said, "let's begin."

Cole watched as he turned the cup over, his eyes drawn to the interior of the vessel and the splotches of black leaves swirling up in a line from the bottom. Cole wasn't sure what he expected – some kind of incantation, or for him to suddenly start talking in

Edgar Cayce's voice – but instead it was very much how Oliver Brooks always was. They might as well have been in the coffee shop downtown, for all that he had changed. His tone was quiet and rough, same as always, and he chuckled lightly as he picked up the cup.

"Well, you've got your wish," he said, shaking his head and trying not to smile, "but I don't know why you wasted a wish on it... I could've told you that'd happen anyhow. God, Ava, you just have to look at the two of you to know that—"

"Dad!" Ava yelped, her cheeks flushing.

Cole dropped his chin, fighting down the urge to smile. He wondered if she'd wished what he'd hoped she'd wished... and imagining what it would mean for them both. The noose of panic loosened slightly, and he brought his attention back to the cup in Oliver's hands.

"Sorry," Oliver said, scratching his forehead. For a moment, he grinned at Cole, then pulled his eyes back to the cup. "Alrighty then... let's see... let's see... the very bottom of the cup is happening right about now..." As he spoke, he gestured with his baby finger, not touching the leaves, but pointing them out as he went. "... and it looks like you've made some big decisions lately. Things that'll affect the rest of your life."

"The National Gallery," Ava prompted, but her father lifted his hand, stilling her words.

"Don't help, please... makes it harder..." he muttered, frowning. "No... no... this is a person. Someone tall, with longish hair. I can see you and Cole... and this guy – pretty sure it's a man – standing just off from the side of the two of you. Cole has no time for him. See here?"

He gestured again to a splotch.

"They have a conflict... it's you, Ava... you know him, somehow... but this guy here... this other guy, not Cole, he's got a whole different path leading off from him. You might've gone that way, I think, maybe at a different time. But in the last few weeks you've decided something, severed those ties, made some decision that had changed all that. It's unravelled it as a choice... he's going away now. That's a good choice. Everything after that point becomes clearer based on the decision. You and Cole here, see?"

Ava had already told Cole about the meeting with Kip when she was shopping with Suzanne. Remembering it, the hair on Cole's arm prickled with apprehension.

'Her dad might've already known that...' his mind hissed, but he couldn't dispel his rising trepidation. *'But why would she tell him...?'*

His thought went no further; Oliver was talking again. Cole's heart was pounding harder with every word. It felt like the floor beneath him was moving, his balance unsettled like a boat on the choppy sea.

"So as the cup goes up, you can see it heading into the future. The next year is very busy. There's a trip coming up; I can see you snorkeling." He squinted, pulling the cup nearer. "The Caribbean maybe? I'm not sure, but I see a sea turtle. Anyhow, there're all sorts of family-related items too. There's a woman here – looks like she's a writer or something." Oliver laughed. "The image here is of a pile of books on a desk... maybe not a writer... perhaps a librarian? But anyhow, she becomes important to you, Ava... and to Cole too.

"There's an older man there too – not me – but he's important too. There's a symbol next to him: it's a flag. He's sort of a father figure, I'd say, but I think he has something to do with Cole more than you... though there's conflict there too. Good Lord, there's a whole mess of it! Just awfully muddy in this one part of the cup... shadows around the two of them... Cole and this man... so much anger..."

For a moment, Oliver stopped talking and looked at his daughter, voice growing serious.

"I don't want you worrying about it," he said, "the conflict isn't because of you, Ava. Don't think that. It's just that there'll be some moments when you need to step in, and you should be ready for it. It's going to be a hell of a fight... but I think you're up to it."

He winked. Across from him, Cole's eyes darted to his own upside-down cup, wondering what Oliver would see in his future.

'Cold calling...' his mind whispered, but the voice inside was less sure than before.

"You've got big events coming next summer... graduation, of course: here's a cap and placard... but there's also money in this cup: dragons and good fortune." He chuckled. "God help me, but I think you might actually be able to support yourself on this Arts degree." He laughed and Ava giggled, and then his voice settled back into its regular pattern.

"There's a show at a gallery... and yes, it's probably the National Gallery, but then I knew that anyhow." He frowned, leaning closer. Cole found himself leaning in, too. "I want you to be watching for someone that night. This sounds foolish, but this image I'm getting is a mandarin orange – whatever that means – who knows, could be nothing. But there's someone there, and he's really, really important, Ava. Remember that. For some reason, that's the image I'm getting with him. An orange."

Ava nodded. In the other room, the music had shifted to another song, low and plaintive.

"Whoever it is, he'll be a kind of mentor to you. Next to him is a plane... and more dragons, and a map of the far East... and

that's almost at the top of your cup. Perhaps a trip or a show...
everything leading into the future... And more dragons...
everything just leading up and away from there. There's Cole
there too. He's standing next to you. The two of you together."

Oliver sighed tiredly, turning the cup over and over again
in the palm of his hand. Cole let out a relieved sigh, his hands
unclenching.

"Now, we could stop here," her father said, "or we could go
forward another year..." his voice grew quiet. "But I don't want to
do either."

Next to Cole, Ava straightened up in concern.

"Why?" she asked warily.

"Well, here's the thing," he said, gesturing to the bottom of
the cup. "There're all these swirls in your teacup. Things I've
never seen before... like knots of rope or seaweed... snarled... not
troubles, per se, but some kind of links to you... and they're all
coming from the very bottom of your cup. All of them tethered
together."

Oliver cleared his throat, his fingers covering his mouth for
a moment, brushing over his lips distractedly.

"I don't know, Ava," Oliver muttered, "but I'd almost say
that what happened to you tonight with Cole's sculpture had
nothing to do with what's going on with you right now at all."

"What do you mean?" she asked, fear creeping into her
words.

Cole glanced into the cup, and sure enough, the bottom was
a web of swirling lines... almost like Ava's painting of the snake
and the coins. These threads reached up from the bottom, touching
bits and parts of the other images.

Entangling them...

"If it's okay with you," Oliver said, "I'd like to do a reading from your past, rather than your future."

Chapter 8: The Snake is a River

"A reading from my past?" Ava repeated.

Her father nodded.

"If that's all right with you."

Ava stared down at the cup, chewing anxiously at her lower lip. The music played on behind the group of them, a single note pulsing for a long moment, a woman's keening voice.

Decision made, Ava looked up.

"Yes."

Her father set her cup upside-down on the napkin in her saucer. He reached forward, putting his fingers on either side of hers, holding her hands tightly. Sad notes of trombone and saxophone rose and fell like waves around them. Cole's heart was in his throat as he watched. He had been pushed to the side. Forgotten for a moment.

'Not sure I like this...'

"There's no number of turns to this one," Oliver explained, eyebrows pulled together in concentration, "just go backward — counter-clockwise this time — as long as you want to, Ava. Let your mind wander if you can, and I'll look if I can see anything that's coming up from there."

'Up from where?!'

Ava nodded. Cole could see she was scared. His body was starting to twitch in anticipation. Ripples from the future he could almost wrap his head around, but the past affecting the present made no sense whatsoever. Tonight had jumped from the realm of science fiction to complete fantasy. He couldn't quite keep up with the script. He reached up for the collar of his t-shirt, tugging it away from his throat. It felt like he couldn't breathe.

"Will it work?" Ava asked.

Oliver laughed, his fingers still on hers.

"It didn't matter what's in your cup," he said, winking. "It already happened, right? So there's no point worrying about it. Nothing to be scared of."

Ava nodded again. The same feeling Cole'd had at the studio when he saw Ava's painting of the swirling clouds – fear and horror – was starting to mesh with his apprehension. For a moment, he considered just calling it a night and walking out. But then Ava set her fingers lightly on the edge of the upside-down cup and began going backward, counter-clockwise. Her eyelids fluttered, then closed. She almost looked asleep except for the endless turning of her fingers.

Cole waited.

And waited.

And waited...

The turning went on for longer than he'd imagined it would, his mind starting to wander. He was tired and strung out from the aftermath of Ava's reaction to his sculpture. Across from him, Oliver watched the motion of Ava's fingers, body poised and waiting.

'Wonder how long this will—'

"Now," Ava whispered, her eyes blinking back open.

Her voice had changed and Cole jumped at the sound, feeling a cold tremor run the length of his spine. There was a strange canter to her words. Like she was speaking with an accent he'd never noticed before. She looked sadder... *care-worn.* The sight of her pursed lips reminded him of something or someone he couldn't quite place.

'Something from a dream I once had...'

Cole cringed at the thought.

"Okay, then..." Oliver said, picking up the cup, and glancing down into the bottom.

Cole could see that more than half of the tea leaves now sat on the discarded napkin in the saucer. The interior of this cup was far more barren and sterile that her first. It looked like a faded map.

"This reading's definitely an old one." Oliver began. "It's the end of a long journey... maybe across the ocean. I can see a group of people going out for a long, long time... travelling so far that they can no longer see the shore of where they'd left from. See here?"

He gestured to a lump in the center.

"Yeah?"

"I'd say that's a ship of some kind," Oliver continued. "An old, big-bellied one, maybe a galleon." He frowned, squinting. "Actually, it's not one boat, it's two. There's a second one there, in the distance... following from behind. They're moving together, leaving one place, going to another. Heading to another land. It's a new beginning..."

Cole's heart shuddered against the walls of his chest, his breath becoming jagged; he felt like he'd been running.

'It's not real!'

"Things had gotten very bad in the place you left from, Ava. People were fighting," he said, voice sad. "Sickness... poverty... The place you were headed was a beginning. You were starting a new life, but it wasn't easy. People were being tested, their faith questioned. You most of all..."

Ava gasped. Cole reached out, weaving his fingers into hers. He squeezed, then let go. (He didn't know how to reassure her when he was fighting the terror, too.)

"But you survived it... both of you, actually…"

"Both?" Ava asked.

"Yes, the two of you. Look, there's Cole there too."

The older man gestured with his finger to a small shape of leaves, but the smudges looked like nothing to Cole, so he simply sat back and listened.

'Could be anything,' his mind prompted. *'Doesn't mean a goddamn thing...'*

He didn't know why the words bothered him so much. Why he was getting more edgy by the second. The record had switched to a new song, the instrumental music slow and melancholy.

"When the ship begins to near this new land, there's so much hope. I can see you standing on the deck of the ship, looking up at the birds. See here, Ava? Yes, that's a bird, and you're watching it, knowing that you're almost there…" Oliver's words suddenly stopped, eyes widening.

"What?"

"It's um…"

"Dad, *what?!*"

Oliver's chin bobbed up, eyebrows furrowing in alarm.

"Before you make it ashore, there's a storm, a terrible storm. The two ships are torn to pieces. There are people in the water, screaming. So much death… so many dying. Oh Ava, I'm sorry."

"And Cole?"

"No, Cole's okay. He's swimming. Wait! You're there too! But something's not right..." He lifted the cup closer, brows low over his eyes. "You're both there at the end – I can see the two of you together ... both of you on a beach but... but..." He frowned, eyes narrowing. "Hold on... Yes, both of you made it to the shore. The storm's ending, and you've made it to safe harbour. I can see you, Ava... you're lying in the grass, looking up to the sky. Cole's beside you... the new land surrounding you... swirling grasses and low rolling hills... And from above I can see something that looks like a snake..."

'The snake is a river,' Cole's mind announced. At the words – coming from someplace deep inside him – his body began to quake.

"Yes... I can see it now... not a snake exactly, but a river leading out to the ocean. You're laying a short ways from the shore, a field of grass all around you... a river in the distance... the sea further on... and trees. You and Cole are together, but you're staring upward... something's not quite right..."

Oliver tipped his head in concentration, his gaze back in the past. Cole's body was frozen in place, his fingers clawing the edge of the table. Heart thudding loudly in his ears.

'This can't be happening...'

Oliver's voice dropped back into its hypnotic rhythm, the words rippling like wind against grass.

"The sun is shining. It's a beautiful place: the shore and the trees, and the river in the distance. There is so much beauty there, so much peace. Cole is talking to you and the wind is blowing... but you already know something..." He frowned. "Ava, you know what's happening to you."

"What's happening?" Her voice was barely a whisper.

Cole could feel something pulling at his awareness. It was so close now he could feel the wind on his cheek. Knew the texture of the grass under his shoes. Adrenaline rushed through his veins, poising him for flight.

'I've been there!' his mind screamed. *'I've seen this!'* His body rioted with the urge to run. It was too much, and the denials from earlier only made this moment all the worse for its intensity.

"You're there, just the two of you. You love him, Ava... I can see that even here." Oliver's voice roughened. "Cole's begging you to stay with him, but you can't…"

As Oliver spoke, distress began to wrap tightly around Cole's chest. Oliver's voice was no longer soothing to him; the words leaving Cole more panicked with each passing second.

'I know this story...' he realized. *'I know how it ends!'*

"He wants this new beginning… this new start for the two of you…" Oliver glanced up, catching Cole's eyes, and with that, ice ran down his spine. Oliver looked worried. "Ava, you're just lying there… and you want to stay with Cole, but there's something wrong, you're hurt… your body is… you're…"

Oliver's voice broke, and he let out a sharp gasp. Both Ava and Cole jumped at the sound.

"Please, Dad," Ava begged. "I need to know."

"Your body it's… it's just *broken*, Ava. You're dying. Cole's there with you, talking to you, and you want to stay with him, but you can't."

His words stumble awkwardly to a stop, and he looked up at his daughter, eyes wide.

"I'm so sorry, Kiddo."

"I died after we made it to the shore," she answered him, her voice oddly calm.

Cole pushed back from the table, his screeching chair tipping over and banging on the floor. He was already on his feet when Ava jumped up. Oliver dropped the cup from his hand with a loud clatter, tea leaves scattering, words disappearing as Cole began to yell.

"No!" he shouted. "It can't be that story! That's my DREAM! Don't you see?! You're seeing my dream!" He was yelling, his body wracked by the onslaught of pain. "The dream I had after Hanna died. I was always being left behind... and it was always Ava who LEFT ME!"

She was beside him, her arms around him, holding him tight.

"It's okay," she said, voice breaking, "I'm here now."

Chapter 9: The Time of the Lone Wolf is Over

They were drinking tea again, this time out of coffee mugs; all the teacups for reading were shoved roughly to the side. Cole had his elbows against the table, his body slumped forward. Next to him, Ava rubbed circles into his back, her arms around him. It had taken a full twenty minutes to get the story out of Cole in any semblance of order, and Ava still wasn't sure what to make of it.

Cole dreamed of her dying… had dreamed it endlessly for many years before he met her that day last Fall outside the art history class. He'd had the dream enough times to describe it with uncanny detail. Remembering her own dream in his own way. There was no peace in his version, only his absolute horror at her loss. Ava was more bothered by this than the fact that he'd recognized her painting, or that he was in her past-life teacup at all. It was Cole's agony with her dying that grieved her. Even now, mug in hand, he was inconsolable.

'No wonder he's afraid I'll leave him.'

Across from them, Oliver had a lit cigarette in his mouth, returning sense to the incomprehensible events of tonight. Narrow bands of smoke wove around him like loosely coiled rope, winding around his hands and arms as he gestured. Ava's father never smoked in the house... never.

Until tonight.

"It's something that already happened," her father explained. "It obviously is affecting you both. But it doesn't mean that something like that's going to happen again. I mean, why should it?"

He took a long draw on the cigarette, and Ava knew she was not imagining the tremors in his fingers. This reading had really bothered him.

It worried her too.

"What scares me," Cole muttered, "is that Kip Chambers dreamed of Ava too."

"He dreamed of my painting," Ava corrected. "Not me, exactly." It felt like a lie, but the truth felt worse.

Oliver frowned.

"Who's Kip?"

Ava fiddled with her mug, weighing her words before laying them out. Things were unbalanced again and getting worse. For just a moment, she flashed to sliding down the steep decking of a boat. *'Another dream...?'*

"He's the other guy you saw in my cup," Ava answered nervously, "the one I had to make a clean break with in order to get things cleared up. The guy Cole has an issue with. He had these dreams – these nightmares – when he was a kid... and it seems linked to me somehow."

Oliver nodded, tapping ash into the chipped saucer next to him.

"Ah, well, that makes sense. He's probably from this other time too. But I didn't see him in your cup at all. Just saw Cole with you there at the end."

"Maybe he was one of the people who died in the storm," Ava said quietly. This wasn't making her feel any better at all.

Oliver shrugged and put the cigarette to his mouth again, lips pursed to hold it in place.

"Could be," he mumbled, "looks like a lot of people died in that storm." He paused for a long moment as he drew the smoke into his lungs, and Ava knew what he was going to say right before he said it. "Even you died, Ava."

Next to her, Cole sat up.

"What the fuck does that even mean!?" he snapped, fury under the surface of his pain.

Oliver frowned, leaning back and setting aside the cigarette. He picked up Ava's discarded teacup and held it in the palms of his hands. His lips tightened as he looked into it.

"There's a figure here. I'd say the figurehead on the prow of the boat. It's a woman – a woman with wings instead of arms—"

"An angel," Ava interrupted.

Oliver nodded, setting the cup down and steepling his fingers.

"What Ava saw tonight at the show, the woman you carved, was an echo of that memory. It must've been something she saw – something that meant something to her, something that scarred her – and after that she… she…"

He left the word unspoken, picking up the cigarette from the saucer with trembling fingers.

"I've no idea what it really means. I don't know anything for sure... but whatever happened, it marked both of you. You're connected – the two of you – and you, and this… this thing between you is still connected. Still wrapped together." He frowned, pointing at Cole with the burning end of his cigarette. "Emily Bronte wrote that *whatever our souls are made of – his and mine are the same.*' I think that's what Ava is to you, and you to her." He sighed. "Your past is tangled together, and it's affecting things here and now."

Cole laughed coldly.

"Look, I don't believe in any of this shit, alright? I don't know how you knew that about my dreams... but I don't believe in past lives. When you're dead, you're dead."

Ava watched as her father took another lengthy drag on his cigarette. His eyes were narrowed and critical. The atmosphere of conflict made Ava feel sick.

"An atheist, huh?" Oliver said curtly. "Well, life might throw some things at you every once in a while to question that." He laughed harshly.

"Doesn't make any sense." Cole grumbled.

Next to him, Ava's fingers found their way to his hand, holding tight.

"No, it doesn't," her father replied, "but there's a lot of crazy shit that happens in life that science never explains... and the ripples of events – past and future – go both ways, forward and back. Most of what we're doing now is our focus, but big events change us. Call it a parallel universe if you want to... or a past life... or just misfiring synapses." He tapped the side of his head as he said it. "I don't really care how the hell it gets explained, but the ripples happen, and they go both ways..." He gestured between them, the cigarette forgotten in his hand. "I think that's what's happened here."

"So what do we do about it?" Ava asked. "I mean, is this a warning? Something that's going to happ—"

"It's already happened," her father barked. "You remember that. Alright? It's done now, Ava. Done!"

She could tell he was upset too. He never raised his voice. It wasn't her father's nature.

"But how could this...?" Ava mumbled, not even knowing what she to ask, just that she was feeling lost, and wasn't sure where to go now. Cole leaned closer, his shoulder pressing against hers. Balancing her.

Across from them, Oliver set the cigarette butt into the saucer at his elbow as he blew smoke to the side. He rubbed his ragged face. There were rings under his eyes, skin waxen. He wouldn't be reading any more teacups any time soon.

"I don't know how it happened, Ava," he said wearily, "but the woman with wings is here, and you dreamed her, and the voyage ended in death." He glanced at Cole, voice hard. "I know what I saw... and if you dreamt about it and so did Cole, then it's obviously done and gone. So it's this life you should be thinking about," Oliver said, knuckles rapping loudly on the tabletop. "What to do *now* should be your focus."

There was an uncomfortable silence and then Oliver glanced to the side as if hearing something. Without a word, he got up and headed into his bedroom, returning seconds later with a dog-eared book. He flipped through the pages as he walked.

Clearing his throat, he began to read.

"This could be a good time. There's a river flowing now very fast. It's so great and swift that there are those who will be afraid. They will try to hold on to the shore. They will feel they are being torn apart and they will suffer greatly. Know the river has its destination. The elders say we must let go of the shore, push off into the middle of the river, kept our eyes open, and our heads above the water. And I say, see who is in there with you and celebrate...

"At this time in history, we are to take nothing personally. Least of all, ourselves. For the moment that we do, our spiritual growth and journey come to a halt...

"The time of the lone wolf is over. Gather yourselves! Banish the word struggle from your attitude and your vocabulary. All that we do now must be done in a sacred manner and in celebration...

"We are the ones we've been waiting for."

He glanced up as he finished. Ava felt a sense of déjà vu... she'd had a dream once about another man talking to her about a boat. He'd told her about the time to head out into the water, and the time to wait out a storm. Her throat was tight, too many emotions under the surface.

'My father died, leaving us all behind… and I had to choose because of it…'

She blinked and the almost-memory was gone.

"Who wrote that?" Cole asked. His voice was raw with emotion.

"No one knows the name of the author," Oliver answered, "it was before the advent of written language. It's a Hopi prophecy about our time."

He sat back down at the table, lifting the cigarette. He gestured between Ava and Cole, ashes swirling.

Set adrift…

"This time around," Oliver said with a nod, "in this life… the two of you are in the river together."

Chapter 10: Polaroids

Ava's last semester of university appeared in a series of flashes. The first were bright and intense: Christmas with Cole's family, the fight at New Year's, the teacup reading with her father the night of the Student Show. Others had the muted golden hue of 1960's prints, poignant and wistful. They were single events that would someday form a nostalgic illustration of the end of an era.

These times reminded her of the photographs now lining one wall of her studio, random moments captured in a blur of light and colour. There were weekends partying with Chim, Suzanne and Cole at The Crown and Sceptre, late weeknights at the university print-making lab, trying to adapt the multi-print zinc plate into ten variations, sharp memories of biting her lip to stay quiet in Cole's thin-walled dorm while he moved on top of her. Individual moments marked the passage of time.

Some of the snapshots on the wall had been developed at the local film shop, though two strips were from the two dollar insta-booth in the mall – one with her and Cole, and another with all four of them, squished together in the booth, Chim's Marley cap down across his forehead. Lately a growing number of these pictures were the oddly-shaped self-developing ones; names and dates scribbled in the band at the bottom. Wednesday at the Crown. Suze and Chim. Hiking in the river bottom. Sunday in the diner...

Chim had located the old Polaroid camera at the downtown thrift shop and they'd all pitched in for film. These quick snapshots had become an impromptu art project; there was a growing collage, supplemented by drawings on napkins and doodles on receipts. Each snippet decorated the space that had become, over the last months, the agreed-upon meeting place for the four of them. Ava couldn't help but feel like she was recording this all for later.

Each week moved her toward graduation and all of its challenges. There were decisions to be made about the future. Chim already volunteered for Amnesty International; his supervisor had offered to extend his role into a paying position starting the following summer. Now the rest of them were beginning to realize that these last few months were, in many ways, their last 'free' time together. Jobs and mortgages and life would soon take over. It was both exhilarating and terrifying.

Suzanne was the one who'd come up with an answer.

She had several friends who were planning to spend their Spring Break volunteering at an animal sanctuary on Martinique. With their help, Suzanne located an inexpensive chateau to rent down the coast from Trois Îlets. The place she'd found was a private residence that fronted a secluded beach. With the change in currency and a split four ways, they would have more than enough money to pay full price for airfare. Cole grinned as Ava insisted that they plan on snorkeling when they were there.

"You're cheating, you know," he said, raising his eyebrow sceptically. "It isn't really coming true if you force it to happen."

She lifted an eyebrow.

"Cole, you don't even believe in teacup reading," she replied, dryly. "Not sure why you care how it works."

Dubious or not, the two of them had been changed by Oliver's words. The story of their dreams, and the sudden awareness of the connection between them, was yet another piece that simply "fit." Ava found herself thinking about it on occasion, bits of dreams – a wooden bird, the two of them holding hands in the rain – coming at random moments. These past echoes gave her comfort, but they weren't the only part of her cup she intended to see to fruition.

Tonight in the Crown, it was the future rising up across the side of the cup she was focused on. Across from them in the booth, Suzanne pulled out a pamphlet from amongst the rest of her travel guides.

"If we do decide to go snorkeling, I'd like to go to the Trois Îlets Wildlife Sanctuary," she said, tapping the paper in front of them. "They're repopulating the Hawksbill Turtle population there."

Ava glanced at Cole and this time she was the one smirking.

"Fine, you win," he said, throwing up his hands in defeat. "Maybe your dad did see something."

Ava turned to him, her voice dropping.

"Maybe…?" she scoffed.

Under the table, one of Cole's hands slid up her leg. Her knee jerked in surprise, bouncing the glasses, and Chim gave them a knowing grin.

"He's right more often than not," Ava said, voice squeaking, "but you've always got a choice about what you decide to do. Nothing's fated. You can change anything, you know?"

Cole grinned, fingers moving higher. She closed her eyes as his hand began tracing over her inner thigh. Across from them, Marcus rolled his eyes, turning back to Suzanne; in seconds, they were lost in their own conversation.

"But how can he see it, if you've got a choice?" Cole teased. "Doesn't make sense."

She thought of her wish – the two of them together – and in that moment his hand slid in the rest of the way, leaving her gasping.

"I don't care how it works," she gasped, squirming under Cole's roving hand. "I just know it does."

It was a Friday night in early February, and Cole and Ava were staying in Frank and Nina's guest suite. The Spring weather was blustery, and with the pressure change, Nina had developed a migraine. After dinner, she and Frank had retired to bed, leaving Ava and Cole to fend for themselves.

Coastal suburbia was dead for a Friday. After a late supper at the downtown pizzeria, the two of them came back for the night. They tiptoed up the stairs, laughing like teenagers before climbing into bed, listening to gusts of wind around the eaves. Ava lay on her stomach on the bed, bare feet propped on her pillow, flipping through television channels. Behind her, Cole lay propped up against the headboard, a black notebook in hand.

"What'cha doing?" Ava asked, twisting to look over her shoulder at him. He'd been scribbling steadily for the last twenty-five minutes, pages turning one after the other. Cole glanced up, raising an eyebrow suggestively.

"Well, if you'd strip down, I'd offer to sketch you... but since you're wearing too many clothes, I'm doing some work instead."

The scratching of the pen returned. Ava flipped through a few more channels, her curiosity growing. The figure drawing suggestion had some merit, she had to admit. It was nice having her dad back in town but his presence had put a damper on Cole's visits. The dorm was no better. His next door neighbour had given her lascivious looks the two times he'd run into her leaving. Ava was definitely too loud for Cole's bedroom.

She rolled sideways, propping herself up on an elbow to watch him.

"What kind of work are you doing?" she asked, nudging his ribs with her toe. He smirked, catching her foot.

"Writing," he admitted, rubbing his thumb along her instep and making her giggle. She squirmed until he let go, turning onto her back, her hands now behind her head. The minute his pen dropped back to the page, her toes prodded him. He kept his eyes on the sketchpad, ignoring her.

"Okay," she said with a grin, "I'll play. What kind of writing, Cole?"

Her toes wiggled against his armpit, moving lower until they hit a particularly sensitive spot and he jumped, snickering. The book dropped and she could see the lines of text filling the white pages.

"Writing for Marta," Cole admitted, reaching out and pulling her up the bed, so that her hips were now next to his. The fingers of his free hand dropped down to her waist, finding the seam between her top and yoga pants, working underneath. He propped his book against his knees, writing once more.

"Marta, huh?" Ava said, eyes narrowing. "Should I be jealous?"

Cole snorted, fingers of one hand tugging at her waistband while he continued to write. The pauses between scribbles were growing longer.

"Depends..." Cole said, grey eyes taunting her, "what would you do if you were jealous? Hmmm....?"

Ava began to squirm as he got hold of the top of her pants, pulling on one side roughly, exposing her panties, then sliding over to the other hip and doing the same thing.

"I dunno," Ava admitted, a line of irritation between her brows. "What does she look like?"

Cole glanced away as if remembering. Meanwhile, the fingers of his free hand slid her pants lower until they were puddled next to him. His other hand was still poised on the paper, but no longer writing.

"She has long dark hair," he said. "Really nice hair, actually. And brown eyes." He smirked. "Very pretty."

Ava scowled as Cole slid his hand up her calves, inching toward her thighs. She crossed her arms, holding in the urge to sigh.

"Hmmph," she grumbled. "Do I know her?"

Cole chuckled as his fingers reached the silken edge of her panties and began teasing back and forth, sliding along the seam toward her crotch.

"I don't think so..." He tapped his pen on the book, watching her, his voice a low purr. "Jealous, are you, Ava?"

He worked her panties off with one hand and they joined her pants at her ankles. She kicked them violently away, abruptly annoyed. Cole stopped touching her altogether, going back to writing, his face distracted.

A full minute passed, filled only by the scratching of his pen.

"I'm *not* jealous," Ava said petulantly.

At her words, Cole stopped writing. He straightened the book against his knees, his face full of mischievous good-humour.

"Cole?"

He glanced up again; this time he winked.

"Hmmm?"

Ava twisted so she could sit up, putting them face to face.

"Seriously now," she said, hoping she didn't sound as anxious as she felt. "Who's Marta?"

She realized that at some point her hands had rolled into fists. That part of her reaction concerned her.

Cole's face lost the smirk and became softer. He dropped the book onto her lap and set the pen on the table. Ava waited, chewing the inside of her lip as her heart pounded. This conversation left her feeling more naked than all of the moments she'd been undressed in front of Cole in the last months combined.

"Marta Langden is the therapist that Dad and I are seeing," Cole said gently; his fingers dropped to her waist, stroking lightly down the naked curve of her hip. His fingers were persuasive, laying a path of feather-light touches on her skin.

"Oh."

Ava knew they were seeing a counsellor. She also knew that Cole was going for an hour before each session, too. She frowned for a moment, trying to remember if the therapist had ever been mentioned by her first name. Ava didn't think so.

All the while, Cole's hand moved lower, dropping overtop her curls, teasing lightly. She shivered. He leaned forward so that his face was close to hers. (He could have kissed her, but he hadn't yet.) Both hands slid under her top, fingers moving against her skin.

"You can look at what I wrote, you know," he said quietly.

He leaned in to drop his lips against her mouth. His thumbs reached the underside of her breasts, fondling her through the lace of her bra.

"What are…?" Ava gasped, her eyes closed against the tender caresses, "What are you writing?"

Cole's hands moved higher. He found the edge of the bra and pulled it down so that his roughened fingertips could reach her nipples. She shivered, the pink peaks hardening.

"It's homework," Cole admitted, his face a hands-breadth away from hers. "Things I remember from when I was a kid..." his tongue flicked out to the shell of her ear, "things about my family and my emotions. Stuff like that."

"Oh..." Ava said weakly. "Well, that's good then."

His teeth grazed her ear lobe, nibbling gently, and she shuddered, but Cole wasn't done.

"Yes, it is good..." he murmured, tasting the hollow under her ear.

Cole's mouth was nipping and licking her neck. Ava couldn't think any further. His hands had grown impatient in their wanderings,. With a groan, Cole pulled his mouth away from her, hands dropping from her breasts to her waist. He pulled her to straddle his lap where he sat against the headboard of the bed. Her lashes fluttered open. He was watching her, face grave.

"I was teasing, you know," he said. "There's no reason to be jealous, Ava. I wouldn't do that to you... *Ever.*"

She smiled at his words, the way he hadn't made light of her feelings.

"Thanks," she said, cheeks warming under his unwavering gaze.

He pulled her closer, grinding her down against his hips. The look in his eyes was shifting again, seriousness and intensity drawn into something needier.

"The writing's a good thing," he added, voice husky with desire. His hands eased the tank top over her head. "It's not fun, exactly, but good to do."

Ava nodded, twisting her arm backward to undo her bra. Cole pulled it slowly down her shoulders, his eyes half-lidded as he talked.

"Although Dad and I aren't really talking to each other yet..."

The curves of her breasts were exposed and she shrugged the bra off. Cole's mouth moved in hungrily to capture one of her nipples in his mouth, Ava's hands tightening in his hair. He paused, lifting his face to look at her, fingers taking the place of his mouth.

"It's still progress..." Cole said, "even if we're just answering questions in the same room."

Ava made a soft mewling sound and he laughed quietly.

"But it's still a start..." she panted.

Then Cole leaned toward her, his mouth slanting hard against her lips, the book of stories forgotten on the bed.

Chapter 11: First Volley

Ava waited in her truck, glancing at her watch. Frank and Cole were seventeen minutes late. That had never happened before. She watched the door, a wrinkle of concern etched between her eyebrows.

'C'mon guys...' her mind repeated. *'Get out of there...'*

Something bad must had happened. Ava was sure of it.

With a bang, the door of the office building swung open, the glass panels shuddering from the impact. Frank Thomas stormed onto the sidewalk. His face was purple with rage, hands balled at his side, stance wide and angry as he stomped toward his vehicle. Ava considered calling out to him; one look at his scowl changed her mind.

Ava waited until he climbed into his SUV, driving away with a screech of tires before she stepped out of her own truck. She headed through the door of the therapist's office, pausing for a moment on the nameplate: *Dr. M. Langden, LCSW*. A grey-haired secretary sat inside at a desk, typing away at a computer keyboard. There was no one else in the waiting room, but she could hear shouting at a distance.

Ava felt a nervous twinge. The sound bothered her.

'Cole...?'

Stepping to the desk, Ava waited until the woman stopped typing, her grandmotherly face breaking into a patient smile.

"Hullo, dear. What can I do for you?" the woman asked cheerily.

"Uh... hi. I'm Cole Thomas's girlfriend," she answered apprehensively. "Has he left yet?"

Ava glanced at the clock on the wall. Cole was now twenty minutes late. The woman smiled benignly, motioning Ava to take a seat.

"I'm sure he'll be along shortly," the woman replied. "He's still in his session, far's I know."

Ava shifted from foot to foot.

"But he's supposed to be done already," she said. "Like twenty minutes ago."

The woman paused her typing for a moment and looked back up at Ava.

"Yes," she said patiently. "Tha's right."

"But he's not."

"No, dear. Not today."

Somewhere, Ava heard another shout. This time she was sure it was Cole. 'Shit!' Peeking into the hallway, Ava took half a step forward. The elderly secretary rose to her feet.

"Oh I don't think so," the woman said. She was calm but there was steel under the velvet.

"Look," Ava argued. "I really just need—"

"You will sit yourself down, dearie, and WAIT!" the woman ordered, pointing again to the chairs.

Shaking her head, Ava headed back to her truck, swearing under her breath.

: : : : : : : : : :

Cole didn't come out for another twenty-three minutes, by which time Ava had chewed her thumbnail down to the quick. Her heart was in her throat as the door of the building opened and Cole stumbled out. He was pale and sweaty, hair dishevelled, his coat unbuttoned. Ava blanched; he looked years older than when he'd gone in. The change shocked her. She watched him wend his way to her truck, face haggard. He wrenched open the door, slumping as he sat.

"Oh my god," she said, "are you okay?"

Cole shook his head.

"No," he choked.

She put her hand against his arm.

"I'm so sorry, Cole."

Cole laughed sadly, his hand coming up to lay overtop hers.

"It's okay," he muttered, eyes closing. "Just give me a sec."

Ava nodded, watching him struggle for control.

"Cole, I came into the office when your Dad left," Ava said quietly. "I, uh... I heard you."

He released a whistling breath, fingers tightening around hers.

"Yeah." His lips twisted in disgust. "Today Marta wanted me to, um... not just answer questions, but... participate with Dad. Insisted I tell him when I didn't agree with what he'd said."

Ava swallowed with a dry throat.

"He didn't take that well?"

Cole laughed, angry and bitter.

"Let's just say that his version of events didn't match mine in the least. He, uh… got right down to business today. Told me I was dead wrong," Cole sneered. "That didn't go over well."

Ava slid across the bench seat, her hand staying atop his, unwilling to break the contact. She put her face against his cheek.

"Want to talk about it?"

There was a pause before he answered.

"Yeah, sometime, Ava." He took a slow breath. "I do… and I will… but not yet, okay?" When he turned to look at her, he was smiling, but it was hard-won, his eyes dark and stormy. "I just… I can't right now."

She nodded, letting go so that she could wrap her arms around his chest tightly, the bits and pieces of Cole's story starting to pick away at her own self-control. For a moment she flashed to Frank's expression as he left the office, face mottled. Ava's heart pounded furiously, temper rising.

Cole deserved to be treated better than that.

: : : : : : : : : :

When they reached the driveway, Cole stepped out of the truck, pulling up the zipper of his coat and heading away from the house.

"Cole…?" Ava called.

He hadn't spoken on the drive back and that worried her. He hadn't pulled away like this in weeks; tonight he was somewhere else entirely. She shoved her keys into her pocket, slamming the door and following him.

"I've got to blow off some steam," he muttered, heading out into the wind. "I'm just going down to the beach to walk for a bit."

Ava jogged to his side, hand going to his arm.

"Can I come?"

He shook his head, his lips grim. His eyes were on the horizon as if watching for a storm.

"Please, just let me go, Ava."

His tone was sharp and angry, and she stepped back, giving him space.

"Oh… okay."

He gave her a weak smile, raising his hand.

"I'll be back soon, alright? Wait up for me." He took a single step, then turned around. "I will come back," he repeated. "Promise."

Ava nodded silently, watching him walk down to the beach, his hands shoved deep in his pockets. Her jaw clenched as she headed into the house. Frank Thomas was going to get a piece of her mind.

: : : : : : : : : :

He was in the den, a glass of whiskey in hand, static coming from the television. Ava paused in the doorway, her father's voice warning her to let herself calm down before she went in. But she didn't care anymore.

'Cole's trying…' a voice inside her roared, *'it's Frank who's being an asshole about this…'*

She stormed in without knocking, throwing herself down into the chair opposite him, waiting until he looked at her. He was no longer angry; his face was despondent and distant. Ava didn't care. She was pissed, and he was going to know it.

"You hear it?" he asked, lifting the tumbler to his lips. His eyes were half-closed, alcohol mixing with melancholy.

"No, I don't," she snarled, words cold.

His expression changed at her answer. She, of course, knew exactly what he was listening for. Those children were long gone... both of them... and his grown son had been forgotten in return.

Frank sat up, frowning.

"What're you doing here, Ava?" he grumbled.

"I could ask you the same thing."

He scowled, gesturing to the television.

"You know what I'm doing..." he muttered, his lips a hard line. *"Listening."*

Ava shook her head angrily.

"No," she snapped, "you're not. You're sitting here, hidden in this…" she nodded to the room, "…this goddamn *tomb* while your son is outside, hurting!" She glared at him, aiming her words to cut. "Cole's alive, Frank. He deserves your time, not her!"

There were a few seconds of silence before he pointed to the door.

"Get out!"

It was the sound of a man used to giving orders and being obeyed. Ava crossed her arms, leaning forward.

"No!" she snapped. Across from her, Frank's eyebrows rose in shock. "You really have no idea what it's like for him, do you?" she continued.

He recoiled as if he'd been slapped.

"Don't you talk to me about my son!" he growled, banging the glass down on the table, amber liquid sloshing over the edge. "You know NOTHING about this family!"

Ava laughed bitterly, voice rising to match his.

"I know a hell of a lot more than you give me credit for."

"Out!" he ordered again, but Ava just laid into him, her words fast and furious.

"You really have no idea what it was like to grow up with Hanna as a perfect fucking ideal that Cole could never, EVER live up to!"

"Don't you DARE!" Frank bellowed, rising from the chair like a shark from the depths, enraged and ready to attack. Ava stood at the same time. He loomed over her, but she wouldn't step back.

"I will dare," she hissed. "Cole is doing this because he wants to fix things with you. He WANTS to get to know you. Can you honestly say you want the same thing?!"

She could see him breathing hard, fighting to control himself.

"So tell me, Frank," she said, voice lowering slightly, "what are you bringing to the table other than your grief?"

Cole's father said nothing, just stared at her. After a moment, he spun on his heel and walked out, leaving Ava alone with the sound of pouring rain and the ghostly echoes of children.

Chapter 12: Legacy

Nina was reading in bed when she heard Frank walking up the wide wooden stairs. There was something about the slow progress and heavy thud of his footsteps that peaked her concern. They'd been married almost a decade now. Little hints like the heaviness of his tread warned her that not everything had gone well this evening.

She'd known this would happen eventually.

With a sigh, she set down the copy of Gloriana's Torch on the bedside table, her fingers tucking a small copper bookmark into its heart, careful as always not to bend the pages. She had read this book more than once, but it soothed her, the epic descriptions of common people drawn into events beyond their control. Dreams and visions of the future guiding the grand events of the Spanish armada.

Nina didn't have a lot of use for the character of Queen Elizabeth, though perhaps, she thought, that was her own issue. She could, at times, see too much of herself in the queen's machinations. After the car accident, she'd had plenty of hours to contemplate that aspect of her character. She wasn't Frank's first wife; he'd been married when they'd met. Nina shook her head at the thought. *'Too much time to think about my own role in the Thomas family's misadventures...'* her mind prompted. Lately she rather fancied herself more in the behaviour of David Beckett, adventurer and soldier. He was a commoner who worked for the greater good. He saw the truth in his dreams, and believed.

She ran her fingers over the worn dust cover, her mind pulled like a snare back to the constant fight hidden in the walls of this house, the thing between Frank and Cole that would not rest. She could feel – much as Beckett had – the danger ahead, the damage about to break free. She wanted to be strong enough to help them, but she was tangled up in it too, and she wasn't sure she'd be able to do much. But now they had Ava; that thought left her smiling. Frank's voice wasn't the only one she'd heard raised downstairs in the den. The girl, with her strength of character and quick temper, would fight to the death for Cole. Nina had known that months ago.

Outside, the slow steps reached the landing, and Nina knew that Frank was pausing outside the door. She could imagine him pulling himself together, the mask coming down. She waited, eyes on the wooden panel for the moment he would walk in.

He cleared his throat and the door swung open. Frank looked tired, but his eyes brightened when he saw her.

"I thought you were already asleep," he said with surprise.

She smiled, reaching out as he crossed the room.

"No," she said smiling, "just reading. I slept most the afternoon, but the migraine's gone now. Feeling better."

"Glad to hear it," he said, taking her hand and dropping a kiss on her forehead like she was a little girl.

He settled himself down next to her, running his thumbs against her double wedding rings, spinning the heavy bands inset with stones again and again on her finger. It reminded Nina of her grandmother. The way she'd carried her rosary beads with her, praying in silence at random times during the day, almost an afterthought after so many years of practise.

For a moment, a line from the book she'd been reading came to mind: *'The gods too had rivalries and enmities...'* Her grandmother prayed for sins long-since forgotten by everyone but her. In the last few years, Nina had come to understand that need. Across from her, Frank's fingers twisted the ring, and she wondered if he was doing the same.

They *all* had sins.

"Cole's out walking," Nina said quietly.

Sound carried in the big house. She'd heard Frank return alone, heading to his den to wander the darkened halls of the past. Ava and Cole arrived half an hour later, though only one set of footsteps had come in through the front door. She knew Cole would be down on the beach now, walking the way he always did when his father's words became too much for him to bear.

The two of them had fought.

"Yes, he is," Frank growled, his face darkening. Nina sighed.

"What was it today?" she asked out of habit, not sure she really wanted to know. "What did he say?"

She knew the question could be flipped. Frank was easily the one who might have started this, but she had learned to handle her husband's temper in their years together. Careful phrasing was the first step. Patience was the second.

Frank lifted his gaze from her thin hands to her face. His knuckles brushed lightly over the papery skin before dropping back to her fingers, wrapping them in warmth.

"Dr. Langden wanted us to talk about Angela."

He didn't hold her eyes when he said it, his gaze wandering to a picture near of his first wife with their children which hung near the door. The four of them together: Hanna, her mother's image, Cole, Frank. Nina had never removed it – *never felt the need* – but she felt her rival's gaze on her tonight. It bothered her.

"Well, Frank," she said, sitting up tall, "that's probably a good place to start. You and Cole do have some issues revolving around her."

"Harrumph," he grumbled, face turning to the side. He hadn't let go of her hands, but he'd stopped fidgeting with her rings.

"You didn't want to share that?" she prompted.

He turned to her, heavy eyebrows drawn together in frustration.

"What's the point of it, Nina?" he sighed. "What's done is done. Open up all those old wounds and Cole and I are right back where we were when Angela died. Yelling at one another and... and..."

He stopped himself, though Nina knew the next word was fighting. She had been there at the graveyard that day. She could remember seventeen-year old Cole in the backseat of the hearse, his cheek purpled and swelling, sitting silently as they'd driven back to a home he now despised.

She cringed in remembrance. (She'd played a part in those events too.) When Frank didn't go on, she pulled her hands from his, straightening the bed linens and smoothing her nightshirt (as if this gesture could straighten everything else undone too). Nina felt like she'd faded since the accident in the fall, like the brush with death had brought everything too close to the surface.

Tonight was no different.

"It all started with Hanna's death," Frank muttered.

Nina paused for a moment, wavering. The easy thing to do here was to agree with him... but there was a young woman downstairs right now who'd stood up to him, and that gave her the nerve to say it.

"No, it didn't," she said firmly. "There were issues long before Hanna died. You know that as well as I do."

Frank's head bobbed up, eyes sparkling with indignation. She felt a twinge of guilt. Looking the way she did right now – still wan and tired from the migraine, dressed for bed and settled in the covers – he wouldn't argue with her. In a way, it gave her an unfair advantage.

One she intended to use.

"I don't... I don't know what you mean by that," he mumbled, his face becoming wary and distant. It reminded her of his son.

She smiled, weaving her fingers into his, raising an eyebrow in disbelief.

"You and I were far more than just friends before Hanna passed away," she said quietly.

"Yes, well," Frank stammered, glancing back to the photo of his ex-wife for a moment, then to Nina, as if worried she would somehow overhear, "Angela never knew about that, Nina. I mean she suspected you and I were more than just friends but—"

It struck her that Frank – a veteran – was blushing. Her fingers tightened on his, pushing his denials aside.

"Even Hanna knew about us, Frank."

She watched as he closed his eyes, his face warring with pain and grief. His daughter's memory was preserved unsullied like her upstairs bedroom, the one with the pressed sheets and lines of school awards, still waiting for her return. Frank swallowed hard, throat bobbing, before he spoke again.

"You don't know that she did for sure," he retorted, voice wavering. "Hanna, she... she thought something was going on, but she never really knew for sure. I never said anything about it to her."

Nina's heart thumped painfully hard, the muted pain in her temple beginning to pulse in time to it. This was difficult for Frank... anything to do with Hanna was... but it needed to be said.

"She *did* know," she insisted.

"No, she couldn't have."

"Yes, Frank," she repeated, nodding. "She could and she did."

"No!" he barked.

It was a command. Nina felt the admission resting on the tip of her tongue, ready to disappear under his words. She'd spent a decade in the hazy fog of almost truth.

That stopped today.

"Yes," she said flatly. Frank's mouth opened to argue, but she pushed on, finally saying what she'd denied for so long. "She came to my apartment and confronted me once. Hanna was a senior in high school then: all teen bravado and indignation." She leaned back against the pillows, sighing tiredly. "God, she was so much like you, then... the same exact temper. Furious with me – the other woman." She laughed . "She stood up for Angela." Her voice wavered. "That girl of seventeen shamed me."

Frank stared at her, wide-eyed, cheeks ashen.

"That's why you left that summer." His voice was incredulous; this had never occurred to him before.

She picked up the corner of the embroidered sheet, fiddling with the hem.

"Well, part of it anyhow," Nina said with a weary laugh, "France was nice too. But the truth is, I needed to get away, to think about things... to decide what I wanted to do about you... and us."

Frank reached for her fingers, his hands around hers once more.

"I'm glad you came back."

She nodded.

"I am too."

For a moment, Frank's gaze rested on the framed picture with Angela and the children. Something dark churned under the surface of his expression, his voice breaking when it finally returned.

"Hanna knew," he said quietly. "Why didn't you tell me that she'd talked to you? I never realized..."

Nina shook her head, throat tight. She didn't know all of the reasons; perhaps there was more to her in Elizabeth's manipulations than she wanted to admit. Once, long ago, she'd been good at reasoning the balance of carefully slanted facts and half-truths, dealing them out carefully like a miser's coins. *'Frank's not happy in his marriage... they've already separated twice... Angela had an affair before he did... it's a marriage in name, nothing else...'*

Now they all felt like lies.

"At first, it was because you and I were... apart." She said cautiously. "Later, when Hanna died and things got bad with Angela, it just seemed unnecessary." She cleared her throat. "And then... and then Angela took her life, and I just... I didn't know how to tell you."

"Oh, Nina," he choked, but she kept speaking.

"Lately with these issues with Cole, and the things you are talking about, I just thought I should say it. Get it out in the open."

Frank's fingers had gone back to the golden bands on her finger. He stared down at their joined fists, crumpling under the weight of her admission like a sail without wind.

"Sorry," she whispered. "I should have told you long ago."

The words lingered between them, only the steady spinning of the wedding rings continuing. With a heavy sigh, Frank looked at her, his face defeated.

"You're not the only one with secrets, Nina. You know that."

She smiled sadly, nodding.

"You need to tell Cole what happened with Angela."

All of Frank's rage was abruptly present on his face. His hands dropped away, pulling back into fists.

"No!" he growled. "I don't think I– …I can't—" he stammered, face growing red. This had never been an easy topic for either of them.

"Yes, Frank," she repeated, reaching out to touch his knee. "You have to."

He stood, anger roiling around him like thunder clouds. He stormed across the floor and didn't look back.

"You can't keep running from this!" Nina shouted, but he was already slamming the bedroom door behind him.

On the wall, the picture of his first wife and her two children shuddered, then stilled once more in its frame. Angela smiled on, indifferent to the family drama. This had always been her house after all.

: : : : : : : : : :

Half an hour later, Frank Thomas was in his den, the television now silent.

He'd wandered the house since his argument with Nina, unsettled and outraged. He stood in front of the wall of framed photographs which documented the early years of his marriage to

Angela Draper and before that, to his parents and grandparents as they passed through the generations. There was a picture of young Angela, her head tipped back in laughter, looking much as she did when they'd first met, long waves of fair hair and a wide smile.

His gaze was trapped by this picture, snared the same way he'd been when he'd first met her.

'I was so in love…'

There were times, like tonight, when it was harder to remember her laughter. During the long years between then and now, he'd tried to focus on remembering her like this, but he wondered if he'd been wrong to do that. He reached out, his fingers hesitantly touching the cool glass in the frame, wondering what she'd say if she could see him. But Angela had died years earlier, and tonight her voice – either in joy or in pain – seemed far, far away.

Frank pulled his hand back, his eyes on the open 'o' of her mouth, the crinkled joy in her half-closed eyes.

"We were happy once," he said to the empty room, then turned and walked away.

Chapter 13: Ripples Moving Back

Ava was in the shower, her body shaking with post-adrenaline jitters. The confrontation with Cole's father left her feeling the same giddiness she'd once gotten after a close call with the police. She let the hot water sluice over her skin, surrounding her in a bubble of heat and noise. Soothing her.

Her eyes drifted closed; a vague image, hazy like the mist filling the bathroom, floated in the back of her mind. It was a dream she'd had, or a book she'd once read. She couldn't quite remember when…

She'd been huddled on the docks for hours when he found her. Unlike her mother and sisters, Thomas knew she came here, and she knew he knew this… The sound of his footsteps had her heart quickening in anticipation.

"Your mam will tan your hide if you don't get home before nightfall, y'know."

His voice came from the distance, warm with hinted laughter, despite the warning.

"Mother can go right ahead and try," she muttered sullenly, voice half hidden by her woollen cloak . "I would rather sit…"

Ava was pulled from her reverie by the sound of the bathroom door opening. She peeked past the curtain in concern, catching sight of Cole pulling off his clothes, kicking them into the corner. He had dark circles under his eyes, the tip of his nose red, fingertips purple, the rest of his skin muted by the cold.

"You're back," Ava said in surprise.

The last time he'd taken off, he'd been gone for hours. He'd hardly been gone forty minutes tonight. Cole shrugged sheepishly.

"Sorry I couldn't talk to you right away," he said bashfully. "I know I should've tried, but I just was so fucking mad, and that always kind of freaks you out."

She nodded. What he'd said was true. It was that aspect of his personality that unnerved her, though getting to know Frank Thomas had certainly put Cole's anger into perspective. Undressed and shivering, Cole pulled back the curtain, letting in a blast of cold air as he climbed into the shower with her.

"I'm glad you're here," Ava said, moving sideways to give Cole room under the stream of water.

"Me too."

He pulled her into his arms. Cole's skin was icy from the winter air, his fingers clammy and cold. He burrowed his face against her neck, warming him while chilling her, the water pouring over them both. Her arms were tight around him. She was surprised he was back with her now, not quite sure what to make of it. But Cole had been trying lately, rather than shutting down altogether, and that made her chest ache with love for him.

She waited in silence, letting Cole's chilled hands, the thrum of the water, the white noise of the shower tow her back into a hazy lull. The almost-memory was there, waiting in the clouds.

Thomas' laughter echoed from the fog as he approached, and for the first time in hours, Ava smiled, despite her dark mood. She couldn't see him through the rain, but his tread she'd know anywhere.

His footsteps turned hollow as he reached the dock. Ava turned, slipping back her hood to look over her shoulder. The sound of steps hinted at his nearness as Thomas came through the soggy blanket of mist, appearing by degrees. First a dark blue shadow, then lighter, then finally just him, smiling down at her despite the bedraggled sight she knew she must be.

He reached her side, dropping nimbly beside her. He was just far enough away to be appropriate, though the thought of that infuriated her. She wanted more.

"You've got everyone worried, Ava," he said quietly. He was staring ahead, looking out over the wrinkled black sheet of the sea, the white crescents rising and falling with each gust. "You've got to go back now. Fight with your mam or no."

Ava shook her head, turning to stare out at the ocean with him. She was glad it was still raining. He wouldn't be able to see she'd been crying .

"If I go home, she'll want to know..."

Cole's hands began to roam her body, leaving Ava's skin rising in gooseflesh under his fingertips. Despite the heat of the shower, a chill had settled into her body, cold leeching into her core. Cole's mouth dropped against the white column of her neck, his hands running up her ribs to cup her breasts.

She shivered, mind drifting again…

The icy hand of rain had soaked through the cloak, chilling her.

"What exactly does your mam want to know?" he asked.

Ava glanced at him furtively from under rain-dampened lashes.

"My answer to Jon," she said quietly.

Thomas knew Jon had asked her, of course. That was no secret. But he didn't know she'd considered it. He turned, moving forward (nearing that space he never entered). Perhaps it was to hear her better, perhaps (she hoped) it was because it bothered him.

"What of it?" he asked. "What answer did you give?" There was a blunt desperation to his question, the joking tone gone.

He'd asked for her hand in marriage too. And she'd waited, so far...

Cole pressed her up against the wall of the shower, his fingers touching her everywhere at once. The cold tiles behind her meshed with the icy pall of his skin, the water from the faucet cooling as the shower lingered on. Cole's mouth was the only point of warmth, and Ava gasped as he dropped lower, tugging one nipple into his mouth, his hands sliding over slick skin.

"I told him I would consider his offer," she answered.

"Consider it?" There was indignation in every line of his face. His hands reached out, taking her by the arms and dragging her forward. "You promised ME!"

The accusation was a lash against bare skin.

"I HAD to!" she yelped. "My mother KNEW he asked me! She... she... insisted I think of things. Think of the future of my sisters and—"

"And what of OUR future?"

His eyes were wild and panicked, another lash of the whip. Thomas had spent every spare hour the last four months working endless odd jobs, trying to save money for passage to America. There, he said, they could start again. It would be their beginning. There it wouldn't matter that they had not a single haypenny between them.

"I... I cannot WAIT any longer!" she cried.

His hands were tight around her arms, holding her in place. Shackling her.

"What of how you FEEL, Ava? What of that?"

"It does not matter what I feel!" she sobbed. "Not when we cannot—"

"It does!" he interrupted. "Does he make you feel like I do? Do you love Jon like you love me?"

"Thomas, please."

He pulled her forward, his mouth angling nearer.

"You tell me THIS doesn't matter," he growled.

Ava moaned as the sensation of his mouth against her breast became too sharp, pain mingling with pleasure. She let her head thud against the wall, her body quaking under each brush of his fingers over her hip, between her thighs.

"Please," she gasped, her mind still caught on the ghostly-memory of sitting in the rain, Cole's mouth overtop hers.

At her plea, he released her nipple, sliding up against her, fingers threading into her wet hair. Her chest was tight with something… throat aching. The room was almost white with steam, his face hazy as he reached her lips.

"Please what?" he whispered, his hips against hers, leaning closer.

She wrapped her arms over his shoulders.

"Kiss me like you mean it."

Suddenly Thomas was kissing her, his mouth hard against her lips. Gone were the chaste summer kisses in the lane behind the church. These were wanton and needful, a man's kisses, not a boy's. Ava gaped in shock. In a second his tongue was pushing into her mouth, dipping in to taste her, his fingers sliding into her hair, shoving back the cowl of the cloak in his haste. The rain against both their faces.

The sound of the shower pounded like the rain, heat slowly spreading between them. His mouth was against her, kissing her breath away. Their teeth and tongues were rough as they came together, need burning away the last of the chill. They were both out of breath when Cole pulled back, his teeth grazing the edge of her jaw, biting her skin and then suckling her earlobe.

"Love you, Ava," Cole growled, his mouth hovering above the shell of her ear. "Always…"

"Love you too," she panted.

In the last minutes, his fingers had finally warmed, lighting a path of fire where they touched her. He slid his hands underneath her, pinning her against the wall. Scrabbling for purchase, Ava hitched a leg over his hip as his body held her in place, connection nearing.

"Tell me what you want," Cole growled against her open lips, punctuating his words with kisses.

She moaned in response. She could feel the heat of his body pressing against her, close but not joined.

"Tell me," he insisted, kissing her, then pulling back to look at her. "I want to hear it."

In the steam of the shower, his hair looked longer, flattened against his face like a cap. A wave of déjà vu had risen inside her, leaving her trembling, but not with cold.

"I… I want you," she whispered.

The kiss was reckless and rough, months of suppressed desires suddenly released. Ava found herself moving into it – every hissed warning by her mother forgotten in an onslaught of need. She ran eager hands over his shoulders, the sodden cloak

*wrapping half over him as he tugged her onto his lap on the dock.
She wouldn't think anymore. Wouldn't decide. She would just let
herself feel... to follow her heart this time and nothing else. Even
the rain no longer felt so cold.*

'Not with Cole here...'

*She blinked in confusion. For a moment it seemed that she
was somewhere else entirely, and then the feeling was gone. This
was Thomas – 'my Thomas' – and he was kissing her – really
kissing her – for the first time. He stroked her face, his eyes intent
on hers, his gaze holding her in place.*

"Tell me what you want of me, Ava," he said.

*Again the sensation rose inside her, that feeling that he'd
said exactly this sometime before. She took a shaking breath,
feeling everything – the rain, his body against her, her mother
waiting at home, furious – all poised on this moment. Like a single
drop of water poised atop a blade's edge, able to go one way or
the other, the moment shifted slightly. The decision changed.*

"I... I want you."

: : : : : : : : : :

They lay tangled in sheets, the steady patter of the rain
outside wrapping them in a staticky buzz. Ava's face was against
Cole's chest, listening to the steady thump. She ran a nervous
hand up his ribs, pausing atop his heart. She should tell him.

"I uh... I should probably let you know I had a bit of a
disagreement with your dad tonight," she said timidly.

"You what?" Cole asked, his voice disbelieving.

"I kind of..." her voice dropped, "told him off."

Cole did nothing at all, his whole body waiting silent, and then suddenly he was laughing raucously. Ava felt him shaking with mirth, the sound leaving her smiling.

"So, uh… that's okay with you then?" Ava asked, shifting to prop herself next to him on the pillow.

"Marta keeps telling me I have to start standing up for myself. So I certainly can't hold it against you."

Ava nodded, tipping her face toward him, but he didn't kiss her right away. He ran his fingers over her face, tracing her features the way he'd done when sculpting her, expression solemn.

"I love you, Ava," he said, the palm of his hand resting against the curve of her chin.

She nodded.

"Love you too," she answered, leaning her cheek into his hand. "I'm really glad you're starting to talk to your dad. Even if it means yelling."

Cole nodded, a pained look passing across his features like a cloud blocking the sun.

"We were talking about the time before Hanna died," Cole began, his voice growing quiet, "Dad was giving the same old line about everything being great... just bullshit, all of it! This time though... this time I just called him on it. Told him I didn't agree. That he hadn't been there enough to even know."

Cole's arms curled around Ava, his face next to her ear, leaning against her as he talked.

"Dad just kind of freaked out. Refused to hear it. I told him how Mom used to be. About the way she was when he was gone… about her staying in bed all day, crying all the time, not being able to function. And then," his voice broke, "Marta brought up the term 'clinical depression' and Dad just flipped. He started yelling, like totally lost it! He stormed out of the office. God, Ava, I was so upset. Marta wanted me to talk to her... about what had happened with Dad and I tried, but I was so fucking angry. I was yelling too."

His words disappeared and he turned his face against her hair. Ava felt his sobs. It was like his chest was ticking as the sound tried to burst out.

"Shh..." she whispered, hands running up and down his back, face next to his. "It's okay. You did good, Cole. I'm proud of you. Love you."

After a minute, his breathing returned to normal. He rubbed his face with one hand, eyes red.

"You're pretty awesome, you know?" he said roughly.

Ava smiled, laying down against him once more, sleep tugging at her senses.

"Together, we're pretty awesome," she answered, lids dropping closed.

Chapter 14: Messenger

Cole's dream started as it always did: he sat next to her body, seconds before her death.

"I love you, Ava," he gasped. "I have always loved you... I always will."

She didn't answer, of course; that wasn't part of the dream. Cole waited for the moment, his gaze on the slant of sunlight in her eyes, like a clear stream slowly dulling with silt. Ava lay still and cold, the shallow rise and fall of her chest slowing with each breath, her hand icy despite the growing warmth of the day. As he watched (as he always did), her eyes dilated outward until they were no longer blue but black, unseeing.

"No... please, god, no..." he cried. "Don't leave me."

Sobs heaved from his chest, the ache spreading inside him until pain was all he was. He had no shell any longer, nothing to hold back the deluge that drowned him where he knelt. She was gone from him. Lost forever.

"Hullo...?"

The voice came from the distant trees. Cole's face bobbed up at the sound. He'd never dreamt that before. A lone figure appeared in the haze of blue shadows, like a diver slowly rising from the depths. It was a woman coming from further up the beach, her steps slow and steady.

She cupped her hand around her mouth and called out to him as she reached the tree line.

"D'you need some help there?"

Cole sat up, wiping his face with his hands, his heart hammering against the walls of his chest. There was something about the woman's build, her fair hair – brown on top, but sun-bleached caramel at the bottom of her braid – and her gait as she walked, half-hidden in the shadows of the canopy that had his chest tightening with anticipation.

"Can I bring you some help?" the woman called.

'It can't be...'

"Can she be moved?" she asked, louder now. "There are others up the beach. I could get some'un to help you."

Cole laid Ava's hand back against her chest with trembling fingers. He climbed shakily to his feet, his voice breaking with grief and hope.

"There's no point," he managed to answer. "She's already gone."

The woman stepped forward, her appearance leaving no room for doubt.

'Hanna...' He'd never dreamt this before. She was new and it terrified him.

She walked toward him, her eyes on Ava's stilled form. As she neared, she lifted her eyes to Cole, the expression so exactly his sister it nearly took him to his knees. It was Hanna Thomas as she'd been in life, the light humour and joy in her features so right that it left his throat aching with tears.

"You came back," he croaked, eyes brimming with tears of grief for Ava, and joy for his sister's return. It made no sense, but she was here. She was alive.

The woman's face rippled in confusion. She glanced over her shoulder as if expecting someone else to be there. When she turned back, she gave him a sympathetic smile.

"Others survived," she said, her brogue the only difference to his sister's voice. "They're up there on the beach now."

She offered her open palm and Cole reached out unsteadily for his sister's hand. She closed her fingers around his hand, squeezing three times. *'I love you…'* Cole opened his mouth to speak, but only a sob came out.

"You're not alone," she said gently, pulling him away from Ava, her fingers tight around his. "There are others who've made it to the shore. Come…"

: : : : : : : : : :

Ava floated above the field, watching the three figures: two standing, one laying, unmoving, on the ground. The snake and the coins were visible below her, the curve of the river echoing with Delft blue, Davy's green in the swirl of the sea grass. As she watched, two of the figures turned and walked down the beach, leaving her – in the air, on the grass – alone.

'Wait for me!' she called. *'Wait!'*

But her cry was only the wind, her voice lost in the calling of sea birds in the sky.

: : : : : : : : : :

Ava woke alone in the charcoal hues of pre-dawn, the bed beside her empty and cold. The room was dimly lit with greenish light coming from the window that overlooked the ocean. Within the window frame there was a silhouette.

"Cole…?"

His shadow turned toward her, but didn't leave his place.

"Sorry," he answered. "I didn't mean to wake you."

Ava squinted, unnerved by his voice. His voice was slightly different. Thicker somehow, like he'd been coughing or crying.

"Cole," she called hesitantly. "Is something wrong?"

He laughed (or sobbed,) she couldn't tell, not without seeing his face. He turned back to the window, putting his hand against the pane. Staring out into the slow bloom of dawn.

"I dreamt about her," he said brokenly. *'Crying then,'* her mind observed.

"About?"

"About Hanna," he said, leaning in to the window. Ava realized he was looking out to the cliffs far beyond the beach, where Hanna had defied death by jumping, and Cole had waited for her at the bottom. "I… I haven't dreamed about her once… not once… since she died." He shuddered, his forehead pressing against the pane. "But I dreamed of her tonight."

Ava slid under the sheets, soft warmth giving way to crisp cold. She took hesitant steps across the room. When she reached the window, Cole dropped a hand down from the glass, reaching out for her with chilled fingers. As with the night before, a hint of memory, hidden in the dark waters of her mind, slid toward the light, like a fish about to surface, fading before she could get a glimpse of what it was. This moment was too pressing, Cole's pain too sharp.

"What did you dream?"

This close, she could see his expression. A smile flickered at the edges of his lips.

"I dreamed of the field after the storm." He gazed at her, then back to his vigil at the window. "I dreamed of the snake and the coins."

Ava felt the other sense tug once more, moving closer to the shallows of her conscious mind. Her eyebrows pulled together in concentration as she following his line of sight to the seascape and the rocky peaks beyond. There'd been something she'd dreamed too, but every time she pulled it forward, it faded once more.

"My painting," she breathed.

Cole's fingers tightened around hers.

"The dream I had after Hanna died. The same one… but this time it didn't end."

Ava turned in shock, her hand slipping out of his fingers, rising in surprise.

"It didn't end?" she gasped. "But… but how?"

Cole's laughed tiredly.

"I dunno," he said with a shrug. "But usually it's the same: me on the grass, and you. But this time, instead of ending, there was more…"

Cole continued talking but Ava's mind skittered feverishly with the news. The thing under the water of her mind was very close. She could feel its scales, could run her hand over the shape of it, and she knew its name: Hanna Thomas.

She'd dreamed her too.

"…and she took my hand, Ava. She squeezed my fingers the way she did when we were kids." He took her hand and squeezing three times. "Then she told me it was going to be okay." Cole's voice broke, and though he didn't let go of her fingers, he turned again to the window. "And then she led me up the beach. I just knew… I knew it was all going to be all right."

"And me?" Ava asked. "Was I there?"

The muscle in his jaw began to jump at her question. After a moment's delay, he turned to meet her eyes.

"The rest of the dream was the same."

"Oh…"

Ava watched the breaking waves on the beach, the pale blue lines growing lighter as dawn neared. She could remember a part of her dream now, and it terrified her.

'He left ME behind this time!'

Ava's heart was pounding even before she spoke. She knew how Cole felt about these things, but it had to be said.

"Cole, I… I want you to let Dad read your teacup sometime."

He made a strangled noise, turning completely from the window, letting go of her hand.

"Uh-uh, no way."

"Why not?"

He paused for a moment, crossing his arms and then uncrossing them again, as if realizing what he'd done. He was either on edge or annoyed. Outside, the first rays of light reached the horizon, bright crimson spreading out under purple clouds that covering the sky.

"Look," he said, running his fingers along her arm, "I just have a hard time believing that stuff. Last time when he read your teacup, it was just kind of... messed up."

Ava put her hands on her hips.

"Well if you don't believe it, then what's the problem?" There was aggravation threaded through her tone as much as persuasion.

"Last time was just a little much," Cole answered , his hands settling atop her shoulders as he moved away from the window.

"But you don't believe it," she grumbled, glaring at him. "So why not?"

"It's just too weird."

"But Cole..." Ava started, "if something's changed, then I want to know what. I want to know how that happened!"

Cole tipped up her chin so she looked at him.

"Yesterday was big for me, Ava. I finally told my Dad my side of things." He released a heavy sigh before continuing, "I've been trying to do that for years. It was fucked-up and awful, but it happened."

"I'm glad, but I still think—"

"No," Cole interrupted. "Look," he said, "It's probably just because of the things with my dad, and the things your father told me about. Mix it all together, my dreams have changed. Because things here..." he picked up her hand and placed it against his chest, "...are changing. So maybe my dreams are too."

"Maybe," Ava muttered, narrowing her eyes like she didn't quite believe him.

Cole's mouth twitched in amusement.

"Haven't sold you on a logical explanation yet?"

She rolled her eyes. Across the dark water, bands of gold and red light filled the sky, making the dark bedroom less ominous. She could see Cole's face clearer now, the anguish fading with the coming of day.

"I want Dad to read your teacup before he leaves for Europe."

"I'll talk to your Dad. No problem," Cole said. "But I am not letting him read my teacup."

Ava scowled petulantly.

"Yet," she added. Her voice was quiet, almost a whisper.

"What did you say?"

She shrugged, a hint of a smirk pulling up the corners of her mouth.

"Did you just say, 'yet'?" he asked, chuckling as he wrapped his arms around her.

"Maybe," she said, the admission muffled against his shoulder. This time, the smirk was definitely there.

Cole chuckled.

"Ava Brooks, you might just be the most stubborn person I've ever met."

"After you," she corrected.

Cole grinned, twisting around to tickle her ribs.

"Oh, you're going to pay for that."

With a shriek, the two of them ran back to bed.

: : : : : : : : : :

They woke to the sound of persistent knocking. It was late morning or very early afternoon, warm yellow light outlining the heavy curtains.

"Fuck!" Ava hissed. "I'm not dressed!"

She pulled the covers up to her chin so that only her face and the top of her head were visible. Cole stumbled out of bed. He searched his duffel bag for a pair of shorts.

"Hold on!" he called over his shoulder.

A few more steps and Cole pulled open the door. He was expecting Nina, but to his surprise, it was his father.

"Dad," Cole said, stepping back.

The older man looked exhausted this morning, the lines around his eyes more deeply etched.

"Yes, uh..." he said, clearing his throat. "Nina's feeling better this morning. She's making a big breakfast for us all. Sent me to get you both."

He waited awkwardly, not holding Cole's eyes, just staring at the floor. He was clearly uncomfortable in the role of messenger. Ava came to the rescue.

"Tell Nina we'll be right down," she called from the bed.

"Right then," Frank muttered, "I'll do that." Without a backward glance he made a hasty retreat down the stairs.

Cole pushed the door closed with a click, confusion colouring his features. Usually he and Frank just avoided each other after a fight; his father's appearance this morning had unsettled him.

"What the hell was that about?"

Ava grinned.

"I'd say that's your Dad making an effort."

Chapter 15: Wednesday's Child is full of Woe

February flew by even faster than its shortened calendar length would suggest. It wasn't long before Cole and Ava left Oliver at the airport, the two of them driving back to the city in the late-night lull of traffic. Ava drove the truck while Cole flipped through the radio stations. Neither was really talking; exhaustion had taken its toll. Instead, they sifted through the fractured channels of late-night talk radio, watching as the distant lights of the city began to near.

The green signs announcing the different multi-lane overpasses began to glow in the truck's headlamps. Catching sight of them, Ava aimed toward home. Cole would be sleeping in his dorm tonight; they had classes tomorrow morning, and they were both exhausted. (Both of them knew what would happen if he stayed at her place.) There was no rush now that her father was away on tour again, and both of them knew Cole would be spending more nights at her apartment than ever. For the first time since her father had said goodbye an hour earlier, she smiled. She was going to miss Oliver terribly, of course, but she liked having the apartment to herself.

Seeing the signs for the main thoroughfare toward the Eastern side of the city's downtown core, Ava moved to the far left lane. Space between the streetlights shortened as they neared the industrial area. Her mind, as she drove, was on her father. Oliver never had read Cole's teacup, though he'd offered twice. True to his word, Cole did talk about the dreams. Her father's take on the difference of the ending was simply that things changed... *they were always changing*. Things from the present were just as likely to change the past as the other way around. Her father's interpretation was that she and Cole's connection now was the deciding factor. Ava liked that explanation, though she selfishly wished that she'd been the one walking away with Cole, rather than his sister.

Cole might not have agreed with him, but they discussed it at length. (Ever the devil's advocate, Oliver argued that Cole's refusal to have a teacup read meant he was actually an agnostic, rather than atheist and Cole, undaunted, laughed it off.) Ava loved watching the two of them: Cole and her father had developed an easy-going relationship built on respect. The three of them had spent several afternoons together in 'their' coffee shop, arguing about books they'd read, ideas they had about life, and (of course) dreams.

Ava's eyes flickered to Cole where he sat next to her on the bench seat, his fingers tapping along to a remixed song on the radio, eyelids heavy. She was glad that he was here now. It was always hard, but she'd never felt her father's leaving with as much poignancy as she did this time. It could have been because university was ending, and at some point, she would be making choices about the next year. Or it could have been because this had been an amazing visit. Either way it hurt.

She followed the paths of the streets, heading back to the university and Cole's dorm, finally pulling into the lot. He kissed her hard – leaving her body throbbing with desire – and Ava reminded herself what a good idea it had been to drive him straight home. Neither one would have slept otherwise. She needed to go to the printing studio before class tomorrow to try to get ahead on the prints. She already had five of the ten completed – two dry point and three etchings – but true to Giulia's description of the project, the multi-print plates were hard to work with. There were several deeply-gouged lines from Ava's first inexperienced prints that had been fighting her attempts to remove them. Tomorrow she was going to switch to the mezzotint rocker and blacken the entire plate.

Once Cole was inside his dorm, (after a discussion of why he should be staying with her after all), she drove home through silent streets. It was after midnight; the apartment building and the hallway leading up seemed particularly barren. Reaching the door to the apartment, Ava's eyes drifted to the end of the hall and the fire escape. The gouged brick was sitting inside, door closed tight.

It made her sad.

She fought to get the keys in the lock, finally pushing the door open with her hip and stepping into the sunken foyer. It felt lonely, as if her father had taken 'home' with him when he'd gone. The decision to leave Cole behind at his dorm nagged at her. Sighing, Ava shrugged off her jacket and headed down the stairs, pausing as a pulsing blue light caught her gaze.

There was a single message flashing on her machine.

With an unexplained feeling of dread, Ava pressed the button. There was a high-pitched beep and a voice echoed on the other end of the line.

: : : : : : : : : :

Cole wasn't sure when he first noticed the difference, but sometime during the start of March, Ava became quiet and withdrawn. There were several times when he found her staring out the window during class, gone to the world. She jumped when he touched her, bringing her back to the present. He asked her about it, but she claimed that she was overwhelmed with her classes. Just had a lot on her mind, and that she missed her dad. Cole accepted that.

It made sense in the beginning.

It wasn't big things at first, just an ever-growing series of small alterations to her schedule that added up to something bigger. Cole was concerned in a way he couldn't explain. Like how she never usually smoked pot, but now, she almost always followed Chim out the back door of The Crown to toke up. How she claimed to be painting almost every night in her studio, but didn't want to share the images with him. That he didn't even know for sure that she was painting at all... because sometimes he drove by and the lights of the studio were all off.

These were the nights she wouldn't answer her phone. There were other things too. Like the way she rolled away from him after they made love, curling into a ball and falling into restless slumber.

Those kind of things.

It didn't seem to be school-related. Besides the printing project that was driving both of them crazy, Ava seemed to be doing fine. Cole's life had developed a stability it hadn't had in years. Nina's continuing attempts to encourage Cole and Frank to spend time together were paying off, and she and Ava had become close during their weekends together. Even the tension in the Thomas household didn't really seem to be much of an issue. Frank and Cole had taken definite steps toward reciprocation. It was a very slow process and there had been another blow up in the meantime. But they were starting to talk.

It was just Ava.

: : : : : : : : : :

He caught up to her as she was hoisting an overnight bag into the passenger seat of her truck. She was dressed in nicer clothing than usual: black slacks and a grey sweater. Her hair was curled, and she wore a smudge of makeup, though her face was wan, dark circles under reddened eyes. It was the clothing that tipped him off: the lack of jeans and leather jacket were a glaring red flag. Cole scowled as he approached, his hand closing the open door with a bang as he reached her truck. Ava jumped at the sound, blanching as she saw him.

"Is it Kip?" he asked, face furious.

There was no preamble. The two of them had danced around this long enough. Her last-minute cancellation of this weekend's trip to Frank and Nina's after doing exactly the same thing the previous weekend had been the final clue. Cole might be in love, but he was not stupid, and he knew he'd seen her truck headed out to the Coast the previous Saturday.

She was having an affair.

"Wh-what?" Ava asked, stepping back slightly. Cole followed, pressing into her space.

"You cancelled... again. I know what's going on. You're screwing around behind my back."

She blinked, eyes glancing to the side and then back to him, confused.

"I'm… I'm not," she said, voice breaking, "I just... I had something to do. I had a meeting about the National Galle—"

Cole laughed bitterly.

"That was the excuse last weekend, Ava! Get your fucking story straight!"

She gaped, her mouth opening, then closing like a fish out of water.

"There's nothing going on, Cole," she gasped, voice barely controlled.

"You're lying!"

She shook her head wordlessly. He stepped forward, a disgusted sneer twisting his face into a harder version of himself. A *meaner* version...

"Tell me, Ava," he hissed. "Do you think about him when we're together?"

For a moment he thought she was going to slap him, because her hand pulled back, but just as quickly, she dropped it, holding it in a fist at her side.

"How dare you!" she spat, breathing hard. "You jealous bast—"

"It IS him, isn't it!" Cole barked, stepping closer.

His hand snaked out, grabbing her wrist in a steely grip. He knew he should walk away, but his calm voice wasn't winning.

His chest was filled with the destructive power of a storm about to break.

"No!" she yelped, tugging away. She could have been talking about Kip, or perhaps she was angry about him manhandling her. Cole didn't know and didn't care.

"Yes," he growled, "it is Kip, isn't it?!"

"Fuck you."

Her eyes narrowed dangerously, stance widening. Cole laughed harshly, dragging her toward him, but she twisted in his grip and freed her arm. She'd tightened her fists until her knuckles were white.

"I saw you leaving the city last weekend!" Cole shouted. "Saw you, Ava!"

He turned away for a moment, because he was fighting the urge to slap her, and that he wouldn't do.

"You… You followed me?" she cried. Her eyes were wide, hurt. "How DARE you!"

She took another step backward, and the movement angered him more than was rational. His jaw clamped shut, the next words coming out in a hiss.

"I was out biking along the coast and I saw you, Ava! I fucking SAW you leaving town!" He laughed coldly. "Wrong direction if you were going to the National Gallery."

That gave her pause. She glanced down, brow furrowed. After a moment she looked up.

"I was out of town but I *wasn't* with Kip..." Her voice shook, face flushed with pain or anger. Cole was so incensed he couldn't tell.

"Kip Chambers has a place up the coast," Cole sneered. "I know that!"

She took another step away from him.

"I had to deal with some unexpected things. A family emergen—"

"You're LYING!" he snarled.

That stopped her.

"FUCK YOU, Cole!" she bellowed. "You don't know a goddamn THING about what's going on with me!"

Her voice was quaking and Cole pushed, wanting to be in her face. Needing her to know how much this hurt him! But the second he moved, she turned to walk away, and resistance was shredded under the riptide of his rage.

"No, fuck YOU, Ava!" His hand grabbed for her shoulder, spinning her around. "'Cause I know Kip Chambers has always had a thing for you and I—"

He saw her throw the punch and he had time to deflect most of the blow, but she still grazed his cheek. For a moment he was caught up in the sheer horror of what was happening: the two of them in a fight in the parking lot of her apartment. He stepped back, eyes widening.

"Don't you EVER fucking touch me again!" she screamed, her body shaking with pent-up emotion. Tears ran down her face, the sight of them shocking Cole into silence. She took a sobbing breath, pushing past him to the door of her truck. "I had to DEAL with things, alright! I DON'T have to explain ANYTHING to you!"

She was inside the cab seconds later, the door slamming shut. Cole watched, unable to answer; she pulled out of the lot, the tires spinning shards of gravel up behind her.

Gone.

: : : : : : : : : :

Cole didn't see her for the rest of the weekend, and he was glad.

She wasn't in class on Monday either. That made it easier.

Tuesday she was still missing.

On Wednesday afternoon, Professor Wilkins popped by the Printmaking class to ask Cole if he'd seen Ava. She hadn't been in class for a couple of days, and he wanted to know if she was interested in applying for a graduate curatorial program next year. He was so impressed by the way she considered art, he thought her unique spin on artists' work could be a real asset to her in a career as a curator. Wilkins left a flyer for Cole and asked that he get Ava to contact him.

That night Cole was concerned enough to go by her apartment and check, but there was no answer. Her truck wasn't in the lot. At that point, Cole went to find Chim.

She wasn't at the studio – hadn't been all week, it turned out – and Chim's anxiety caused Cole's fear to skyrocket. Suddenly he was admitting to the whole argument and his accusations. Marcus listened, hand on Cole's shoulder, assuring him she was probably okay, then immediately suggesting they start calling their friends while they checked out Ava's usual haunts. Suzanne was the first one who showed up to help them search. They were an hour into the process when they got their first lead.

Talking to the Crown's bartender, a heavy-set man named Mike, the trio discovered that Ava had been at bar yesterday afternoon. She'd been drinking heavily, refusing to talk. Mike gestured to one of the waitresses doing rounds. In minutes, the young woman was describing the incident, while the three of them stood listening. The waitress had just gotten to the part where Ava told her to put the bill onto her tab, when Cole's phone began to ring. He stepped to the side, glancing down at the number. It was the police station.

Cole took the call, his voice abnormally calm when he said hello.

"Hi there..." a chipper young woman said. Not Ava then. "Is this Cole Thomas?"

For a moment, a horrible image of Ava dead somewhere flashed into Cole's mind. It was the image from his dream, her eyes wide and black. Body broken.

"Yes..." he managed to force out. He couldn't go any further. At the table, Chim straightened up as he caught Cole's tone.

"Cole," the caller said, tone businesslike and practical, "this is Lieutenant Elizabeth Alvarez calling from the fourteenth precinct police station. I'm contacting you in regards to Miss Ava Brooks..."

Chapter 16: Extenuating Circumstances

The three of them drove down to the police station in Suzanne's older-model Mazda hatchback. The small vehicle was overloaded with their combined weight and she scraped it heavily on a cement block as she parked.

"Nice job," Chim said, winking at her. "Think we only lost half the bumper on that one, Suze. Want me to drive next time?"

"Better yet," Suzanne said cheerily, "you could get your lead ass out of my car, and then we wouldn't be over the weight restriction."

"Nice," Chim said, laughing, "very, very nice…"

The two of them continued joking while Cole stared forward blindly, waiting to bolt. Suzanne and Marcus seemed content that Ava had been found but Cole had none of their comfort. Once Chim climbed out of the car, releasing the seat so Cole could get out, he pushed past, heading straight into the building, not waiting for either of them.

Inside the main foyer, he gave his name and ID at the front desk, shuffling nervously as he waited to be called to the back. Cole had no idea what was going on other than Ava was alive, but stress now fought with relief and the residual effects of jealousy.

'Goddamn Kip Chambers!' his mind repeated

He was almost entirely sure that Kip and Ava had been caught tagging tonight… and since it hadn't been Ava who'd called him, he didn't know how she would react to him being here. His chest ached with a confusing mess of conflicted emotion. He needed to know she was okay, but he wasn't done being angry about the affair with Kip. The door opened, and Chim and Suzanne crossed the floor to his side.

"Any word on Ava?" Marcus asked.

Cole shook his head.

"Still waiting to be called in."

At the desk, the receptionist glanced up, motioning to the chairs behind them.

"Lieutenant Alvarez will be out as soon as she can. Feel free to grab a seat."

Cole didn't move until Chim took hold of his arm, steering him to the waiting area.

"C'mon, man," he said quietly. "You're not getting called any sooner by standing here lurking."

Cole nodded, allowing himself to be led. Suzanne sat on one side of him, Chim on the other, leaving Cole feeling like a child. Angela and his father had used the same tactic when he misbehaved. For a brief moment, he wondered what kind of parents Chim and Suzanne would be someday... good, he'd guess.

"Here," Suzanne said briskly, handing him a magazine. "Keep yourself busy."

Cole flipped through the pages. It was a celebrity gossip magazine and the pictures flashed by in a rush of saturated smiles, his mind lost elsewhere. They were essentially sitting in the same position Cole had been in when he was here earlier this year, when he'd come to pick up Ava the first time. At that time, Cole thought bitterly, he'd been excited to have her back. Happy that she was okay. By that time his temper had already cooled when she'd been making her final report to Lieutenant Alvarez.

He wasn't settled like that tonight.

Deep inside him, like jagged rocks under dark water, sharp edges of jealousy fought with his relief that Ava was okay. Cole knew she'd been doing something when she cancelled plans two weekends in a row. He knew he'd seen her driving out of town and down the coast and he thought he'd known where she was going... but then again maybe he hadn't. His chest tightened as guilt began filtering its way into his relief. Tonight, and the sudden terror that Ava might have been hurt, had left him unmoored. Cole frowned as a young couple walked out hand-in-hand, and with their passing, a memory floated forward.

This image was of Kip and Raya. They'd argued on their way out that long ago morning. Cole remembered Simpson's face seething with envy and then Kip's face when she'd accused him. He'd been shocked and incredulous.

"She's no goddamn 'kid'! And don't think I haven't seen the looks you give her. God, I'm so fucking mad at you I could just—"

"You're jealous..."

"And you're an asshole!"

Guilt rose up in a wave inside him. *'Perhaps,'* Cole's mind prompted, *'it's nothing to do with Kip at all...'* The thought left him squirming. Uncomfortable, he shoved it underneath his impatience and went back to flipping the pages of the magazine.

The phone beeped at the desk and the young man glanced up.

"Cole Thomas," he said, motioning him forward. "Lieutenant Alvarez will see you now."

Chim put a heavy hand on Cole's shoulder.

"Look Cole, I know Ava," Marcus said quietly. "Something's gotta be up, but if you want my honest opinion – and I think you should listen here, man, – I really don't think she'd cheat on you. Ava's a lot of things, but she's not that."

Cole nodded as Suzanne added in her two cents.

"Let her do the talking, okay? She'll be pissed that they'd even called you."

Cole nodded again, feeling like he'd sudden had two parents watching his every move.

"Thanks guys," he muttered, heading up to the desk, acutely aware of the eyes following him.

: : : : : : : : : :

Cole sat in the uncomfortable hard chair while Lieutenant Alvarez closed the door to her office and sat down.

"Thanks for coming, Cole," she said with a grin, shaking his hand.

Cole nodded, wondering how old she was. She had ponytailed hair, a thick fringe of bangs, and a happy smile. Maybe her early twenties at most, though the paperwork he just had to fill out, certainly suggested thoroughness.

"Can I ask what's going on?" Cole asked. He was irritated. No one had told him anything yet, though he'd had to provide plenty of documentation of who he was in the meantime.

"Of course," she said, opening a drawer in her desk and pulling out a pen and photocopied papers. "A squad car picked up Ava walking out in the river bottom tonight," she said glancing up at Cole. "There's no law against being out... but public drunkenness is an offence. She was pretty intoxicated."

Cole wrinkled his nose, feeling the prickle of annoyance. 'Drunk, too...'

"Ava had a pack on, but she obviously wasn't out on a nature hike, not in her state." She chuckled. "Not with what she was carrying."

"Fuck!" Cole snapped, his temper flaring. He knew she'd been out spray-painting.

"Please watch your language, Mr. Thomas. Do I need to remind you where you are?" The woman's tone was sharp; she suddenly looked more than old enough to be a police officer.

"Sorry," Cole mumbled contritely.

"Now, if you'd just hear me out," Lieutenant Alvarez said, pulling out a manila folder and closing her desk drawer with a metallic bang. "I've had some time to look through Ava's file, and have decided not to press charges."

Cole blinked, taken by surprise.

"Why?"

"Well, the thing is," the officer continued, hands playing with the edges of the folder in front of her. "There are extenuating circumstances with Miss Brooks."

At her words, Cole's temper dropped, guilt replacing it.

"Our fight," he said quietly.

She shook her head.

"No... not that." She was watching him now, appraising. There was a long pause in her words. "Did I do the right thing by calling you, Cole?" she asked, voice brusque.

He blew a gust of air from his lungs, leaning forward, dropping his elbows against his knees.

"I honestly don't know," he said, frustration sharpening his words. "Because I've got no idea what's even going on!"

She didn't say anything for a few seconds, fingers drumming on the desk as if deciding something.

"I remembered you from the last... *incident,*" she said. "I had your character witness report – that's how I got your number." She eyed him suspiciously. "It said you were close friends."

Cole sighed, running a hand over his face.

"We are friends. More than friends. I just have no idea what's been going on with Ava the last couple weeks. She's been away a lot... distant."

Lieutenant Alvarez shrugged.

"Makes sense."

She watched him, then reached into the folder and pulled out a sheet of paper. She slid the upside-down scanned document across the desk. Cole could read the header: *'Ocean View Detox and Rehabilitation Centre.'* He stared down at it. Things weren't making sense.

"What is...?" Cole stopped, not sure what he wanted to ask. "Who?"

Ava's words were suddenly in his mind: *'I've been dealing with a family emergency...'*

The officer nodded at the document, her face softening.

"Ava's mother came in for treatment of a meth addiction about a month ago. I understand she and Ava had been estranged for many years. That's in her file, too. As part of her treatment she'd requested, and been granted, contact with her daughter. They'd been talking for a few weeks when the incident happened."

"Incident?"

"According to Ocean View, Shay Brooks left the facility, unescorted, Wednesday the fifteenth. She OD'ed two days later, though her remains weren't located until the following Sunday."

"That was the first weekend Ava cancelled..." Cole muttered under his breath.

"Once everyone knew what had happened, her daughter, Ava, was notified and an autopsy performed. Last week, Ocean View contacted Ava regarding Shay's remains. There was a small, private memorial this weekend," she added. *'The day she left, and we fought,'* Cole's mind noted in horror. "One of the items we found in Ava's backpack was an urn of her mother's ashes..."

: : : : : : : : : :

Ava lay on the hard mattress in the cell, staring at the cinder block wall a few inches away. The lines of mortar swirled and danced before her, leaving her brain feeling unhinged, a boat without a keel. She closed her eyes, forcing herself to breathe in through her nose and out through her mouth, quelling the wave of nausea.

The cell stank, partly from when she'd been sick an hour ago. The toilet in the corner had come in pretty handy. In fact, the police had taken her blood alcohol levels twice, concerned that she might've had alcohol poisoning. She didn't. It was just a good old bender.

Ava coughed, wincing as the noise stabbed into her brain. Her stomach was empty now, though she wished she had a glass or mug. Cupping water in her fingers at the small sink attached to the wall made it hard to get enough to counteract the alcohol, especially as she could hardly stand. Now that she was no longer vomiting, she didn't even have the strength to get up and try to drink again. It was easier to stay here and wait it out. She wanted to curl up into a ball and go to sleep forever.

'She's dead,' her mind chanted. *'Gone...'*

It still didn't feel real.

Ava felt wrung out, tired beyond exhaustion, as if she was only a shell and nothing else. The reaction she was having was shock (she knew that in some part of her logical mind,) but that didn't change it.

'*It's finally over,*' her mind assured her.

That thought left her close to tears, though she couldn't tell at this point if they were anger at her mother for fucking up rehab, or simple grief that the tentative peace they'd forged in the last weeks had been torn away. She wondered if there was even a difference any more. She took a breath, waiting through hot tears, swallowed again and again, closing her eyes and remembering the message that had changed everything.

"Ms. Brooks, this is Terrence Colby from the Ocean View Rehabilitation Centre. We have a patient here by the name of Shay Brook: your mother. As part of her ongoing treatment, she's requested a meeting with you..."

There'd been a phone number from the facility and details on how to contact the counsellors. There'd been nothing from Shay at all. No "I love you" or "I'm sorry" or anything like that. Just a statement of fact: her mother was in treatment for meth addiction and she wanted to see her daughter.

The choice had been Ava's alone.

A sob heaved from the interior of her chest, fighting its way out like a trapped animal. She gasped for air, feeling the ache settling once more. '*Over now. All over...*' the voice repeated soothingly. Ava could distantly hear the guards on shift changing, people talking in the hall. It was late, near midnight for sure. Time lately had had no meaning.

She hadn't called Ocean View back for days. She'd spent a full week thinking about it, in fact. Distracted. There had been at least fifty times she'd almost told Cole, twice that many times she'd picked up the phone to dial her father, then changed her mind. She'd had her reasons, though the logic in them now eluded her. For Cole, it'd had to do with his own progress with his own father; he'd been trying so hard to get past his own issues that she felt guilty burdening him with her own. That, and the shame. Her mother had never featured in regular conversations with Cole, and Ava liked it that way.

She hadn't wanted to share that dark part of herself with him.

The reasons for not telling Oliver had been far more complicated. He'd known the whole story. He'd been the one to come back from his tour to fight for (and win) sole custody during the divorce, to change his whole life to be at home with her. Ava curled tighter, pain mixing with homesickness. *'Should've called Dad,'* her mind hissed. *'He would have understood.'* But that was the thing. She didn't know for certain that he would, because even Ava had difficulty explaining why she'd wanted to see her mother again. She just knew that she had.

She'd driven the hour up the coast to meet with her mother for the first time in over a decade in early March. The meeting had... *changed things.*

Ava rolled onto her back, throwing her arm over her eyes as she did. *'Why the hell do they leave the fucking lights on all the time?'* her mind snapped irritably. Her head would hurt less in the dark, and that's where she wanted to be, to have a few minutes of peace now that the turbulent push-pull of fear and need, guilt and love, was over. She'd been icy cold walking the trails of the river-bottom, numbed at her mother's unexpected death. *Inexplicably relieved.* She winced at that thought.

Ava had gone to the train yards for one last night of painting, her mother's ashes in the backpack with the spray cans. It had seemed like a fitting memorial, since Shay had been the source of so many of Ava's early, angry pieces, but she hadn't gotten far.

A jogger had seen her stumbling along the road to the river bottom (and then up to the train yards beyond). She'd apparently looked distraught enough that he'd called the police, and two officers had met Ava along the trail and brought her in for questioning. She'd known they couldn't charge her with anything except public drunkenness, but she was angry that they'd stopped her. They'd offered Ava her one phone call, but she'd declined. She intended to sleep this off first, then call Chim tomorrow; she refused to think of Cole. It was too painful to consider him.

It still was.

Ava heard the metal door opening at the end of the line of cells. It scraped inside of her skull like rocks along the bottom of a hull, her eyes squeezing shut in pain. In a flash, Ava was back in the detox centre, looking in the doorway of her meeting room...

She sat in a chair next to Terry, an open book in her lap. Shay's body, always lean, was skeletal from years of hard living. Her arms had withered down, like the cordwood you find on the beach. It was the drugs, Ava knew, eating her body from the inside out. The difference between her own mother and Nina Thomas was thrown into shocking contrast as she stared at her. Ava knew – the way her father sometimes did – that, clean of drugs or not, her mother didn't have long to live.

She hadn't realized how close the vision was to coming true.

Her mother glanced up, placing the novel she'd been reading into the large pile of books on the side table, sitting taller. While her body had whittled away to nothing, her face was much the same. It was younger than Ava expected, now that the flesh had been worn away. Her eyes seemed preternaturally large. She had the same fair blonde colouring as Ava, though her eyes were brown. Her cheekbones were high and wide. She might even have been pretty in her day. Her stature was probably no more than Ava's height, her body almost childlike as she sat in the chair, an oversized hoodie and worn blue jeans swallowing her small frame.

The sight of her mother shocked her. In her memory, Shay had always been so much larger.

Ava waited at the door, hesitant to step into the room. Terry was the first to move.

"Ms. Brooks," he said gently, "I'm Mr. Colby – please call me Terry. I'm so glad that you made it." He stepped forward, shaking her hand. "Come in, come in."

Ava waited, unwilling to step into the room, to put herself near her. Her whole body was pulsing with the primal need to run.

"I didn't think you'd come," her mother said. As much as everything else had changed, Shay's voice was exactly the same.

"Neither did I..."

Chapter 17: Letting Go

Cole followed the guard and Lieutenant Alvarez to the holding cell. All was quiet except for the sound of someone coughing wetly. As they made it to the end of the row, Cole's body flooded with déjà vu. This was so much like the last time he'd picked Ava up from the police station... except that she hadn't called him tonight.

She lay in the bunk with one arm flung over her face, body perfectly still. He knew as soon as he saw her that she wasn't sleeping; there was a tautness to her posture that made him long to step inside the cell and touch her. The guard moved forward, putting the keys into the lock, and Ava dropped her arm at the sound, squinting to see who was there.

Her face flared with colour as she saw Cole. Without conscious intent, he smiled, impossibly happy she was okay. Since Lieutenant Alvarez had told him about Ava's mother, he'd had time to come to terms with the fact that he'd been wrong to accuse her. Chim had been right; Ava wouldn't do that... and though he was frustrated that she hadn't told him about her mother, he was appalled that he'd assumed the worst about Ava without asking first. He needed to rebuild some bridges here. (He and Marta had talked about this skill at length.)

Cole intended to start tonight.

"Thought you might need to be busted out of here," he said, stepping up to the bars. "You know I'm your guy for that."

He couldn't keep the grin off his face, and Ava glanced at him nervously, walking to the cell door. He could tell she was tense and wary as she wrapped her arms around herself. Her gaze flicked to Lieutenant Alvarez.

"I'll need you to fill in some paperwork, Ava," the officer explained, "but you're free to go. We've dropped the charge, given a very..." she smirked, looking at Cole, "...glowing character witness report you had on file, and based on your mother's recent death. I talked to Mr. Colby from Ocean View, too. He explained what happened last week." Her voice grew softer. "I'm sorry to hear about your loss."

"Thank you," Ava answered, her eyes on the lieutenant first, then Cole. With a screech, the door finally swung open and she stepped out.

Cole pulled her into a tight hug the moment she was out with them. Her body was motionless as he pressed his face to her hair. She smelled of beer and smoke and day-old sweat, but Cole didn't care. His hands rubbed up and down her back as he breathed her in. He could feel her hands hovering lightly on his back, like the wings of a bird, uncertain if it should settle down to stay.

"I'm so glad you're okay," he said, hands kneading her tense muscles. "God, I was so worried something happened to you."

She didn't respond, but Cole could feel little hitches in her chest warning at the nearness of tears.

"Ava, I'm sorry," Cole whispered, his mouth almost against her ear. "So sorry about what I said and did. I was wrong... I know that. All right?"

"'S'okay," she mumbled.

"No... no, it's not," Cole said, pulling back to look at her. He stroked his thumb against her cheek. "But I want us to be okay. Can we... talk about this sometime? Just you and me?"

Ava nodded, eyes glittering with unshed tears. Cole reached for her hand, and this time her fingers tightened around his, holding on tight.

: : : : : : : : : :

Chim and Suzanne were waiting in the lobby when Ava was released. Chim rushed toward them the moment Ava and Cole walked out together, hand in hand. He pulled Ava into a hug, then released her, his eyebrows dropping in annoyance, nostrils flared.

"Goddammit, Ava," he chided, "I can't believe you'd PULL something like this again. I mean, you really fucking SCARED me this time!"

His voice had the older brother tone he sometimes used with her; responsibility and frustration wrapped up in love.

"Chim," Cole said, hand on his arm, "it's okay."

"No," he barked, shrugging off Cole's touch. "No, it's not!" (The calm from before, Cole realized, had been an act for his benefit.) "Seriously, Ava. You can't keep pulling shit like this! You've gotta grow up!"

His cheeks were blotchy with colour.

"Sorry," she muttered. She stared at the floor. Voice empty.

"Not good enough," he grumbled, stepping toward her. "I swear to God, Ava, if your dad knew tha—"

"Marcus!" Cole snapped, stepping between the two of them, "her mom died!"

Chim stopped, his face draining. He hugged Ava again, holding her tight to his chest.

"Oh god," Chim gasped. "So, so sorry. I didn't know..."

: : : : : : : : : :

They drove back to Ava's apartment, the high-pitched buzz of the little car their only sound. It was just after midnight and all of them had classes in the morning. Cole offered to stay with Ava, and Chim and Suzanne quickly said their goodbyes. Ava didn't quite know what to do with Cole's offer... or whether she wanted him there or not... but she said nothing, and that was taken as yes.

She didn't want to decide anything anymore. She was too tired.

"Thanks for letting me stay," Cole said as they walked up to the front door, his hand on her lower back.

Ava saw him watching her and she dropped her eyes again. Things were still weird, and she wasn't sure how to get back to normal. She needed time to think... or sleep... or finish sobering up. *'All of them probably...'*

"Yeah," she muttered, punching in the code and leading Cole inside.

In minutes they were at the entrance to her apartment. Ava dropped her backpack on the floor while she fiddled with the lock. After two unsuccessful tries, she leaned her cheek against the door, wearily closing her eyes. She couldn't get her key to fit. She jumped as Cole's hand brushed her arm.

"Hey," he said gently, "I'll go, alright? I just wanted to make sure you were inside, safe. I'll, uh... I'll call you in the morning."

Ava turned to him, eyes shining in the dim light of the corridor.

"No," she answered, "I want you here, but I think... I think we should talk now, not later. Okay?"

Cole nodded, expecting Ava to pass him the keys, but instead she pulled out a mostly-empty pack of cigarettes and a lighter from her bag.

Cole frowned.

"You don't smoke."

Ava laughed tiredly.

"I do tonight." With a sigh, she hefted the bag back onto her shoulder, heading toward the fire escape. "C'mon," she called.

: : : : : : : : : :

They sat side by side, Ava talking through the events of the last weeks. Her voice rose and fell in a quiet tempo, trying to make sense of the blur of time. She described the first meeting with her mother after so many years apart. How Ava had gotten angry enough that she'd raged at her during the session, finally telling her everything that she'd felt as a child. How much she'd hated her. How terrible Shay had been. How much of the abuse she actually remembered.

Ava laughed bitterly.

"I didn't think Terry would ask me back again after that." She took another drag on the cigarette in her hand, holding the smoke in her lungs before blowing it away. "But she... she wanted to get well. She did, Cole. And Terry said that this was part of that process for her, so..."

The sentence ended mid-thought. Ava turned to Cole. There was an odd expression on his face, not quite sad, but somehow hurting.

"And so you went back," he prompted.

She nodded, letting the taste of the cigarette smoke bring her father to mind as she inhaled.

"There was another message from Terry when I got home. So I went back the next night, and she was waiting." Ava paused, lifting her hand up, thumbing her eyebrow, the low-burning cigarette dangling. "Didn't expect that, I guess. I just kind of... talked to her. She – my mom, I mean – she never said sorry. Not that I expected her to. I mean she hadn't really changed, even though I had. Addiction's a funny thing."

Ava laughed angrily and Cole's expression grew uncomfortable.

"She never said sorry?"

Ava shook her head.

"Nope... but that wasn't what I was looking for, anyway. I just wanted to have my say. To be able to tell her: *'this was the fucked up shit you did to me, and it was never EVER okay'.*" She lifted the cigarette with shaking fingers, rubbing away a tear with her free hand. "And then... and then she went and fucked it all up anyhow. Took off and OD'ed in an alley downtown. Just an addict, screwing up one last time." Ava took a sobbing breath, cheeks shining with tears. "That was it. She was gone."

"God, Ava, I wish you'd told me," Cole said, sliding closer. She nodded, flicking ashes into the wind and watching as they swirled down into the night.

"Yeah, well, me too." She gave a short, harsh laugh. "But here we are."

Cole put his arm over her shoulders.

"Yeah, here we are."

Ava drew the warm burn of smoke into her lungs, coughing and blowing it away before continuing.

"Part of me wants to say it was just a fucked-up waste of time to even meet with her. She didn't get clean, after all. But there were all these things that I got to talk about. These things I'd never said to her, or anyone. Things I was sure I couldn't say... and I'm... I'm glad for those." She reached down, tapping ashes onto the stair's grate. "I mean... I got to tell her about Dad, and how amazing he was when I was growing up, and how I turned out just fucking fine without her. I needed to say that." Ava dropped her face down, lips twisting into a cynical smile. "For a while she... she just kept trying to rationalize it all. About why the abuse happened... why it wasn't her fault."

Cole's arm tightened on her shoulders.

"God, baby, I'm sorry."

Ava shrugged.

"Yeah, well, people are people. This thing that Terry set up," Ava said, ashes rising as she gestured, "it was supposed to help her get clean, but the truth is, Cole, it was never about her... it was about me. So I just kept talking, and whenever she'd start in on her shit, I'd walk out the door."

Cole laughed.

"Sounds like me."

Ava sniffled.

"Well... a better choice than punching her, which was what I wanted to do," she admitted.

She smiled morosely.

"I kept thinking one day I'd show up and Terry would say she wouldn't see me, or she'd tell me to fuck off, that she was done, but she never did. I just talked... getting it out... letting go of that pain and anger... and when I couldn't deal with it anymore, I'd come home and paint—"

"You painted?" Cole asked in surprise. Her hair hung down in strands and he reached up, brushing it back behind her ear so he could see her eyes.

"Yeah... my studio's packed with them," Ava said wearily. Cole kissed her temple.

"I'd like to see them sometime."

She reached over, crushing out the cigarette on the metal grate. She flicked it into the night with a shower of sparks.

"I'm not sure you would. They're dark. And, uh... not all of them are on canvas."

He grinned.

"Boy, Chim would have had your ass if you'd been caught at the train yards."

Ava snorted, rolling her eyes.

"I can handle Chim just fine," she said with a tired chuckle. Her smile wavered, and she turned to him, the wariness returning. "It's *you* I'm not so sure I can manage."

Cole nodded.

"Fair enough."

She swallowed hard, closing her eyes.

"I know I should have told you about my mom... *I get that.* But I needed to do this... do it for me." She looked back to him as she spoke, holding his gaze. "I needed to find forgiveness."

Cole's mouth hardened at that, jaw tightening angrily.

"How can you talk about forgiving her, after what she did to you, Ava?" He grabbed hold of her hand, squeezing hard. "She fucked up your childhood! How could you ever get past that?"

His tone was outraged and hurt, and Ava turned her hand over, lacing her fingers with his. This, right here, was why she hadn't told Cole.

"In a way, my forgiveness has nothing to do with her," she explained. "I needed to let go of that anger I was carrying around. Because forgiving didn't mean you're saying that what the other person did was okay."

Her fingers tightened in Cole's hands, eyes on his face. A muscle in his jaw was jumping, his eyes bright and unsettled. It hurt her to see it.

"What my mother did to me," Ava continued, "is never EVER going to be okay! But forgiveness is about me moving past what happened when I was a kid. Learning to be okay with myself, and letting those emotions go."

"But, *how?*" Cole cried. His face was raging with unspoken hurt, anguish in his eyes.

"I needed to let that anger out of me to get past it," she said, her voice breaking, tears starting to draw wet lines on her cheeks. "She doesn't get to own me, Cole... not ever! Not anymore any way. She has no more control. It's my life now. I'm done with hating her."

Ava took a shuddering breath, her face sad but peaceful.

"My mother may have fucked up her detox. She may have screwed up rehab and died in the end. But I don't have to feel bad about that. I tried for ME, Cole. Does that make sense? I let her go on my terms. And the truth is, I'm glad about it. It's over... the pain is gone. And I'm glad."

Next to her, Cole pulled her into a painful hug, his body quivering. He was breathing harshly, almost in tears himself. Ava could barely make out his words when he whispered them.

"So what do you do if the person you need to forgive is already dead?"

Chapter 18: The Darkness Between

There was a long moment after Cole said it... admitted to the anger he'd been feeling for years. Ava just stared at him in confusion. In the dim haze from the security light, the blue of her eyes was so dark it seemed almost black. Dreamlike.

"You're angry at Hanna?" she asked, perplexed.

Cole sighed, shaking his head. It came to him that he'd never really said this aloud... not in years. Not since his mother's funeral. Even then, he didn't get to say it clearly. (His father hadn't wanted to hear it.)

"No, not Hanna..." he admitted.

Ava's expression shifted as the rest of the story appeared. He could actually see the moment she understood.

"Your mom." This time it wasn't a question.

The secret hung between them like the mist from their breaths.

Cole nodded.

"Yeah. You can't believe how angry I was at her..." He stumbled. "...how angry *I am* at her."

Ava reached for his hand. She was frowning like she was trying to solve a difficult equation without a calculator.   Cole realized that though he had told her about the facts of his childhood, he really hadn't said much about what he felt like when it was happening.

"You ever talk to Marta about it in your sessions?" she asked. "Or the ones with your dad?"

The suggestion was disconcerting and he choked, the cold air turning his breath into white clouds.

"Twice," he muttered. "Dad freaked out."

She nodded, her thumb rubbing circles into the back of his hand. She chewed the inside of her lip, eyes unfocused, as if gnawing away at an idea. He had the urge to kiss her, here on the grated step of the fire escape. His heart ached with all the things he wanted to tell her... needed her to know and understand about him.

"What do you talk about in your sessions with your dad?" she asked gently.

He shrugged.

"Hanna mainly... Dad has lots to say about her."

Ava's smile was pained, as if the thought hurt her. Somehow that made Cole feel better, that she wasn't making light of this. He leaned in, kissing her chastely, then pulled back again. He hadn't let go of her hand.

"How do you feel about Hanna?" she asked.

Cole made a low, whistling sound as he exhaled, his body growing heavier as he thought about her. Hanna's memory had been with him for so long; until recently, Cole hadn't known how to think of himself without the perspective of his older sister. (The person he wasn't.) In the last two months of counselling, he'd come to realize that much of who he was had been shaped by Hanna Thomas. As a result, his perspective had changed about her.

"What is she to you?" Ava prompted.

His eyes drifted out to the snow-covered city beyond the steps, velvet black lit by golden pools of light, coins thrown atop an ink-soaked sheet. That, he realized, was how he remembered Hanna: individual bright moments lighting the darkness. The group were linked together in a chain of meaning.

"I dunno," he began. "I used to kind of idealize her like everyone else, but in the last few months... writing about my feelings, and talking about it with Marta, that's changed. The shit Hanna used to pull... always taking risks she shouldn't have..." He shrugged. "You know, that stuff has consequences, but she didn't really care. I guess I've come to realize that she was just a messed-up kid like me."

Ava slid closer, her body tucked tightly against his side. She leaned her head on his shoulder as he talked.

"Everyone's messed-up, Cole... everyone."

He chuckled.

"Hanna was great in a lot of ways… an awesome sister. I mean, I miss her... I love her." He slumped lower, his limbs like an anchor, drawing him down to that darkness inside himself. "She was the cool older sister who kept care of me. When I was a kid, I used to get so angry with being compared to her, but Marta and I have been talking about how that's more my Dad's problem than mine. I never really wanted to be Hanna. Ever. It was Dad's thing. I'm okay with that now."

Ava turned to look up at him, her hair brushing his cheek like a paintbrush on canvas.

"But your issue with your mom…?"

Cole's smile disappeared, like the sun going behind a cloud.

"Yeah, Mom…"

His voice disappeared. He stared out into the night. As much as memories of Hanna were points of light, memories of his mother were darkness. The emptiness between.

"You're going to need to talk about your anger with her sometime," Ava said quietly. "You're got to deal with it, or it'll never go away."

She turned his hand over, tracing letters into his palm.

I...L.O.V.E...Y.O.U...

Cole glanced down at her fingers, smiling.

"Yeah," he answered, "I am. But it isn't going to be good, Ava... it's just not."

She moved away from his shoulder to look him in the face.

"Why?"

He winced, trying to put it into words.

"Dad just... he has this thing about Mom. They might've divorced and all, but she's a really sensitive topic for him."

Ava shrugged.

"Maybe it's because they divorced."

"Maybe..." he answered, voice wavering. There was something else there. Cole had sensed it for years, but he wasn't entirely sure he wanted to know about the thing in the darkness that no one spoke of.

Lost in his thoughts, Ava's voice startled him.

"You need to push the issue, Cole," she said firmly. "Tell him how you feel. Make him talk!"

He wondered for a moment where she got the strength to not give a damn about the consequences. Cole had spent his whole life running from conflict; Ava was always running toward it. He closed his eyes, imagining what would happen if he did tell his father about his feelings. If he pushed the issue as Ava'd suggested. His chest tightened at the thought.

There would be consequences.

"You have to," she insisted.

He nodded.

Ava tipped her head to the side like a bird examining a crumb, her face losing the seriousness of seconds earlier. She winked and brightened.

"Your dad's not so bad some days, you know... I've told him off and still walked away from it."

Cole made a scoffing sound.

"Yeah well, Dad's a little soft on you for some reason."

She poked him in the ribs with her elbow.

"Maybe that's because I call him on his shit and no one else does." She raised an eyebrow. (It was the look of someone who'd just walked out of the candy store with their pockets full of candy.) "You ever think of that?"

Cole smirked.

"Yes, actually, I have." He leaned closer. "I told Marta about it."

Ava's expression softened.

"You did...?"

"Yeah, in my sessions... not the ones with Dad."

Ava watched him, her lower lip caught in her teeth, a wrinkle of concern between her brows. Cole chuckled, his smile widening.

"Of course I did. Why?"

She ducked her chin into the collar of her coat, looking away with embarrassment.

"I dunno... just seems, serious?"

Cole could see she was blushing, a line of pink rising up her neck. He reached out, touching her chin so that she turned back toward him. She looked scared.

"We are serious," he whispered. (It felt too important to say aloud.) "I'm sorry, Ava... about accusing you—"

"Cole," she interrupted.

"No," he said, taking Ava's fingers with his left hand, and slinging his right arm around her shoulder, "No, I need to say this. I'm sorry about what I said. I shouldn't have assumed anything... and you don't have to tell me what you were doing." He shrugged. "I wish you had... but you didn't have to. I do trust you." He shook his head. "Yes, I know I'm a jackass sometimes, but when it comes down to it, I really do trust you. This is my issue. Not yours."

She smiled at him.

"Thanks for understanding, but the blame goes both ways...." she tightened her hand around his. "I should have tried harder, but I just... I had to do it myself, Cole. Can't explain it better than that. I couldn't even tell my dad."

Cole nodded, then leaned in, kissing her lightly once more. This time Ava's lips moved under his, and their embrace grew more charged. Like a night with a storm brewing, the smell of ozone sharp in the air. Their mouths slanted together, growing rougher, all the pent-up emotions of earlier rising to the surface. He bit her lower lip, tugging her mouth open, and she gasped. Her hands slid around his neck. Legs numb from the cold, she tugged him down, pulling him against her.

The kiss dragged on. They were divers refusing to surface. This here, this now, was all they needed, both of them fighting to stay together, refusing to be the first to let go. Teeth and tongues and mouths slid together, nails scraping on cold-stiffened jackets until finally – breathless and lightheaded – they fell apart. Their emotions churned like the rush of turbulent water still pressing against them.

"Missed you," she panted.

Cole laughed raggedly.

"Me too..."

He was about to lean in and kiss her again, but Ava reached out for his chest, pausing him.

"Cole, if you don't mind... I had something I wanna do."

"Okay...?"

"I though... maybe... you'd want to be part of it." She frowned, dropping her eyes. "Can I ask you something? Like a favour?"

Cole could see she was nervous; her face was guarded.

"Sure."

Her lashes settled closed, chest rising slowly and falling. He waited. When she opened her eyes, the fear was gone.

"Could we have a bonfire the next time we go out to your place?"

He grinned, not quite understanding the request. It seemed like a pretty easy thing to make happen.

"Sure, I guess. But why?"

Ava turned to the side, staring out into the dark. In profile, her face was suddenly tired and sad, and Cole felt the urge to wrap himself around her. To protect her from whatever was dragging her down. He watched her throat bobbing as she swallowed back tears, her knuckles coming up to rub angrily at her eyes.

"I've got some paintings I want to get rid of," she said roughly. "And my mother's ashes.

Chapter 19: Blacking the Plate

Ava scowled at the zinc plate; one-tenth of the surface was pitted with the fine-toothed grain of the mezzotint rocker, but the rest of the image was perfectly visible. Her arm burned; she was never going to get this done.

"Goddamn motherfucker," Ava growled, massaging her bicep.

Cole snickered, glancing up from his seat across the table from her, writing in his notebook for Marta. It was late, and the studio was empty, except for the two of them. Cole's eighth plate had been finished since yesterday while Ava was struggling to make up the missed time from earlier this week. It might be Friday night, but they wouldn't be going out to The Crown with Suzanne and Chim.

"You want some help?" Cole asked, dropping his pen.

Ava grimaced.

"I don't want to waste your time," she mumbled. "You have stuff to get done too."

"True..." Cole admitted, his eyes devious, "but you could always make it worth my while."

Ava snorted in response.

"As fun as a little 'quick and dirty' in the print lab sounds, I'm going to say no..."

Cole set down his book, leaning across the table. His wolfish grin left Ava fighting the urge to giggle (or run).

"You know," Cole murmured, "they don't have cameras in the studios, so, uh..."

A barking laugh rose from her chest in an explosion of sound. She cackled again, covering her mouth with her hand. When the giggles subsided, she pointed the rocker at him.

"Look, if I'm not done with this plate, then I have to finish my essay for Wilkins. It's due on Monday and I haven't even started yet."

"Shit!" Cole hissed. "I almost forgot..." He rummaged through his backpack, pulling out a pile of crumpled papers.

"What?" Ava asked, peering at his hands.

"Wilkins asked me to give you this. I totally forgot," he answered, unfolding and flattening a glossy brochure with his hands. "There's some kind of curatorial program being offered next year. Graduate level. He thought you might be interested."

Ava sneered in disbelief.

"Really...? Me?"

She waited for the punchline that never came.

"Yeah, really," Cole said with a grin. "He likes the way you think. Called it 'unique.' Wilkins said to get in contact with him if you want. It actually sounds kind of cool."

Ava gave the brochure a sceptical once-over.

"Huh. Didn't see that coming."

Cole shrugged.

"I think I might apply."

Again, Ava grinned and waited for the rest of the joke, but it never came. The two of them had argued endlessly about the flaws of the gallery system. She'd never imagined Cole going into that line of work.

"Yeah." Cole said, winking at her as he picked up his book and pen.

Ava put her palms on the table, her hips against the side as she leaned in. Cole's eyes flickered to her face, then down to her breasts, before going back to the notebook. She smirked.

'Cole Thomas has a very one-track mind...'

"You don't think that's going over to the dark side?" Ava teased. "Becoming a curator..."

Ava hummed a few bars of the Emperor's Theme from Star Wars. Cole chuckled, and again there was the flicker of eye movement. Face. Breasts.

"I prefer to think of myself as a revolutionary," Cole said.

Ava raised an eyebrow.

"Uh-huh..." She grinned, leaning forward to give him a better view down her shirt. Cole reached out, trying to grab her hand, but she pulled it back out of reach.

"Yeah," Cole said, lifting his chin, "trying to change the system from within."

Ava paused, imagining the changes Cole could make if he actually became a curator. It was a very political move in the art community, but Cole was already an artist, and that was a good start. He really could make a difference.

"Honestly? That's pretty cool."

His smiled grew hungry. He dropped his voice to a purr.

"I could get you a show," he said, eyes moving up and down, "for a price."

Ava harrumphed, standing back up again, the distance returning.

"Yup," she said dryly. "I see where this is going."

Cole laughed and Ava turned back to the zinc plate. She leaned into the motion and began blacking the surface once more. For another twenty minutes, they worked in silence only broken by the dull grind of the rocker and Cole's pen. Shifting the plate sideways, Ava hissed. Her arm pulsed with fatigue once more.

"C'mere," Cole said, smiling patiently. "Give that thing to me... You can owe me one later."

Ava eyed him with uncertainty.

"You serious? I could really use the help here." She worried the inside of her lip, undecided.

Cole tapped the edge of the table with his pen.

"Let's pretend that this is Warhol's Factory and I'm the cheap labour."

A smile tugged up at her mouth.

"Which makes me…?"

"Oh, you're the brains behind the whole thing." He put out his hand. "C'mon. Give it over. This is a limited time offer, y'know."

She giggled, sliding the plate across the table, checking him out.

"Well, you do have the arms for it."

Cole coughed.

"Thanks."

She leaned forward and passed him the mezzotint rocker.

"This sounds like a pretty good deal for me."

"Yeah, well, you're Warhol," Cole said, winking.

"And you're the eye candy," she teased. "I'm imagining you as Edie Sedgwick."

Cole laughed, reaching out to snag her wrist, tugging her toward him. Ava squealed as her hips hit the edge of the table and she slid forward.

"A socialite!" Cole scoffed. "I'm hurt!"

Ava roared with laughter as he grabbed her other arm, pulling her closer. Halfway across, she knocked his bag to the floor, pens and art history books scattering. Her cackle echoed through the room.

"At least let me be Basquiat," Cole argued. "Badass rule-breaker. Counter-cultural free thinker!"

Suddenly she was in his arms, her body half-sitting, half-laying on the tabletop. Cole's mouth dropped to Ava's grin. They were stretched out across the tall printing table, his hand on the back of her neck. His tongue moved over the crease of her lips, teasing, then invading her mouth, tasting her. The edge of the table dug into Ava's hips, but she didn't care; her entire focus was on the play of his mouth on hers.

After a long moment, Cole pulled back and Ava ducked out of his grasp, demurely picking up her Art History book as she slid back down.

"I've thought about it and I get to be Basquiat too," she said archly. "I'm the graffiti artist after all. Not you."

With an exaggerated sigh, Cole dropped the mezzotint rocker, then stood up and walked around the table. Ava squeaked as he picked her up, setting her on the edge.

"What ARE you doing?!" she shrieked.

Ava was giggling so hard she could hardly breathe as Cole positioned himself between her knees. His hands tugged at the bottom of her shirt, mouth sucking and nipping his way to her collarbone.

"Stop. STOP!" Ava laughed.

His hands slid under her shirt, reaching her breasts.

"Not a chance," Cole growled in her ear. "If you're claiming you're the badass rule-breaker, then I want some fucking proof."

Ava shivered at the sound, dropping her fingers to the buttons of his jeans.

"You've got it."

: : : : : : : : : :

By Saturday, the Spring weather had warmed. Nina and Frank drove into the city to see the show, and the four of them met at the university gallery. Ava's oil painting was the first they looked at as they walked through the Student Show and she was gratified to hear both of Cole's parents compliment it. Frank had grumbled his way past the most controversial pieces, confused as anything by Suzanne's container sculptures.

Ava almost burst into laughter as he commented on her contribution.

"Now this is my kind of artwork."

Next to him, Nina nodded appreciatively.

"And some other time, dear," she said, catching Ava's eyes, "we'd like to see the rest of your artwork, too."

Ava beamed, feeling a warm wave of acceptance. She really liked the Thomases.

They continued toward the alcove housing Cole's sculpture. Ava was nervous of her own reaction to the piece, but standing with Cole and his family, her anxiety wore away, and she found herself enjoying the moment. Her dream of the storm and winged death seemed far away when they were all together. Now she was almost able to appreciate the skill it took for Cole to create this. Almost...

The limbs were smooth planes, Modernist in approach. Cole had carved exaggerated angles which hinted at musculature rather than perfectly mimicking it. It wasn't something she'd put in her living room, but she recognized the beauty inherent in the piece.

"This is just lovely," Nina said. "You've really come a long way."

"Thanks."

He shifted uncomfortably under his stepmother's praise.

"Cole's quite a perfectionist when it came to getting things right," Ava added with a smile. "I had to pose for this thing for almost a week straight."

Cole smirked.

"Yeah, well, I made that up to you. I think I posed longer, actually."

Nina looked at them in surprise.

"Oh, did you paint Cole? I'd love to see it sometime," she said with a wide grin.

Embarrassment painted Ava scarlet from chest to cheeks.

"Uh, yeah... sometime."

Cole laughed at her discomfort and Ava dropped her eyes. *'That WON'T be happening any time soon,'* she thought with chagrin.

"Proud of you, Cole," Frank said, placing a heavy hand on Cole's shoulder.

Ava glanced over to see Cole watching his father... face tense and wary. His hesitancy made her heart tighten in grief.

"Uh... thanks, Dad."

"Hell of a lot of work to get this much detail and... and... life, out of stone," Frank said, dropping his hand and stepping forward. "Must've taken you ages."

Cole nodded. Father and son were side-by-side, but not touching. A small smile framed Ava's mouth. They were trying... both of them. Marta's advice was obviously helping.

"The way you've caught the bird... or woman... in flight. The detail... that's just amazing," Frank said, nodding to the wings. "Don't know where you get the talent from."

Cole smiled at him, uneasy but clearly happy.

"I'm guessing Cole got it from you," Ava said, drawing both of their attentions.

Frank frowned.

"Oh no, I don't—"

"But I've seen your photographs," Ava insisted. "The ones in the den and library. I guessed – from pictures of Angela and your children – it must've been you taking them."

Frank's expression shimmered, his eyes moving almost too fast to be seen from Ava to Nina, and back again. If she hadn't been watching, she might have missed it… an emotion akin to guilt.

"Yes, dear," Nina said, clearing her throat. "I've always thought that myself. Frank does take lovely photos."

Ava turned to her, wondering at the unease she'd sensed from Frank.

"There's one of you on the landing, Nina," Ava said. "You're sitting on a chair on the porch. The sunlight's just gorgeous."

Frank seemed to relax at that.

"Yes, well," he muttered. "It's easy if your subject's as beautiful as Nina here."

Nina preened, brushing her fingers through her hair, eyelashes fluttering in amusement.

"Oh Frank," she said with a laugh, "you do know how to sweet talk, don't you?"

"Now, what do you say we all grab something to eat?" Ava suggested. "We could have supper before you leave. It's nearly five now."

"I'd rather just grab something on the way out of town." Cole's father groused.

Nina laughed ruefully.

"Frank's not one for fine dining, Ava," she said. "I swear he'd eat macaroni and cheese every night of his life if I let him… straight out of the pot it was cooked in, at that."

Frank ducked his chin.

"Less dishes," he muttered.

Ava laughed gleefully. The logic made sense to her.

"Then I have the perfect place!" she announced, nodding to Cole.

He winked as he answered.

"Crown and Sceptre?"

Chapter 20: The Many Lives and Secret Sorrows of Josephine B.

Ava sighed, her face pressed against Cole's back as the sway and pull of the motorcycle set her body adrift. They were taking an early morning ride, Cole showing her different haunts of his youth. The two of them were spending the weekend with Nina and Frank. A large number of Ava's paintings – some canvas, many unstretched – were now piled in the back of the Beast, her bags covering the passenger seat, so Cole had brought his ride as well. She loved the feel of the bike, had been considering how to buy herself one for months now. Even after paying for student loans, living expenses, and a little bit of cash tucked away for later, there would still be a few thousand dollars left over. The idea of a motorcycle had an undeniable appeal. She couldn't wait.

This morning, she and Cole were exploring the coast, heading to an area where Hanna and Cole used to cliff dive as children. Cole laughed off the dangers, but a very real part of Ava hated that Hanna Thomas would drag her kid brother along for these kind of outings. One wrong move and she might've been taking this ride alone.

The thought was stuck in the no-man's land between fury and terror.

They needed to be back in two hours, so Cole could make it to his session with Marta before a session with his father. Ava closed her eyes, letting the wind in her ears and the heat of the sun against her leather jacket lull her into a sense of calm. It was like floating, only the shift and sway of the chassis hinting that any other forces of nature were at work, so perfectly separate from everything else that Ava's heart ached. She and Cole were alone in the rush of movement; her arms curled around his chest, her thighs on either side of his.

Together.

The bike slowed, and Ava's eyelids fluttered open. Cole pulled to the side, getting ready to turn off onto a smaller road. They were almost there.

While Cole was away later, Ava was looking forward to spending a few hours alone with Nina. The two women always ended up laughing at something, talking about crazy things that Ava swore she'd never tell anyone. A very real part of her was considering sharing the nude painting of Cole with Nina (though she knew Cole would be horrified if she told him that).

Cole shifted in his seat and Ava unconsciously moved with him. She smiled as it happened: this synchronicity. While she would miss Cole this afternoon, she was proud of him for taking therapy so seriously. His small black notebook was now full of memories and thoughts. Cole shared them with her as he wrote and they'd discovered a new understanding of each other as he did.

Ava was a bit nervous, as Cole had decided to bring up his mother during today's session. Ava knew it was for the best, but she also knew there would be hell to pay for this one. Cole planned to take his bike downtown so that he could leave if he needed to.

Eyes still closed, Ava felt the jitter of gravel rising through her feet resting on the frame of the bike, up through her legs, all the way to her torso. The tang of salt air sharpened her senses. She forced herself to wait, eyelids tightly closed, wanting to have the full experience of this place.

The motor of the bike shifted down, wheels rolling to a stop.

"We're here," Cole called.

Her eyes opened to a sight so bright and sun-drenched it left her blinking.

They were at the top of a wide cliff, the water below like a shimmering sheet beyond the rocks, waves crashing loudly. Ava felt the back of her legs tighten as her body reacted to the height. The image of fourteen-year-old Cole cliff diving with his sister flashed through her mind and her chest tightened in dismay. But it was the water that drew and kept her gaze. Seen from above, the endless expanse rippled and moved like...

Ava shivered.

...The ripples of grass in her dream.

: : : : : : : : : :

Ava perched on a cream-coloured couch in the upstairs library, Nina nearby at the bookshelf. While the den reflected Frank's masculine tastes, this room was definitely Nina's domain. It had heavy oriental rugs, velvet drapes, and elegant furniture laden with multicoloured throw pillows. Nina insisted on flopping down onto chairs like they were thrift store rejects, kicking her feet up onto the narrow-legged coffee table while she read.

Ava smiled seeing it, knowing she'd have felt uncomfortable otherwise.

Right now, Nina was searching for a book, tapping her manicured fingernails on the shelf in front of her.

"I thought it was The Rose of Martinique..." she said irritably, "but that's not right. This one was non-fiction. Something else. Hmmm..." She moved to another shelf, chattering quietly.

"Don't worry about it," Ava answered, glancing up from her phone. Suzanne had texted her with the updated information for their flight. They were leaving for the Caribbean – Martinique to be exact – next Friday afternoon. Their week in the sun was suddenly a reality.

"No," Nina said, pulling out another book. "I'm sure it's here, I just need a better filing system than by size."

Ava grinned.

"Really, it's no problem. I can just grab a paperback from the airport."

Nina scoffed, raising a thin eyebrow in disdain.

"Really dear, this would be much more appropriate, given your destination."

With a decisive nod, she stepped to the next shelf, her fingers dancing along the books. She knew them by feel as much as title.

"You know," Nina said as she moved through the volumes, "I was thinking of throwing Cole a graduation party at the end of the year, but I wanted your opinion. I know Frank and Cole had been making strides." She glanced back at Ava. "Honestly, they are talking for the first time I can really remember. A party might be nice... unless you think it'd be too much."

She ran her fingers nervously along the books. Ava chuckled.

"I dunno about Frank," she answered. "But I could ask Cole if you want."

"Please... I would like to do something, but I don't want him to feel obliged." She peered over her shoulder. "Is your father going to be back for the grad ceremonies?"

Ava nodded.

"He made his itinerary last year with that in mind." She closed her phone, and stood up, stretching. "I can't wait for him to get back."

Nina smiled wistfully.

"You have a good relationship with your father..." her face rippled briefly. "I don't even know him," she added, waggling a finger at Ava, "I can tell by listening to you."

Ava grinned at the truth of the statement. She walked up to the shelf, hands on her hips.

"Alright, Nina," she said. "Let's stop pissing around. What am I looking for here?"

Nina burst into laughter.

"You know, if you and Cole have kids someday, you'll have to learn to watch your language."

Ava felt the blush rush up her face, but she stepped toward Nina with a veneer of indifference.

"Stop changing the subject and tell me what the hell I need to find. Title... colour... author..." Ava listed brusquely. "I want this book you keep harping about."

Nina's hands dropped from the shelf.

"It has a picture of Josephine on it... an old painting of her on the dust cover, on a chaise lounge, I think. She's young in the image. A little sad..."

"Josephine who?"

Nina smiled conspiratorially.

"Why Josephine Bonaparte, dear. You are going to Martinique after all. She was born there."

Ava laughed.

"Really? I thought she was French."

Nina clucked.

"French by heritage, but born in the Caribbean." She turned back to the shelf as she talked. "The author's name starts with 'G'... Garren... Gorum... something like that."

Ava went through the books in sequence, searching for an image of a young woman on a couch. Nina talked as the two of them worked.

"She was born Marie-Josephe Tascher," she explained, speaking in a warm, gossipy tone (as if Josephine was coming for dinner tonight, not some faraway figure from history). "Her father was a dandy and a wastrel, but she married up." She laughed. "Sadly her husband wasn't much better."

"Napoleon?" Ava asked, pulling out another book.

"Oh no, her first husband." Nina's voice dropped as if she was telling a scandalous secret. "You know, they say he was the author of Les Liasons Dangereuses... though of course no one really knows for sure. It was published under the pen name of de Laclos and caused quite a scandal in its day!"

"And Josephine was from Martinique," Ava said quietly. "Huh. Small world."

Nina nodded.

"The book is excellent. It talks about the predictions that an old slave-woman made about her future when she was a child... that she'd wear the crown of France."

Ava's eyes widened.

"Really? Someone predicted that?"

Nina nodded.

"When she was a badly-dowered girl from the colonies with few hopes of marrying well. It's a very good story. Full of romance and adventure..." Nina paused, frowning. "... though the author does tend to see Josephine's story through rose-coloured glasses."

She stopped, fingers on her lip, eyebrows pulled together.

"Gull-something... Gullen... Gallen..." she clapped her hands in triumph. "Gulland! That's it! The author's name."

"So it's a cleaned-up story of Josephine? Like the PG version," Ava prompted, giggling.

Nina brushed her shirt, removing imaginary flecks of dust.

"Yes, well, affairs of the heart don't make the most wholesome heroines or the cleanest sort of adventures."

Ava's fingers caught on a well-worn novel, spine broken, pages frayed. She pulled it out, holding her breath. There was a dark-haired woman in a long empire-waist dress on the cover. She wore a circlet on her head, the dark canvas making her pale skin glow. It reminded Ava of the paintings of Ingres... though less stilted. More informal... perhaps more like the court paintings of Vigée LeBrun. Josephine was staring to the side – *'worried? waiting?'* – her hazel eyes wise beyond what her years suggested. The sharpness of her gaze alongside the beauty of her setting reminded Ava of Nina.

"People forget sometimes that love doesn't always come at the most convenient moments," Nina continued, "and that when you find love, it isn't necessarily with the person you're married to..." Her words became quieter, "or meant for..."

The words set the hair on Ava's scalp crawling. Her hands tightened around the book. Her mind went back to Cole and Frank, talking right now in Marta's office.

"...Life's messy sometimes, and it's the privilege of the writer to clean that up." Nina straightened, rolling her shoulders tiredly and catching Ava's eyes. "I, on the other hand would rather have the real story."

Ava nodded warily.

"The whole truth, no matter who gets hurt?" she asked.

Nina paused, as if considering her words. A smile lit her face.

"Why, Ava," she exclaimed. "You've found the book!"

Chapter 21: Burned in Effigy

Cole looked from his father to Marta and back again. The three of them sat in a circle, taking turns talking. They'd been doing this for most of the hour, chatting about various topics – some guided, some naturally occurring – easing their way into deeper waters.

Cole was just starting to get uncomfortable with the discussion.

Marta had followed this routine for several sessions, gradually letting Cole and his father become adept at sharing. Frank had learned to listen far more in the last few weeks, and Cole had learned not to shut down when things got difficult.

Marta nodded.

"Frank," she said, "you and Cole have both been doing some writing for me in the last few weeks. Both of you have different things you'd like to work through, and we've spent the last couple sessions talking about your daughter, Hanna. I know that's been very important for you."

Frank nodded wearily. Next to him, Cole shifted. As much as he knew this issue needed to be released, he still wasn't sure he was ready. Marta caught his eyes, smiling in support.

"Cole's also been working on his own challenges. He has an issue he'd like to discuss today." She paused. "I've left my next session open so if we would like to talk longer, we can. There's no rush."

Cole swallowed hard. His hands were clammy, heart rioting against his chest.

"Cole, would you like to begin?"

He closed his eyes, thinking back to Ava and their talk on the step. He knew without a doubt that she'd be running straight into this. She'd already told his father off more than once. The thought gave him strength. Cole opened his eyes, turning to look directly at his father.

"Dad, I know we've talked about Mom in our previous sessions…" His father's face became suspicious and cool. "I know that we have different memories of our time with her because we all see and experience things differently."

Marta nodded, urging him on. Cole could see that his father's face had darkened. Usually, that would have been enough warning for him to retreat.

This time he didn't stop.

"I was a kid when you two got divorced, but—"

"I don't see how this is supposed to change anything," Frank interrupted. "Angela and I had our troubles, but that was a long time ago."

Marta smiled patiently.

"That's true, Frank, but issues can come from numerous sources, and if Cole would like to talk about this, then you owe him the chance to talk it through." She paused, voice hardening. The smoothness was gone, the steel underneath appearing. "He has been more than willing to talk about your perceptions of Hanna for many sessions now."

Frank sat back in his chair, stone-faced.

"Alright then," he grumbled.

Cole stared at the black notebook, his fingers tight and bloodless around it. His body was reacting in panic long before his mind had formed thoughts. He nervously cleared his throat.

"Um... so I... I know the stuff with Mom isn't something you and I have ever talked a lot about. But I had some questions."

"Hmmph."

"I, um... I wanted to ask you about Mom... about her depression."

He wavered at the edge. Sunk deep into his chair, eyes hooded and furious, Frank listened wordlessly. *'Progress,'* Cole's mind added. The last time that word – depression – had been mentioned, Frank had exploded. Right now he was just a mine floating in dark water. *'Waiting to go off...'*

"You had some questions, Cole," Marta repeated, easing him through the silence.

Cole struggled for coherence, his mind fishtailing from thought to thought. There was so much he wanted to ask his father, but the real questions were the hardest ones... they were tangled up inside him.

"Yes, well... I've never really understood," Cole began again, voice strained, "what happened... why she went out of control. I wanted to know if you—"

His throat constricted. This felt like the moment in his childhood before he'd jump off the cliff, hoping against hope that Hanna had chosen the spot right, that he wouldn't be killed by landing on the rocks below.

"Go on, Cole..." Marta prompted. "Frank's listening."

His father's narrowed eyes were angry, ready for a fight.

Cole jumped...

"Dad, the summer before she died, Hanna told me you were cheating on Mom. Is that true?"

Walking back from the bookshelf – which had been halfway reorganized in the attempt to locate a single book – Nina handed Ava a novel. It was by the same author as the first. The image on the front was a woman standing with her back to an open balustrade. Josephine. She was older in this painting, stronger. There were lines around her eyes and mouth, a weight to her figure. She was worldly and a little more weary.

The resemblance to Nina was even more striking.

"Here's the second in the series," Nina said, "Tales of Passion, Tales of Woe. It's also a very good read, though the first was my favourite... so full of hope. Josephine young and bright."

She sighed, settling down into a wing-back chair.

"Thanks," Ava said with a smile. "This way I'll have something to read on the flight back."

She was about to say more when the buzz of an engine caught their attention. It was getting louder as someone gunned the engine. *'Cole's motorcycle.'* Ava frowned at the wall clock. He was back early.

"Don't they usually go a bit longer?" Nina asked in concern.

Ava headed down the wooden stairs, Nina was at her side, their footsteps a staccato beat.

"They were going to talk about Angela today," Ava said anxiously, catching Nina's eyes. "Cole wanted to know what happened before she died."

Nina's hand darted out to Ava's wrist.

"Did Frank know Cole was bringing it up today? Did he offer to talk about what happened?"

Ava shrugged as she heard Cole's tread hit the front steps.

"I... I don't know. I'm sorry."

Nina stood uncertainly on the stairs, her hand slowly rising to cover her throat. Her eyes dropped nervously. Footsteps crossed the porch; Cole was just about to reach the door. Nina spun on her heel, jogging up the stairs, leaving Ava staring after her. The front door opened just as she disappeared around the corner. Ava turned to see Cole, his face haggard.

"Hey," Ava said, walking toward him. "You're back early."

He nodded, but said nothing. As she reached his side, he pulled her forward, burying his face against her hair and wrapping his arms around her.

"Cole?" she asked, rubbing his back. "Is everything alright?"

Cole was shaking; his whole body was alive with it. He pulled back to see her, his throat bobbing as he struggled to find words.

"I, um... I am alright... or at least sort of..." He coughed, shaking his head like a dog trying to free itself of water. He looked shell-shocked. "Dad kind of blew up after I asked about what happened with my mom. He's still there with Marta... God, Ava, I've never seen him so out of control. Yelling and shouting... and... and..." Cole's face crumpled. "...and crying, Ava... I've never seen him like that. Not ever. Dad stayed with Marta. They're talking right now."

"What was it? What set him off?"

Ava asked, knowing what secret had been unveiled. The memory of Nina and her description of another woman's choices was pressing into the conversation like the voices of children hidden in static. Cole shook his head, scrubbing his hand over his face, rubbing out wayward tears.

"He admitted he cheated on my mom before Hanna died..." Cole's voice dropped. "With Nina. What Hanna told me was true. Dad admitted to all of it."

Ava pulled him tighter, her face against his shirt, breathing him in. He seemed calmer now that he'd shared it.

"It's over," Ava whispered. "You know the truth now."

Ava felt him nod, his cheek brushing against her jaw as his hands dropped down to her waist.

"Yeah, I do."

They didn't speak, just stood in the foyer, holding one another. Cole broke the silence.

"I think it's time we went down to the beach and had ourselves a bonfire."

: : : : : : : : : :

They sat on the sand, the heavy dome of the night sky above, the ocean an audible, unseen expanse beyond. The house's windows glowed faintly in the distance, sparks from the fire shooting into the air like fireworks. Among the embers were remains of wooden frames; the pile of paintings and canvas was reduced to ashes, Shay Brooks's last remains pulled out to sea by the lapping waves.

Cole and Ava were warmed by the fire, his arm over her shoulders. It was dark; they both knew they should head back to get some supper, but neither wanted the moment to end. Every once in a while, one of them went to pick up more driftwood, adding it to the blaze. The beach was scattered with it and the bonfire burned long into the night.

Cole stood up, pulling in another branch, then settling once more. Ava watched the frugal movement of his limbs – spare and sharp, even in these simple actions – his body in monochrome. The shades of his skin were like the softened shadows and light produced by a burin, capturing shapes but freed of colours.

"You look like a sculpture in this light," Ava said with a smile. "All beautiful and golden."

Cole snorted.

"That seems a little pretentious."

She grinned, sliding closer. His arm dropped back over her shoulders, the flames rising higher.

"No really... you do," she insisted. "Like one of the Renaissance sculptures. All perfect musculature and Classical forms."

She reached out, running her finger along his jaw, following it down to his shoulder. Cole turned, raising an eyebrow.

"You'd better not tell me I look like Donatello's David," he scoffed.

Ava leaned forward, her lips teasingly brushing his before pulling back to answer.

"Not a chance," she laughed. "The sculptor that really gets me off is—"

"Me?"

Her grin widened.

"Besides you, smart-ass, would be Bernini."

Cole's expression darkened wickedly.

"Oka-ay…?"

"What?" Ava asked.

Cole laughed.

"Let's just say, I know Bernini's work, all right?"

"What…?" Ava's eyebrows rose in confusion.

Cole smirked.

"Nothing."

Her lips pursed.

"No, seriously now – you do look like a Bernini in this light, the way you were frowning." She sat up, arms crossing her chest in frustration. "You know, Bernini's sculpture of David with the slingshot."

Cole chuckled, his arm wrapping tighter, his mouth brushing her ear.

"Oh I know that one, all right, but that's not the one I was thinking about…."

He moved in, pushing Ava against the sand, rolling in to cover her, his warmth a sudden weight on her skin. He dropped his mouth to her neck, suckling his way to her collarbone. Ava gasped, eyes drifting and then slowly closing.

"Which sculpture," she panted, "were you thinking of?"

Cole's answer was muffled against her skin.

"The Ecstasy of St. Theresa…"

Chapter 22: Ripples Going Both Ways

'Where am I...?' Ava's mind asked in concern.

She hadn't gone anywhere. She just suddenly *was...* and she didn't know how it had happened.

Ava eyed her surroundings with concern. She was standing in a bustling shipyard, her thin grey cloak soaked with mud. There were people everywhere. *'Too many people,'* her mind hissed as they shoved and jostled her. She lifted her gaze to the ship's tall masts overhead. Ava caught sight of a single bird wheeling in the sky, as a thought began pushing at the edge of her awareness.

'I know this place...'

Something about it that rang to her... that's what her father Oliver would have said... some resonance that echoed with her own. Her eyes focused, looking further into the press of the crowds, the unwashed children, the threadbare clothing of adults, the toothless grins of the elderly. Sharp thrusts of distant buildings angled into the bright sky: *'azure blue,'* she thought, *'mixed with a touch of white.'*

A smile pulled up her lips as the pieces fell into place... *'It's the colours,'* her mind whispered. She'd painted this before. With an odd prescience, Ava realized she knew exactly how to mix the pigments to match the variegated tones in the darkened structures surrounding her. A base of Titanium white lit from within by Raw Sienna for the broad planes of the sooty buildings, a hint of Davy's green for the moss on the lintels, the shadows blended in tones of Delft blue and Burnt Umber.

Under her cloak, her hands itched to try it.

She turned in a circle, watching the people moving around her. There were people packing two boats, as she knew they would be. (She'd seen this play out a hundred times before.) Everything was familiar. The way that the dim alleys reflected the opposite spectrum: purple bands under the golden light.

'Where am I going?' Ava's mind wondered. Her answer wasn't ready anymore.

A man pushed through to her side. *'Jon's returned...'* her mind announced, and then the screen of people parted, revealing the spare, sharp motions of the person striding forward. She could imagine him gathering wood the same way.

She stared in shock. It wasn't Jon, as she'd expected, it was Cole.

'No, not Cole...' a voice inside her corrected. That wasn't his name; not here, not now. She knew that much. This was Thomas – *'her Thomas'* - and they were going to be married today by the captain. They hadn't had time to post the banns, and it seemed improper to ask Jon to do the ceremony... not after what had happened. They'd marry here on the wharf and leave the next day.

"Ava!" Thomas shouted, "the governess has agreed to give us her berth. I've got us passage!"

"Passage?"

He reached out for her hand and she put her fingers into his, confusion rising. *'Something's changed.'* She flashed to another time. Cole and Kip fighting in an alley. Ava frowned; she couldn't place that either. Thomas watched her in concern. Ava's eyes scuttled warily from the boats to the sky and then to him. Around them, the wind rose and swirled, lifting pieces of her strangely-long hair.

"Sorry," she said shakily. "I don't... I don't understand."

"Passage," he repeated, "to the Americas." His smile faltered. "The woman I mentioned... the governess – Miss Brown – she's agreed to give us her berth, and she'll stay with the children she's travelling with. It's what I asked you about last night."

"Oh," she whispered. "That's right."

Her chest was tight; the noise around her loud and confusing. *'What's going on here?!'* her mind screamed. She realized now why she knew this place. She'd been here before. *'I've painted this before...'* But everything had changed.

"Ava," Thomas said, stepping closer, his voice dropping low. "Is... is everything all right?"

"I don't know..."

The noise and the light and the crowds were smothering her. Everything was different. She didn't know what was happening. Hadn't seen this part before.

"Ava, tell me honestly," Thomas whispered, his other hand coming up to hers, "are you having second thoughts? It's not too late. I could take you back home to your mother. Do you...?"

He left the rest of the question unspoken.

Ava lifted her gaze to the ships' masts, the buildings darkened with soot, and the glittering sea in the distance. They were all the same... but something had shifted inside her, leaving her trembling. She could imagine a voice – her father's – speaking words he'd never said in life.

'It's a shadow of something that's coming from the future... Nothing's ever set. It's only ripples of what can be. You always have a choice.'

She smiled at the thought.

"Everything is fine, Thomas," she answered. "I was just thinking on things."

He grinned lopsidedly, more certain now, the wrinkle between his brows smoothing out. He lifted her hands between them, pressing a kiss against her knuckles, his face fervent like when he'd kissed her on the dock. He lowered her hands, but didn't release them.

"Tell me, love, what were you thinking?"

"Of the beginning of a journey…"

: : : : : : : : : :

Ava woke with a start in the oily darkness of the guest suite bedroom, her body warm under the heavy coverlet, warmer still where Cole's chest was pressed tightly against her back. He was awake, Ava realized. His lips and teeth moved against her neck and shoulder, urging her impatiently to awaken.

She fought against the loss of her reverie. She'd been dreaming a moment before. *'It was something important…'*

His hand roved over her breasts and hips, kneading and grasping.

"Cole…?" she murmured groggily.

He ground himself against her, the heat of his body spreading through her thin panties and tank top. She could feel his arousal nudging her as he moved, brushing the curve of her ass as he pulled her closer.

"Want you," he murmured against her shoulder.

He pushed her flat on her back, dropping his lips down her neck while his hands impatiently rucked her top up. In the darkness, she felt rather than saw him drop his mouth to hers, the kiss sudden and needy. Ava's hands rose to his shoulders, clutching onto him even as her mind scrambled backward, struggling to hold onto the disappearing thread of the dream. *'It was about one of my paintings…'* Cole's lips let go of hers for a second so that he could pull the shirt free, then moved to her breasts, sucking hard against the raised peak of one before moving to the other. His hands shoved the thin fabric of her panties away; his fingers slid downward, hinting at the path his mouth would follow.

She was still struggling to awaken under the onslaught of his caresses. It seemed like there was something she was supposed to tell him... but it was a wash of colours now. *'Davy's green?'* Ava wondered... *'or was it Burnt Sienna...?'* The message was no longer clear. Her attention was drawn to the burning spots of pleasure where his mouth and fingers focused. His lips dropped from her breasts to her ribs, moving across the flat plane of her stomach over to her hips and inward, nuzzling against her curls before angling her leg over his shoulder. Finally he leaned in and tasted her.

Ava gasped as his tongue began lapping against her, desire coiling tight in her core. Flashes of her dream appeared behind closed eyelids as waves of ecstasy rode over her. There was the shipyard... and the shore beyond... and then the field and the sea. It was like her painting, but different. She moaned as his tongue moved faster, his shoulder pressed against her thighs, pushing wide. *'The dream's changed...'* she realized, but now Cole's fingers were inside her in time with his mouth, and the only thing she could say was his name.

Her body was tensed and shaking as the motions grew faster, her moans rising in intensity until he finally pulled back, sliding into her. The feel of him, thick and tight inside her, left her crying out for more. His tongue pushed inside her mouth, possessing her. She could taste herself salty on his lips, his kisses leaving her breathless as he moved in an ever-increasing rhythm.

Wave after wave of sensation lapped against her, blotting away the pressing need to tell him what she saw. It felt too goddamn good: one of his hands wrapped tight in her hair, the other pulled up her knee while he drove into her. Ava moaned, eyes shut; the colours were there again. This time it was in the shadows... Delft blue sharpened the focus of the light in a too-bright sky. The memory loomed nearer. *'Something changed!'* her mind shouted, while her panting increased. The agonizing coil of desire was tightening like a spring, focused on the spot where their bodies were joined, thoughts emerging as sounds of pleasure.

Cole moved faster now, hips thudding against her. He slid his hand in between their writhing bodies to reach the point where they joined. Ava cried out as he brushed the spot and his body shuddered at the sound of her ecstasy. He paused mid-thrust, gasping against her ear until he regained control.

Seconds later he was moving again. His hips pumped faster while her moans built to cries of desire. The flashes of colour and memory quickened. The shipyards, and the feel of the wind on her face, the Azure blue of the sky, gold in the light, the hint of purple in the shadows, all flickering together... reminding her. Cole's fingers were moving faster, leaving her legs jumping in desire, sensations meshing with the rush of memories.

She wavered near the peak, her body writhing in time to his rhythm, the importance of this dream hanging just out of reach. Cole's body distracted her from all thought. With a ragged cry, she tumbled over the edge, her body breaking around him. Shudders left her limbs rubbery and weak as Cole thrust twice more, gasping her name as he collapsed atop her.

For a few moments, he didn't move. She smiled against his hair, feeling the moment he realized he was probably crushing her and quickly slid to the side. He pulled her toward him, so that she lay in the tight circle of his arms. Cole's breathing began to slow.

"That's a nice way to wake up," Ava said with a giggle. "Some special occasion I should know about, or is this just a kink about being in your parents' house?"

He laughed tiredly, turning so he could kiss her again.

"I had a dream," Cole said.

Ava froze. She could feel her own dream again, wrapped tight around her.

"W-what?" she stammered. With shaky fingers, she reached out for the bedside lamp, filling the room with hazy light.

Cole watched her. When she lay back down, he dropped a light kiss on her lips.

"I had the dream I always used to have... the one with the storm, and then the field. The one I told your dad about that night after the Student Show when he was reading teacups."

Ava nodded.

"Yeah... I remember." Her voice was wary.

Cole's face was on the pillow next to hers, close enough that he could hold her eyes without straining.

"Well, I had it again... but it changed."

"The part about Hanna?" she asked in worry.

"Not Hanna," Cole laughed. "The thing about everyone being in the water together."

Ava pulled herself up on her elbow. She could remember something else, but hers was wrapped up in the painting of the dockyard.

"I don't... I don't know what you mean," Ava muttered. Every time she tried to remember her dream she got a wash of colours: *Delpht blue and Burnt Sienna.*

"The Hopi proverb," he said with a grin. "You see, the ending changed." He leaned forward, kissing her again. "This time you were there in the water with me too..."

: : : : : : : : : :

There was a faint sound of tapping.

Ava slowly emerged from the cocoon of sleep, itching with the swirl of warm breath on her neck. Cole slept behind her, one arm stretching around her ribs, his fingers cupping her breast in sleep. Sometime in the night, his legs had tangled with her own. She smiled and let her eyes close.

She had just begun to drift when she heard it once more.

Twisting, she glanced at the curtains. It was daylight, a rectangular corona of light marking the edge of the window. She wasn't sure what had awoken her. The quiet sound of hesitant knocking returned.

Easing herself out of Cole's arms, Ava grabbed one of his t-shirts, pulling it atop her naked chest, and donning a pair of sweatpants. She tugging her clothes into place as she crossed the floor to the entrance, hoping not to awaken Cole.

She pulled open the door. Nina stood on the landing, wearing a camel hair coat and knee-high boots. Seeing her, Ava frowned, stepping onto the narrow landing and closing the door behind her.

"You okay, Nina?"

The older woman's eyes were red, face tired and drawn. *'The older Josephine…'*

"Long night," she answered with a wan smile. Before Ava could ask, Nina pushed a small pile of books into Ava's open hands. "You forgot these in the library," she explained, "and I found the third of the trilogy this morning." She gave a tight smile. "I wanted you to have them before you left."

Ava glanced down. The final image was one Ava recognized from Wilkins's class last semester. It was a painting of David's, Josephine being crowned by Napoleon. She no longer looked like a woman, Ava thought, but like a doll dressed up for display.

"Thanks…" she said, gesturing to Nina's coat. "Are you leaving or something?"

Cole's stepmother gave her a brittle smile, fidgeting with her buttons.

"Frank and I had a bit of a…long night." Nina ran her fingers through her curls, leaving them dishevelled. "We're going to go for a drive this morning. There are a few things we need to do, and talk about. And, um…" She glanced at the closed door. "I'm sure Cole has a few things he'd like to…think about too."

"Do you want me to wake him up?"

Nina's eyes widened.

"Oh no!" she said too quickly, "let him sleep. I just wanted to give you the books. No need to bother him."

She turned, ready to start back down the stairs, but Ava's words stopped her.

"Yesterday you said the whole truth," she said quietly. "Did you mean it?"

For a moment, it seemed like Nina was going to say something, her mouth half-opening, but then she shook her head. Instead she gestured to the volumes in Ava's hands.

"Read the books." she said earnestly. "And enjoy your trip… there'll be plenty of time to talk when you return."

Chapter 23: En Route

Cole and Ava headed back to campus later that day without seeing Frank or Nina again. Ava was lonely by herself in the truck but blasted her music, singing loudly as she drove. She followed Cole's bike along the looping curves of the coastal highway, heading toward the city. Watching the easy movement, her daydream began again: she wanted a bike.

The next week rushed by in a blur of preparations for Spring Break. Suzanne had organized the itinerary, but Marcus was event planner; he spent evenings fussing over details, driving Ava crazy with his checklists and last-second questions. Cole was her tether to sanity, teasing her about Chim's antics and insisting that she buy a bikini for the vacation.

Their trip to Martinique was about to occur.

: : : : : : : : : :

Cole Thomas was a nervous airplane passenger. It wasn't something he ever really talked about (or had much experience with), but as they reached the airport, he started worrying. This flight would be the longest he'd ever taken. A niggling voice in the back of his mind kept warning him to come clean… that Ava should probably know, just in case. Before he could, Suzanne and Chim started arguing over the best place to park her car for the week, distracting Cole from his admission. Suzanne ground the bumper against a cement parking block in the long-term parking garage in her haste; Chim raised his eyebrows at the sound.

"I offered to—"

"Don't even say it," she snapped. Everyone burst into laughter, Cole included, the fear temporarily forgotten.

His worry returned at the sight of planes landing outside the floor-to-ceiling windows. His palms were sweating when the four of them reached the arrivals lines, his breathing rapid by the time they plodded through customs into the main terminal.

"You look green," Ava said, dragging him out of his spiralling thoughts. "Are you okay?"

"I should probably let you know," Cole answered, "I get a bit freaked out by planes. Uh... sorry. Thought I'd give you fair warning."

Ava grinned up at him. Her hair had grown long during the school year and she had it pulled back into a ponytail, wayward strands framing her face.

"Really?" she asked, perplexed. "Why?"

Cole shrugged, walking faster, moving his carry-on baggage to the other shoulder. A blush rose up his neck. He didn't want to talk about it.

"Not sure," Cole mumbled. "I just...I dunno, kind of like being in control of things and when I'm stuck inside a plane, I have none."

The excuse sounded lame to him, but that was as clear as he could make it. Next to him, Ava quickened her pace, her strides matching his. She grinned mischievously and grabbed his hand, dragging him toward the restaurants and lounges that lined the mezzanine.

"What...?" Cole asked nervously. He recognized the impish look. She giggled, raising her eyebrows and pulling him into a bar.

"Sounds like it's time to get primed for the trip!"

: : : : : : : : : :

Cole was happily buzzing when they reached their gate. He was warm and content... and not just a little bit distracted by Ava standing at his side. There was something about the way she kept laughing and leaning into him, her fingers reaching up to brush her lips that made him want to push her up against the wall and fuck her right here. He grinned as the thought came to mind.

'Yup, definitely drunk,' his mind observed dryly. *'...drunk AND horny.'*

They wandered up the aisle of seats, hand in hand. They had just reached the end of the line when Chim's eyes lifted from the book he was reading: *The World is Flat.* He eyed Cole suspiciously.

"What's up with you?"

Ava giggled, pulling Cole along with her like a little boy. She'd been drinking too, though she'd had one drink for every three of Cole's. His hands found the base of her shirt as she stopped in front of Chim. Cole ignored Marcus and all the other people waiting for the plane. He focused on the smoothness of Ava's skin and the thought of all of it, exposed to him... soon.

"Cole and I just figured we'd get a head start on things..." Ava explained. He dropped his mouth to her neck and she giggled, squirming out of his grasp. "Get the party going a bit early."

Suzanne muffled a laugh behind her hand. Chim scowled in irritation, nose flared. He looked like Frank Thomas when he did that. Cole snorted with half-suppressed laughter.

'Not feeling so bad anymore...'

"I'm not sitting next to him on the plane then..." Marcus warned. "He looks like he can hardly walk."

"He's fine," Ava drawled. "I'm sure Cole can handle a few shots."

She pulled him back against her, her hip bumping against his. Suddenly that was the funniest thing that had happened all day. Cole began to laugh while other passengers glanced up in concern. Chim began rummaging through his bag. He stood up, handing Ava several air-sickness bags.

"You started this, Booker," he growled. "You deal with it."

She rolled her eyes.

"Don't need a dad, Mar-cus," she taunted. "I've got one. A'right?"

Chim pushed them into Cole's hands instead.

"Here," he insisted. "Just take 'em."

Cole fumbled, dropping the bags onto the floor. Ava laughed and then so did he. (Marcus grumbled before sitting back down and hiding behind his book.) Cole pulled Ava into a sudden kiss. She tasted of tequila, hot and burning on his tongue. There were people around them, but he didn't care. He wrapped his arms around her, grinding her against his hips.

Cole was vaguely aware of someone coughing.

"Uh... you might want to tone that down kids," Suzanne chided, "I'd rather we all were allowed onto the plane."

Cole let go of Ava, noting how dark with desire her eyes were.

'Yup,' Cole's swirling mind thought. *'Damned good way to start the trip...'*

: : : : : : : : : :

An hour into the flight and Ava's plan had dismally failed. Cole was very sick and she was next to him, helping with the air sickness bags while the contents of his stomach came back up again and again.   She glanced up to see Marcus peeking over the headrest ahead of them with a 'told-you-so' look that made her want to punch him.

He peered down at Cole, opening his mouth to say something. Ava interrupted.

"Say it and you're a fucking dead man," she hissed, eyes dangerous.

For the first time since high school, she really did want to punch Marcus Baldwin. He rolled his eyes instead.

"Go. Away. Chim." Ava growled. Next to her, Cole heaved again.

"You know," Chim said cheerfully, "I think you guys have reached the next level in your relationship. Pretty cute, you know: you holding Cole's hand while he pukes."

Ava swore under her breath, glaring at the passengers watching her and Cole with wary eyes. Cole groaned and Chim laughed, dropping back down to his seat. Cole vomited loudly and Ava looked away, catching the gaze of a steely-haired woman watching them with wide-eyed indignation.

"WHAT?!" Ava shouted, furious.

Around her, people averted their eyes. She heard giggling coming from the seat in front of her and she slammed her fist against her thigh, fighting the urge to beat the shit out of Marcus right then and there. She could just imagine the phone call to her father…

'Yeah, hi, Dad. I'm in jail. They had to turn our flight around because I freaked out on Chim….'

Next to her, Cole opened his eyes, skin grey under the overhead lighting of the plane.

"God, Ava..." he mumbled, "I'm so sorry."

He swallowed convulsively. Ava handed him a can of ginger ale.

"Drink the soda and stop worrying, Cole," she said with a tired sigh, squeezing his shoulder. "I'm sure you'd hold my hair for me."

He nodded, and the second hour of the endless flight began.

Chapter 24: Postcards from Martinique

They arrived at Trois Îlets after nightfall and awakened to a world transformed. Their sense of being out of place was enhanced by the French language. Suzanne was the only one who spoke it, so she became their official translator and guide, leading them through their days.

They'd rented a rural chateau. It was in poor repair, with cracked mortar and water-stained wallpaper, but there was still an air of grandeur to the place. Ghosts lurked in the wide hallways and palm-shaded rooms, faint chamber music sneaking into their dreams.

Chim and Suzanne had set up in a bedroom at one end, Cole and Ava at the other. The chateau provided plenty of room for hanging out without getting in each other's way. The weather in Martinique was not so hot that they had to escape it midday, and balmy enough that they spent late nights on the patio drinking beer and laughing.

Chim teased Cole mercilessly about spending the first night of their vacation sick as a dog. This continued until the third day when they went out for dinner and Chim ordered out-of-season clams.

Revenge was sudden and sweet.

They all spent their days sunbathing, exploring, and snorkeling. Mid-week, when Ava and Cole were swimming in the crystalline water, he grabbed her hand, pointing excitedly beneath them. There, in the shimmering blue depths, was a large Hawksbill turtle. They watched until the animal disappeared into a forest of seaweed, their hands clasped together. Beneath them, the light through the water pulsed to some beat no one could hear.

'Ripples…'

Ava had intended to start the books that Nina had given her, but every moment seemed filled with activity. She dragged the novels from spot to spot, but ended up becoming distracted in the best possible ways. One afternoon, lounging on a quiet beach, she decided to begin. They'd come in by catamaran. Chim and Suzanne were out snorkeling, but Ava stayed back, determined to get through the first few chapters.

Cole, of course, decided to stay too.

Ava lay out her towel, flicking through her mp3 player to find a playlist for the beach: Bob Marley and Jimmy Buffet and some harder rock tunes. She had just laid down on her back, sighing contentedly, when she felt Cole bump up against her. He was smiling down on her, his face in shadow, only the white of his teeth visible against the brilliant light.

"I think you need more sunscreen," he said.

He waggled the bottle. Ava smirked.

"Reading today, Cole... you know Nina's going to ask me about the books when we get back."

He laughed, pouring the liquid into his hand and positioning himself at her feet.

"Go ahead and read then," he murmured. "Just ignore me..."

She nodded, but didn't move to pick up the books. Ava closed her eyes, smiling as Cole's fingers dropped to her calves. She relaxed, body melting as he moved past her knees to her thighs, his fingers tugging at the string tie on her black bikini.

"Cole..." she warned, opening one eye. "Public beach." Her voice was stern, but she was grinning.

He shrugged, letting go of the strings, moving to her other leg. This time his fingers dug deeper, leaving Ava sighing with pleasure. Cole Thomas knew how to use his hands. As he reached her inner thigh, his thumb slipped under the edge of her suit. Ava gasped.

"Cole, please..." she said quietly, voice wavering. She hadn't even lifted the book yet.

Her lids fluttered open to find Cole backlit, his body blocking her from the rest of the people. He moved forward, bracing himself on either side of her, his face a few inches from her own.

"No one can see, Ava..." he whispered, voice husky. "Just don't make noise."

She let out a huff of frustration and desire at his words, her eyes closing as Cole continued to massage sunscreen into her skin. He spent a few minutes at her thighs, going up to her hips, then teasing inward until she began to writhe. Grabbing his hands, Ava squinted, chest heaving.

"Cole, seriously... you need to stop that right now!"

He grinned, pulling back and Ava relaxed under his ministrations. Cole shifted to her stomach and then up her chest, fingers sneaking under the edge of her bikini top, rolling her nipples. She moaned and Cole chuckled.

"Quieter, Ava..." he warned. "The creepy guy by the palm trees just looked at you."

Ava blinked, head tilting to the side and laying back again. There was a pink-skinned tourist peeking over a New Yorker magazine, wide-eyed and curious.

"This isn't helping with my plans to read," she muttered.

Cole leaned in again.

"Forget the book... let me touch you." The sound of his voice was the same one he used in the dark, telling her what he wanted her to do. A shiver ran the length of her body.

"Alright," she whispered, closing her eyes, body humming in anticipation.

Cole worked her arms and shoulders first. He had sculptor's hands, strong and deft, finding and working out the knots under her skin. She'd almost fallen asleep when he asked her to turn over. He massaged her back, moving down to her buttocks and legs, the buzz under her skin returning. His fingers kneaded and traced the lines of her spine. With his knowledge of anatomy from figure drawing classes, he accurately followed the striations of her muscles, leaving her moaning with relief and pliant beneath his fingers. She was half drugged by sheer pleasure when Cole finished.

She turned back to him, shocked by the expression on his face: frustration so intense it was pain. Ava licked her lips, nodding to the water.

"You want to swim for a bit?"

Cole scowled.

"Baby, you know what I want."

Ava sat up, her mouth next to Cole's ear.

"You remember that place just up the beach that Suzanne pointed out as the catamaran arrived?" Ava asked breathlessly. "The one that's hidden by the rocks on either side."

"Yeah."

Ava shrugged.

"Well, let's go... the catamaran doesn't leave for another three hours; we've got time."

Cole's eyes widened. In seconds, he was on his feet, grabbing her hand and pulling her up after him.

"Lead the way," he said with a grin.

: : : : : : : : : :

They wandered along the edge of the forest where the overgrown brush met the water, heading toward the hidden section of beach. There was no one sunbathing here, as the creepers and lush plant life reached almost all the way to the water. Cole had a towel wrapped around his waist and so did Ava. They were hand in hand when they finally made it past the last jetty of rocks, finding the alcove. Ava and Cole tossed their towels onto the narrow band of sand, stepping into the water together.

It was a sheltered tidal pool, the size of a small swimming pool, and just as clear, brilliant azure blue. It was sandy on the bottom, protected from the ocean beyond by a small ring of rocks that broke the surface of the water. With high tide scouring the bottom on a daily basis, and separated from the ocean at low tide, the pool was completely clear of any plant life. Ava sighed happily as she sank her toes into it.

"Oh god, that feels good," she murmured. "So warm."

Cole's eyes were on her mouth, body throbbing in anticipation.

"Where?" he asked, eyes heavy-lidded, intense. Ava smiled, glancing around. They were completely alone. She took his hand.

"In case anyone comes up the beach," she explained, breath quickening. "I mean we saw this place... someone else could have, too."

He nodded, following her further into the tidal pool. Partway out, she pulled him down to a crouch, their bodies floating in the salt water.

"Love you," Ava said, her arms over his neck.

His mouth crashed down like a wave as his control disappeared. She floated next to him and wrapped her legs around his waist to tether herself to him as his lips and tongue worked her mouth. His fingers were insistent, shucking the bikini top up under her armpits, leaving his hands free to roam her breasts. Ava gasped, breaking the kiss as he reached her nipples, rolling them roughly between his thumb and forefingers.

"Tell me what you want," Cole ordered, voice dark and low.

She giggled, turning her face away from him in embarrassment.

"You know," she muttered, leaning in to kiss him again. His hands moved up from her breasts to her chin, holding her face steady, forcing her to look at him.

"Tell me..." he said quietly, voice raw. "Tell me what you want me to do to you..."

"Cole..."

"I want to hear you say it. Out loud."

She moaned, body aching with need.

"Kiss me first," she said, wavering nervously. It felt odd giving him directions in the bright light of day, rather than in the darkness of her bedroom.

He kissed her. It was almost brutal in its intensity, over as fast as it began, like being sucked into a tidal wave and thrown back out again. Ava groaned in desperation as he pulled back.

"Tell me how you want to be kissed..." Cole prompted, one hand dropping to her waist, grinding against her. The frustrating barrier of their swimsuits left little to the imagination.

She tightened her arms around his shoulders, whispering in his ear.

"Cole, I want you to kiss me… hard, on the mouth… and I want your fingers…" she giggled again, dropping her face to his neck.

"Where...?" he asked, teeth grazing the lobe of her ear. "Where do you want my fingers, Ava?"

She looked back up at him, mouth parted with desire.

"Inside me…"

: : : : : : : : : :

The week was over too quickly and they boarded the plane sated with sun and surf. Chim and Suzanne slumped down in seats on one side of the aisle. Across from them, Ava and Cole followed suit.

Cole was completely sober this time, and though he squeezed Ava's fingers painfully during takeoff, he made it through without incident. He grinned as the plane levelled off, releasing her hand from his grip, then lifting it gently to his mouth to kiss.

"Thanks," he said shakily. "Not so bad this time."

"Not nearly as dramatic though," she teased.

He laughed at her answer. Ava reached down to pull Nina's books from inside her carry-on, determined to give them at least a partial once-over in case Nina asked her about them. While Cole looked out the window, she opened the first page.

A piece of paper fluttered to the floor.

Ava leaned over, picking it up from between the seats. She stared down at it for a long moment, her eyes tracing over the text once and then again, her fingers starting to shake.

"Cole...?"

He turned back toward her, face anxious, hearing her tone.

"What's wrong?"

She handed him the paper without answering. His face blanched, eyes drawn to the neat cursive text, written in a looping hand. Picture perfect, just like her.

"This is Nina's handwriting."

Ava nodded.

Cole stared, a line of concern appearing between his brows as he read the message. His eyes lifted to meet hers. She could see the pain and confusion in them.

"I think you're going to need to talk to them both when you get back," Ava said.

With a sigh, Cole handed back the piece of paper, staring back out the window. Seeing Cole's withdrawal into himself, Ava was desperately glad she hadn't opened the book until just now.

Her eyes dropped down to the note once more:

Ava,

I can only tell you that the affair was just the start. There's far more to the story, but Frank will have to be the one to share the rest. He isn't ready yet, but I'll talk to him again today.

I wasn't kidding when I said I believed in telling the whole truth, no matter who got hurt in the process. You and Cole both deserve to know.

I'm so sorry for all of this.

Nina

: : : : : : : : : :

For the rest of the flight, Cole sat in angry silence, melancholy and distant. Ava flipped through the book, unable to focus on the storyline at all. With a sigh, she shoved it back into her bag, the paper tucked inside. *'What a fucking mess...'* her mind prompted. She flashed to her father reading her teacup, the earnestness on his face.

"There'll be some moments when you need to step in and you should be ready for that. It's going to be a hell of a fight, but I think you're up to it."

Ava twirled her hair nervously between her fingers, over and over, playing with it the way she had as a little girl. Cole's anger made her edgy and nervous; that reaction, in turn, was making her want to run. All of the good feelings from their vacation were now soiled.

'Thought I was past this...' she thought in dismay.

As the silence stretched on, her thoughts went to her father. It was moments like these that she really missed him. These were the times when she needed someone to talk her down, to give her perspective on managing the stress. She couldn't wait for Oliver to get home; four weeks until graduation suddenly felt like a lifetime.

Partway into the second hour of the flight, Suzanne fell asleep, so Chim began chatting with Ava and trying to lure Cole into conversation. Cole muttered monosyllabic answers for a few minutes, then turned to the window. When Cole headed to the washroom, Marcus stepped across the aisle, taking the empty seat next to Ava.

"What's up with Cole?" he asked. She shrugged, not knowing how to explain. "You guys have a fight or something?"

Ava sighed, twisting the ribbon of hair between her thumb and forefinger.

"No," she muttered. "Not us."

"Well, what, then?" Chim asked again. "He looks like he's gonna start a fight with someone. He hasn't said two words to me in the last hour."

With a weary sigh, Ava leaned forward, pulling the note from her bag. She handed the paper to Marcus, waiting while he read it. His face, usually easygoing and content, grew cool and contemptuous.

"Cole's stepmom?" he asked.

Ava nodded.

"What's her angle?" he grumbled, nose flaring in annoyance.

"What do you mean?"

Marcus sat back. This was the Chim she knew who talked himself out of arrests, who could end a fight with carefully chosen words as quickly as with fists. He had a gift for reading the intricacies of a situation. It was one of his strengths, and Ava trusted his judgement.

He drummed his fingers along the armrest, then cleared his throat.

"What is she getting out of this?" he asked quietly. "I mean why drag you into this at all?"

"I... I dunno. 'Cause we're friends, I guess." Chim's tone that bothered her, and she shifted nervously under his gaze.

"What, Marcus?"

Chim gave her a half-hearted smile.

"She's using you, Ava. Find out why."

Chapter 25: Fallout

It was nearly ten o'clock when the plane set down, though it took them almost an hour to get all of their baggage and load it on a trolley. The group piled into Suzanne's hatchback to head into the city. Chim told stories, embellishing them all the way that only he could.

Cole sat in silence.

He was irritated by their laughter, infuriated by the easy banter. There was too much going on inside him. Too much he couldn't control.

Rage.

Ava reached over to take his hand but he pulled away, staring out into the wet darkness. The city streets were slick with rain, a perfect companion to Cole's dark thoughts. He clenched and unclenched his fists, fighting to rein in his temper. The calm of the vacation had been destroyed by Nina's revelation.

'The affair was just the start... There's far more to the story...'

By the time they reached downtown, Cole's body pulsed with the need to hurt someone or himself. He needed to get out of the car ... the laughter... the companionship... Ava.

Suzanne slowed down as they neared the building where the shared studio was located.

"I'm just gonna pick up a couple things since we're here," Suzanne explained, pulling the car to a stop, and tugging the emergency brake. "I hope you guys don't mind the—"

Cole was out of the door before she finished.

"Thanks for the ride back," he growled, storming away without looking back, "I'm outta here."

Chaos erupted. Chim yelled for him to wait, Ava argued to be let out, Suzanne asked what was going on. Cole ignored them all. He headed away, crossing the busy street in a half-jog. He could hear Ava calling, but he dodged the oncoming traffic, heading toward the main thoroughfare. There were any number of questionable bars there. There would be an easy place to find a fight.

He'd done it before.

Cole had been walking for a few minutes when he located the right locale. It had dingy, dirt-covered windows, loud heavy metal music buzzing the grated door, and a neon sign flashing "op–n.". Cole was just about to duck inside when he heard pounding footsteps behind him. He smiled coldly as he spun around, hands rolled into fists, wondering who else was looking for a fight tonight.

He stopped in his tracks. It was Ava, and she was furious.

"Where the HELL do you think you're going!?" she snapped, striding forward until she was chest to chest with him.

She was breathing hard from running. Bright pink blotches coloured on her cheeks. It struck Cole that he'd never seen her so angry before.

"I needed to take off," he ground out, face stony. "You *know* why."

Her fingers rose to his chest, poking hard. His temper rose – abruptly focused on her – and he pushed the monster back down under the surface. He couldn't let it out... not here... not with Ava!

"You don't have to do anything!" she shouted.

Cole sneered.

"You don't understand a fucking thing," he snarled, turning back toward the bar.

She was at his side before he'd gone two steps, grabbing his arm and pulling him roughly to a stop. She was really strong when she wanted to be... but he didn't think about this for long, because he was too full of fury.

He needed a fight to release it.

"You do NOT get to run off on me, Cole Thomas," she bellowed. "Not now! Not after all of the SHIT we've dealt with!"

She was in his face, breathing hard. Cole tried to turn again, but she grabbed hold of his wrist. This time she didn't let go. His eyes flicked down to her hand, the muscle in his jaw jumping quicker and quicker.

"Don't," he warned. Ava's hand on his wrist infuriated him in ways he could not explain. Not even to himself.

"Don't what?" she hissed, pushing into his space so that they were standing only a hands-breadth away from one another. "Don't care? Don't say anything? Don't touch you?" She was red-faced, her voice bitter. "Since when do you get to give ME the fucking rules, after all the crap you've pulled, huh?"

Cole watched her, ready to react. If he'd already been inside the bar, his hands would've been ready to throw the first punch. But this was Ava, and that had changed the rules. A tiny voice inside him screamed at him to calm down. She stood on the rainy street, waiting for his reaction. He could see it in her face and posture. Her hand was still clenched tight around his wrist. She expected him to try something.

"I want an answer!" she yelped, her voice breaking sharply.

Like a splash of cold water on a raging flash fire, a number of things were abruptly clear. First, that her hand was shaking where she held him. Second, that her lower lip was quivering as if she was about to cry.

She was scared.

At the realization, his temper dropped down to a steady blaze. He didn't move or change his stance, but suddenly he was listening.

"This isn't about you!" he barked.

He wanted to be out there where the lines of bars and one-night hotels lay... to drink and fight and cauterize the gaping wound in his chest with the physicality of pain. He wheeled on Ava.

"I'm just fucked up... okay?!" he roared, the sound echoing loudly off the brick wall behind him. "I'm just so goddamn MAD at everyone and I..." he shook his head, not knowing how to make sense of it. "I don't know how else to DEAL with this right now!"

She nodded, her lips pursing.

"Yeah, I get that."

Cole's temper still burned, fury and disgust and resentment wrapping around him. The rational side of him was telling him to listen to what she was saying, but the pain was too deep. He glanced at Ava's hand on his wrist again. She still hadn't let go.

"I'm just so fucking mad." Cole rasped. "Just pissed off at...at everyone! Okay?!?"

"At me?"

He frowned.

"No... Yes! I don't fucking KNOW, all right" He shook his head in frustration. "God, I just have all of this... rage... I can't even think straight. Fuck!"

She nodded, stepping closer. Her hand on his wrist stayed, but the other hand went to his chest.

"It's okay to feel that way, you know?" She grimaced. It was almost a smile, just devoid of happiness. "I get that, Cole... I really do."

"No, you don't," he retorted.

She frowned, eyebrows pulling together in annoyance, voice rising.

"Yes, actually, I do!"

He looked down at her, his body warring with emotions. Ava was there, and he couldn't bring himself to shove her away. She stared up at him.

"So what do I do then?" Cole asked.

She exhaled shakily, fingers dropping from his wrist to hold his hand tightly.

"Let's go paint."

: : : : : : : : : :

Ava power-stapled a swath of canvas to the wall of the studio with unsteady hands. Cole stood just inside the door, jittery with the need for release. He rocked back and forth on the balls of his feet, hands clenched at his side. His face was closed and dark... *furious*. Ava could almost see the waves rising around him like the heat off pavement in the summer, as if his ire was slowly released in the frustration of the repetitive motion.

This was the side of Cole that scared her, but she wasn't leaving tonight. *Not this time.*

The makeshift canvas covered one entire wall, the raw linen stretched as high as she could reach. If the two of them had been five years younger, she would have suggested spray-painting a building, but she'd had too many close calls lately... and she wasn't risking it with Cole's mood. If the police came, she was almost sure he wouldn't run. *'He'd TRY to start a fight,'* an inner voice warned. Ava knew, with certainty, that Cole didn't care about the consequences of his actions right now... and that worried her.

It reminded her of her younger self.

Pulling open her black painting kit – a large metal toolbox – Ava scooped up tubes of acrylic paint. Oils were too slow-drying for this process. Cole needed something immediate and intensely pigmented. *'Paint sticks!'* her mind suggested. She nodded to herself, grabbing a handful of them too.

She spread them across the shelf of the easel and on the nearby table. Two of them rolled and tumbled to the floor, another following seconds later, but Ava didn't notice. She was filling a coffee can with water from the sink at the back. Returning to the studio, she slammed the can down onto the table, water sloshing over the edges.

With one last look at the supplies, she turned to Cole. He was still scowling, his mind somewhere else. Lifting his fist, she pulled open his fingers one by one, pressing the handle of a brush into his palm.

"Paint it out," she instructed, eyebrows rising.

Cole's lips curled like a dog about to attack.

"I'm NOT a painter like you are!"

There was challenge to the snarled words, and insolence. It irritated her. She tugged the brush from his grip, grabbing a paint-stick and slapping it into his palm.

"Fine, Cole," Ava muttered, refusing the bait. "Draw, then! I know you can do that!"

He stared down, face darkening.

"What am I supposed to do with this?" he growled.

Ava dragged him to the canvas.

"I don't fucking care WHAT you do," she replied angrily. "I just need you to start. Do anything, Cole. Just do it. Make something. PAINT!"

He stood before the blank canvas, body taut with anger. Unmoving. Ava leaned in, her words harsh. Letting her own fury come out in the sharp hiss of her words.

"Just start," she taunted. "Destroy it, Cole! Make it dark! Cruel!" Her voice rose, growing angrier. "Do whatever the hell you NEED to do! Just GET. IT. OUT!"

He'd been scowling at the wide expanse of unprimed fabric while she talked. She saw the wrath just under the surface of his control, rising like flood waters. Dangerous... she took his wrist, holding his fist and the paint-stick next to the wall. Hovering it over the canvas.

"Fuck off!" he barked.

Ava leaned in, her lips in a cruel smile.

"What's pissing you off, Cole?" His eyes met hers. "Is it your dad? Nina? ...your mother?" Ava paused, stepping closer still, breasts bumping against his chest, her intonation almost sexual. "Is it me?"

"Stop it!" Cole roared. His face was flushed; he was breathing rapidly.

Ava smirked icily.

"So how angry are you, Cole?" she taunted. "Show me..."

Like a dam breaking, he was suddenly in motion. He tore his hand out of her grip, her nails scoring his arm. As she watched, a line of expletives smeared across the canvas in a single broad stroke. Fury and rage spilled out into words and obscene scribbles as the minutes passed, the rage given voice in the dark. Ava stood beside him as he worked, watching as he was pulled into the process. Disappearing under the black surface.

Cole moved with surprising speed, his anger rising up out of him in waves. Ava handed him new medium as he used up the old. She switched him to paint when Cole could no longer cover large enough areas with the narrow lines. His actions became bolder. The storm was unleashed.

"More black!" Cole demanded, reaching back to her.

Ava loaded another brush with acrylic, standing back and watching as the pale canvas altered and changed under his assault. It was fascinating and horrifying... she was seeing the physical representation of Cole's demons emerging onto the wall of her studio. Pain. Fury. Hatred. Fear. All growing into a larger whole, blurring together to form something more.

The canvas on the wall slowly filled with released rage, the texture of the words fuelled the raw flow of emotions. Ava glanced at her cell phone, shocked to see that two hours had passed. The streets outside were silent and empty, raindrops steadily slapping against the windowpanes. It was well past midnight, but Ava didn't interrupt the process. She'd gone through this too many times herself. Instead, she watched in awe as Cole's words morphed into hatch marks and then finally into renderings... shapes drawn in searching lines coming out of the canvas toward her.

Another hour passed.

Coming back from changing the can of water, she realized, with a start, what the image was. There were two people struggling to cling to a broken piece of wood as waves crashed around them. Ava stood in place, swallowing again and again as bile rose in her throat. The figures were cut and bleeding. The waves threatened to drown them both.

Cole's arms moved ceaselessly across it, adding colour and detail: blood running down the limbs, water soaking the clothing, dragging them under. There was something she recognized about the image... something impossibly familiar. Only one thing had changed.

'Last time, I was the only one in the water ...'

At the canvas, Cole reached backward, groping blindly for a brush. Ava was too lost in horror to notice. He grabbed the tube of paint from the easel, squeezing it directly onto his fingers, rubbing it directly into the canvas. A glimmer of light appeared over the dark blues and greys, pulling the image into relief. Two people – a man and a woman – were caught together, grappling with impossible forces. Fighting hard to stay afloat.

'That's me and Cole...' Ava realized in shock.

A frisson of fear ran up her spine. This was her dream... the one where she died. She knew, somehow, that the winged woman – the figurehead of the ship – was nearby. But this time, it was going to come down on both of them. They were both dying in this image.

"No... it can't be," she whispered in terror. "He's supposed to make it to shore."

Her words were drowned out by the rain on the windows, the thrumming of the roof above. Cole painted like a man possessed. *Unstoppable.* The image emerged from the darkness, highlights deepening the illusion of depth, the watery grave that surrounded them. A quote from Renoir popped to mind: *"I've been forty years discovering that the queen of all colours is black."* The canvas was leaden with it.

Standing next to the easel, his clothes completely destroyed by paint, Cole altered his approach again. He rubbed pale skin-tones into the grain of canvas, obscuring the written words, pushing them under the surface of the water with acrylic glaze. The liquid character of the painting splashed over the edges. The speed of his fingers edged toward care. Violence was tempered by detail. Cole moved the male figure's hand so he was grasping the woman next to him. The water surrounding them was changing.

'We're not going to make it...' Ava's mind announced.

Ava noted the subtle change as Cole's anger began to recede. She could see it in the way he moved. He no longer was attacking the canvas, but selecting colours now. He switched back to brushes, the edge of a split lip and the purple swelling of a black eye appearing in careful strokes. A crimson line of blood dribbled across a cut cheek like a flower on snow.

Ava swallowed hard as the image shifted into focus. *'That's definitely the two of us...'* she thought as Cole smeared his nose in the image, breaking it in the process. *'But Cole's drowning with me...'* The man in the self-portrait was struggling to stay afloat, his hands wrapped tight around the image of Ava. His face was torn in anguish, body flagging with exhaustion. There was a hint of beauty under the destruction. Tenderness appearing on occasion.

'Dying together...'

It made her want to cry.

Ava wavered on her feet, eyes darting to her cell phone again. She realized in shock that they'd been here all night. Cole was painting even now, though his arms had slowed, and he paused, panting tiredly every once in a while. Outside, the sky had lightened to a greenish blue, promising the coming of dawn.

Stumbling to the couch in a daze, Ava pulled off her shoes, slumping down on the cushions, her mind buzzing with lack of sleep. Cole worked on; he turned around at one point, surprised to see her watching him.

The image – larger than life – had transformed again. Their embrace – a death grip – as they went under the water, no longer held rage and exhaustion. There was comfort in death. Ava noted that Cole's painting style was much more representational than her own. She watched in awe as he shifted the curve of the lips on his self-portrait, so that he was half smiling, as the water rose to cover his face. Pain on his visage, but relief in the expression.

'Together, at the end.'

As if reaching a pre-defined point, Cole stopped, his body going perfectly still. He stood before the canvas a long time, anger finally dissipated. Fatigue and relief were visible in the relaxed lines of his posture, his body close to collapse. Exhausted, but whole. He dropped the brush into the water-filled coffee can, turning back to where Ava waited.

She smiled, lifting her hand, gesturing him to come near.

Cole joined her on the low couch. Ava lay down near the back, pulling him close. He faced toward her, his paint-stained hands between them, together as if in prayer. She tightened her arms around him, her face next to his on the crumpled drop cloth. Cole caught her eyes as she relaxed, and for the first time in hours, he gave a weary smile.

Ava reached out, petting his hair, then running her fingers down his back. He didn't speak, though he groaned tiredly. Her fingers brushed his forehead, rubbing away a smudge of paint. Cole's body was limp in her arms, weak after the lengthy process. She recognized this from her own nights of explosive anger as she waited for his breathing to finally slow. Her hands moved over him again and again in comfort. Her eyes were riveted to the canvas on the far wall.

'It's over…' her mind announced.

Finally Cole slept.

Chapter 26: The Terms of Parley

Cole was in the water, one arm wrapped around her chest, the other slung over the broken mast to which he clung.

"Swim!" he roared, but Ava wasn't answering any longer. Her face, half-submerged, was ghostly pale, eyes closed, lips faded to blue.

His fingers tightened around her limp hand.

"No, Ava! Stay with me!"

His gaze dropped to their joined hands, white against the solid black of the water-soaked mast. Ava's wedding ring glinted, a single bright star in the darkness. It was the one he'd placed on her finger only weeks earlier, the day before they'd left on the journey. He took a breath to shout again, just as another wave rose up like a mountain above them. He could hear the sound of wood breaking, echoing like musket shot.

"Dear God, preserve us both," he gasped in horror.

There was something dark rising on the cresting wave, a winged figure looming above the two of them...

Cole jerked awake to the sound of someone coming up the wooden stairs. He was completely disoriented, not sure where he was or how he'd gotten here. There was a colour-flecked sheet over him that reminded him of Ava. He blinked against the light, twisting sideways and groaning. Running a hand over his face, Cole noticed that the skin on his fingers was stiff with dried paint. He squinted, turning his hands one way and then the other.

'*She was wearing my ring...*' his mind whispered as if from a dream, but he had no idea what that meant.

Pushing himself up on his elbows, he peered back over his shoulder. He froze at the sight that greeted him. There was a painting on the wall – his painting. Death in the water.

With a rush, the rest of the night returned.

The footsteps on the stairs were getting louder. Cole sat up as memories of yesterday's plane ride and their trip ran through his mind. Martinique seemed more than a day away... almost like a different lifetime. Seconds later, Ava walked through the doorway balancing two cups of coffee in one hand, a paper bag in the other. He jumped up to help as she came in.

"Good to see you're awake," Ava said with a grin, leaning in to kiss him lightly on the mouth. "If you're looking for it, the washroom's downstairs on the main floor. Second door on your right. You have to jiggle the handle on the toilet sometimes."

Cole nodded and jogged down the stairs, returning minutes later. Ava had laid out breakfast on a clean section of drop cloth on the floor and she sat cross-legged beside it. Cole dropped down next to her, reaching out to touch her cheek.

"Thanks..." he said quietly, "for last night."

She smiled as Cole settled in beside her. Somewhere Ava had found warm muffins. His stomach rumbled in anticipation. She leaned toward him, offering him a cup of coffee.

"Your painting is amazing," she said quietly. "Painful, but still beautiful."

"No," Cole muttered, "it's not."

"It reminds me of Gericault's *Raft of the Medusa*... all the people from the shipwreck waiting for rescue." She smiled again. "I'm sorry I didn't have a stretched canvas for you. You might have a career as a 2D painter after all."

"Thanks, I think."

His voice was wary; Ava sighed at the sound.

"It's a compliment, Cole. Take it..." she frowned. "And stop feeling so self-conscious about this."

He gave her an embarrassed smile, ducking his head and taking a sip of his coffee.

"I do this all the time," Ava explained, gesturing at his work. "I *get* this..."

Cole stared down at the coffee before his eyes sought hers.

"Thank you."

The words didn't feel like enough, but he didn't know how to keep going. He lifted the muffin and began to eat.

"So, what do you feel like doing today?" Ava asked after a bit. "It isn't quite two and we've got the rest of Saturday waiting for us. You want to go for a ride? It's already pretty warm out there."

Cole's face grew distant.

"I'm going to drive out to my dad's place today," he said coldly. "I want to hear the rest of Nina's story."

The muffin dropped from Ava's fingers.

"So what," she asked, voice frustrated. "You're just gonna burst in, guns blazing, and call him out?"

Cole laughed mirthlessly.

"Uh... yeah. Something like that."

She blew out an angry breath.

"God, Cole, that's just gonna cause a huge fight, you know? It won't solve a goddamn thing!"

He scowled, turning his attention back to his food, dropping bits and pieces of the muffin onto the cloth. Ava waited for him to answer. When he stayed silent, she touched his knee.

"Hey," she said quietly, "look at me." He eyed her warily. "What do you want out of all of this?" she asked.

Cole turned to stare at the painting on the wall. The feelings it invoked – being out of control and not knowing how to get back to solid ground – were exactly how he felt.

"Cole...?"

"I want the truth," he said tiredly.

"You sure about that? Or do you really just want to hurt him... 'cause there's a difference."

His jaw clenched until his teeth throbbed. (Cole hated that she knew him like this.) Ava pulled her fingers from his knee and rubbed her thumb over the back of his knuckles in silent comfort. Outside the window, a car's tires hissed through the puddles, silence following it.

"You have a right to know what happened, Cole," Ava said. "You do. But you need to decide if you're ready." Cole lifted his eyes, weighing her words against the pain inside him.

"Think about it," she continued. "If you go out there today, there won't be any coming back from it. Some things you just can't undo..."

Cole pressed her hand against his cheek.

"So what do I do, then?"

"Call Marta. Get her opinion on it."

: : : : : : : : : :

Marta Langden set the phone down into its cradle, eyeing the scribbled notations on the yellow pad.

Nina gave note to Ava... admitted something more than affair... Cole wanted to know... Frank not talking to him... Angela's depression part of it... Ava thinks Nina has ulterior motives. CHECK OLD SESSION NOTES!

Marta tore the sheet off, placing it next to her keyboard to be typed out. When Frank Thomas had called her last week, panicked and wanting to restart his private meetings, she knew that things were starting to spiral out of control. His behaviour in the four sessions since had added to that conviction. The phone call from his son had confirmed it beyond question.

Everything was going to come out.

Marta leaned back in her chair, tapping her toe as she mentally shuffled through the years since she'd counselled both Frank and Nina Thomas. She could recall the challenges of those times, the subtle and not-so-subtle manipulations between the couple. She clicked open the laptop's folder of clients, opening their file. Marta frowned as she read. There was no more room for secrets now.

Her fingers drummed once more and then stopped. Decision made, she picked up the handset, dialling the Thomases' number. The phone rang twice and then connected with a crackle.

"Hello?" It was Nina Thomas, her cultured voice recognizable after all these years.

"Hello Nina. It's Dr. Langden calling... how are you?"

"Fine, Marta, just fine... and you?"

"Oh good, just busy."

Nina chuckled.

"Well, Frank's certainly taking up all your spare time. It's hard having him away so often. I don't know if you've heard, but we've started in early on the yard. Trying a bit of xeriscaping near the driveway."

"Xeriscaping?"

Nina continued on happily, describing the plants and minimal watering. Marta waited, making small noises of agreement, her eyes on the clock. At the one minute mark she interrupted.

"Ah… I'm sure with your green thumb, it'll be lovely," Marta said, then abruptly changed tack. "Nina, I'm actually calling you today for another reason."

There was a short pause, and the voice on the phone returned.

"Ava found the note, didn't she?" Her voice was sharper, less pleasant. Nina on guard.

Marta sighed. If there was anything she knew about Nina Thomas, it was that the woman never did anything by accident.

"Yes, she did."

"I thought Cole should know about that," she said brusquely, "and I wasn't sure Frank would ever willingly share it."

Dr. Langden's toe had begun tapping under her desk again. She waited. (Nina might do things for her own reasons, but she almost always blurted them out if given time.)

"So do you want me to had Frank call you back?" Nina asked.

"Well, that's the thing…" Marta said, forcing her voice to stay neutral, "Cole told me he wants to meet with you both of you now." The tempo of her tapping increased as she spoke, irritation rising.

"Oh!" Nina squeaked. "I didn't... I thought that…" Her voice had lost something, grown breathier. "Well, I'm really busy with the landscaper this week. And we're having the soil brought in Saturday. I mean I can't just drop everything…"

Her words trailed off.

"I can sympathize with your scheduling issues, Nina," Marta replied, "but seeing as you were the one who brought this up, it's only fair that you be part of the discussion."

There was a long pause. Dr. Langden was just about to ask Nina if she was still there when she finally answered.

"Alright then," she snapped. "I'll come too."

: : : : : : : : : :

It had been a long two weeks since the return from Martinique. Busy with exams and culminating projects, Cole and Ava hadn't visited the Thomases. University was winding down and both of them were overwhelmed as the countdown to graduation began.

The last of the intaglio multi-prints had been printed. The remaining images were blacked away from the zinc plates under the dark grain of the mezzotint rocker. Ava's final image was created of light and shadow, like ripples seen underwater, the image revealed through the use of oil and burin. Cole's was as different from hers as it was similar. It was a landscape. The cliff with the rocks below; the silhouette of a single person walking the shore. Ava had never asked Cole who the person was… whether the tiny figure was Cole or her.

Somehow it seemed better if she didn't know.

Family life for the Thomases was tenuous at best. Cole had had two stilted phone conversations with Frank and Nina, though the details of the note and what it entailed for all of them had never been discussed. Everyone was cautious of unsettling the precarious balance. There was a flurry of preparatory emails with Marta Langden and half a notebook full of writing for Cole, all of it an attempt to mitigate the explosiveness of the eventual meeting. No one knew exactly what secrets would be revealed when the tide receded.

As the weekend neared, Ava felt completely unsettled. Conflict was coming like dark clouds on the horizon hinting at a coming storm. She struggled with her wariness by calling her father's hotel room at random hours. He never complained. Instead, they chatted about empty things, small moments from school, and old memories until Ava finally admitted to her real fears. Oliver calmed her nerves, assuring her things would work out, no matter how the discussion went.

"It's all choices, Ava... just do the right thing, and don't worry. Nothing's set."

She smiled into the receiver.

"That's the part that worries me, though."

Her father made a coughing sound. (Ava knew he was trying to hide his laughter.) The low rumble of his voice returned seconds later.

"But Kiddo, what'd be the point, if there wasn't a choice...? Where's the fun in that?"

Ava snorted.

"It'd be nice to just know, Dad. To just have this idea of 'do this' and everything works out... to just have that guarantee.... not knowing scares me."

Her father paused, and the low buzz of the trans-Atlantic connection filled her ear.

"You say that now," he said gruffly. "But if you had no choice, if that was taken away from you, you'd probably feel differently."

His voice sounded hollow and sad. Ava sighed, wishing again that he wasn't on tour.

"Yeah, Ollie... you're probably right... but I hate feeling like I'm gonna screw this all up."

Her father chuckled.

"Then trust me on this. I saw the end of your cup, Ava." He paused, and the hair crawled over her scalp. "It was dragons all the way down."

She grinned.

"Maybe when you come back you could—"

"Read your teacup?"

Ava laughed, closing her eyes and imagining him sitting next to her on the couch, cigarette in hand.

"No, Dad. Read Cole's teacup..."

: : : : : : : : : :

They were heading out for the first meeting with Frank and Nina. Ava drove the truck as they wove along the road that wrapped the coast like a ribbon, Cole in the seat beside her. He took her hand, pulling it over toward him. He'd been quiet for the last half hour, his jaw set.

"You okay?" she asked, peering over at him.

Cole's smile didn't make it to his eyes.

"I will be."

He flicked on the radio, ending any further conversation; for a time, the coastal highway moved past in a flicker of bright Spring colours. Ava knew what Cole was feeling. He'd worried about the meeting for weeks, tension building until he'd begun waking at night, lack of sleep leaving him irritable during the day. Cole had spent the sleepless hours writing thoughts and ideas as they came to him, sometimes staying up until dawn.

Ava knew this because Cole had been sharing her apartment ever since they'd gotten back from Martinique.

Things had shifted between them, permanency coming with a new level of intimacy. They found comfort in their own connection as things around them began to unravel. Frank and Nina, Ava had reminded him, were not their issue. They were strong. The meeting with them was to provide necessary closure for Cole, something that would close that chapter of his life, and let him start the next.

That was why Ava had agreed to attend the counselling session, too.

: : : : : : : : : :

They sat in Marta's office, chairs in their usual inward-facing positions. Frank and Nina had arrived early and as Cole and Ava walked into the room, they stood up nervously from their recliners. Without pause, Cole went over to his father and hugged him. Tears prickled Ava's eyes at the gesture.

'He's trying...'

Frank muttered something to Cole and both men smiled. Seeing it, the first bit of tension eased from Ava's chest. Father and son stepped away from each other, talking about unimportant things: the weather, plans for the house, the end of university, graduation and applications for grad school. There was an unspoken agreement to talk about things that were safe.

While they chatted, Ava took surreptitious glances at Nina. She had changed since Ava had last seen her, her skin waxy, smile tight and anxious. She was watching her husband and stepson, hands clasped tightly before her. It was the speech posture that Ava knew so well.

Stepping toward her, Ava reached out for Nina, pulling the woman into a warm hug. Despite her frustrations with the note and the havoc it had unleashed, Ava actually liked Nina. That hadn't changed. She just wished she understood her motivations.

"Good to see you, Ava," Nina said as they stepped away from one another. "I'm glad you came today." Her lower lip quivered, eyes growing bright. "I've missed having you coming to visit..." Her gaze flickered to Cole and then back. "Both of you."

"Thanks."

Ava wasn't sure what else to say, but she was saved by the arrival of Dr. Langden. Marta carried two industrial chairs from her waiting rooms, making the space seem tinier than it actually was. Dr. Langden offered to sit in one of them and Cole went to take the other, but Ava stopped him. Instead, she dragged him over to one of the large recliners, urging him to sit down. Cole sat and she perched on his lap, the two of them sinking into the deep cushions, his arms circling her waist. Marta smirked, but said nothing, and the session began.

After a few minutes of small talk, Dr. Langden launched into the plan for their discussion. Cole was the one who'd requested the meeting, so he would start by explaining his concerns. She turned to Frank and Nina.

"You will certainly have a chance to explain your side of the story. That's why we're here, after all. But it's important that we let Cole share his thoughts without interruption."

She waited until Cole's father looked up at her.

"Frank, we've spent the last couple weeks working on your reactions. I need you to focus on your breathing today. All right?"

He nodded, reaching up to squeeze the bridge of his nose as if staving off a headache. Across from him, Marta smiled sympathetically before turning to Cole.

"Alright, Cole. You told me that you'd made some notes."

Ava could feel Cole tense as his hands tightened against the spine of the black notebook, flipping through the pages, one after the other. Ava turned her head, putting her mouth near his ear, dropping her voice.

"It's okay," she whispered. "You can do this."

He held her eyes. There was determination there, something Cole had fought hard to discover over the last months. He wasn't running anymore; he was ready to stay. Ava smiled, trying to will resolve into him. Giving him strength to do this.

Taking a harsh breath, he began.

"When Dad and I met last time, we talked about the affair that he and Nina had before Hanna died. I knew that Mom suspected it, though Dad had always denied it..."

Frank Thomas was staring down at the carpet as his son talked, his face a mask of pain. It struck Ava how sensitive he was about any mention of his ex-wife. It seemed odd. She wondered what else lay under the surface.

"...I kind of figured, at that point, that I knew why Mom became so depressed over the years. It was her fear and anger... and then, of course, Hanna's death... all coming together at the same time. It was just too much for her."

Cole's words disappeared.

"Go on, Cole," Marta prompted. "We're all listening."

"Hanna had told me some stuff when we were teens. Things that Hanna thought had happened, though I never knew if this was just her take on it, or if she really knew something for sure." Cole's voice wavered. "The last time we met with Marta, Dad admitted that he'd had an affair with Nina while he and Mom were still living together. And..." Cole's voice broke. "and it felt good to me, to know how it had happened back then. To finally know what Mom had been going through... I felt... settled... somehow... but I don't have that feeling anymore."

Cole stopped, closing his eyes, breathing raggedly. The uncomfortable silence stretched out, the calm before the storm. Nina's face was white, her hand clasped tightly in Frank's. Frank's face had changed. He watched his son struggling, expression grave. Ava was surprised by the lack of reaction so far... she knew he'd had two weeks to get to this point, but Frank Thomas's volatility had always worried her.

Cole cleared his throat, ready to continue.

"Before we left for Martinique, Nina lent Ava a couple books to read."

Cole's eyes jumped to his stepmother as he talked, and Ava saw a bright flash of anger. It was almost like a bolt of lightning, the way it came so quickly. Nina shifted nervously in her chair and Frank's eyebrows pulled together in annoyance.

'Careful... careful...' a voice inside Ava chanted.

"In one of the books," Cole continued, "Nina had left Ava a note. It said that the affair was just one part. That there was more to the story. Nina," Cole said, focusing on her again, his voice dropping into a growl. "I want YOU to be the one to explain how—"

"Cole, I can't!" Nina interrupted, her eyes wide and anxious. "Frank knew, he could—"

"I want to know!" Cole snapped, his temper flaring abruptly.

"I'm so sorry," she yelped. "I just don't know if I can—"

"NO!" Cole bellowed, his voice echoing through the room, silencing her. "YOU brought this up and I want to know the rest of it and I want to know it NOW!"

Chapter 27: Old Wounds

"Cole! Stop it!" Frank commanded. He leaned forward, positioning himself to shield Nina. Defensive and angry.

Cole gasped, closing his eyes and trying to pull himself into some semblance of control. Ava pulled the notebook out of his grip, setting it between the cushion and the side of the recliner. Cole felt her wrap her fingers tightly around his, squeezing three times like he'd done so often with her.

'I... love... you...'

Cole focused on that warm point of connection. Feeling the balance tipping back in his favour, he let out a sigh, opening his eyes.

"We are all going to keep our voices down," Marta warned. "All of us." She had a calm voice, but there was a backbone of steel in every word.

"Cole is going to finish saying what he wants," she continued. "And then you two may respond to him... appropriately." She turned to Nina, dark eyes flashing. "Please do not interrupt again, Nina. You'll have your own chance to speak."

There was a murmur of assent and Cole began again.

"Nina," Cole said. "You were the one who gave the note to Ava. So I want you to tell the story. The whole story..." he paused, his face sharp with anger and pain, "... please."

Her gaze dropped, guilt and shame and something else flickering over her features. He felt almost bad for doing this... but he knew his father could hardly speak of his ex-wife without an explosion. Frank Thomas wasn't going to be much help.

Nina took a wheezing breath, her free hand coming up to rest on her throat.

"Your father and I met years before he was divorced..." she said, voice wobbling. "We were friends at first, but we grew close over time." Her chin lifted, voice growing stronger. "Sometimes you can't stop things like that from happening. Things just clicked with us."

Cole's arms tightened around Ava sitting in his arms. He understood that part of Nina's story... because that's exactly how he felt about Ava.

"The two of us just had this bond," she continued. "Like we just knew each other somehow… understood things that no one else did."

She paused, looking over at Frank, eyes shining. Cole could see how much she cared for his father. There was love and genuine respect in how she looked at him. Feeling like he was intruding on a private moment, he stared instead at Ava's fingers, noticing how well they fit together with his own.

'She was wearing my ring…' a voice inside him whispered, but he couldn't remember why.

"It... uh... things with us...the affair, I mean," she stumbled uncomfortably over the word, "it had been going on for some time when Hanna found out. I don't know if she just suspected, or what, but she came to my apartment and confronted me. And for a while, I left the city."

Cole's head bobbed up in shock.

"What?"

"I had to make some choices," Nina explained. "I went to France for a time, and when I came back, I kept my distance. Things with Frank and me just sort of... stopped for a while."

Next to Nina, her husband was watching her sombrely. There were sorrow and understanding in his eyes. Nina nodded to Cole, continuing.

"I think you were in Junior High then, Cole, and Hanna had just finished high school." Her voice was wistful. "Hanna was so determined to follow in her father's footsteps."

Next to her, the Sergeant Major laughed bitterly.

"Headstrong, foolish little girl."

Cole blanched. He'd never heard his father say anything like this before. Not about Hanna: the golden child. It unnerved him.

"Later that year," Nina continued, "when Hanna died—"

"Wait."

Everyone's eyes jumped back over to Frank. Marta had opened her mouth, ready to chide him about interrupting, but there was something almost visible about the unspoken communication between Frank and Nina. Dr. Langden waited for him to continue.

"There's more," Frank said grudgingly.

Nina smiled, weary.

"You don't have to do this," she said. "It isn't really part of Angela's story."

Frank shook his head, gesturing to Cole.

"No, I do. Cole said he wanted to know it all." He winced. "So he should."

"Yes, Dad, I do," Cole answered in a strangled voice.

Frank sighed.

"Well, your sister suspected the affair. She came to me... accused me of it." Frank's voice was aching and sad. "And I... I lied to Hanna. I..." He coughed. "I told her it was all in her head, and that she was..." Frank ran a trembling hand over his face. "She was just taking your mother's side, the way she always had when we used to fight."

Frank's voice broke and Cole could see him swallowing again and again, trying to pull himself together. Fighting down tears.

"Breathe," Marta said quietly.

After a few long seconds, he continued.

"We had a terrible fight, Hanna and me. God, I just... I said awful things to her. Hanna decided then she was leaving. She said she wouldn't stay at home a day longer than she had to. Her marks weren't high enough for a really good college... but she'd always had excellent reflexes... was good at sports, and the military seemed like the next best choice. A choice I supported."

Frank's face dropped as he stared at the carpet, his voice ashamed. "She joined up to get away from me. I knew she was probably too young really – younger than I was when I joined – but... but I..." He coughed again, eyes glittering with unshed tears, "I figured it'd help her grow up, you know? Get rid of some of that daredevil attitude of hers."

Frank looked back up, face ragged and worn. Across from him, Cole nodded, his own throat aching.

"She really pulled some dumb shit sometimes," Cole said with a tearful laugh.

His father nodded.

Nina squeezed Frank's hand, clearing her throat as she picked up the story.

"Frank and I became close again after Hanna's death." She looked over at Cole, her gaze bright with tears. "Your father was changed by losing Hanna. He blamed himself for her death, and he needed someone to talk to, and I was—"

"But Mom—"

It was Frank who answered him.

"Your mother was broken by Hanna's death, like we all were. She couldn't get past it. She wouldn't let me in... wouldn't let anyone in. She just wanted Hanna back."

"She was always Mom's favourite," Cole whispered, voice breaking.

Ava turned, watching him fight through the emotions. His father nodded, chest heaving with half-suppressed sobs.

"It was hard for Angela," Nina said quietly. "She'd lost a child, and now was faced with divorce. I can understand that in some ways, Cole, but she..." Her voice cracked, lips pursing tightly. "She did things, Cole. You have to realize that. She tried to hurt Frank. To hurt me. She used to call me late at night. Showed up at my office. Left angry notes on my car. She threatened me... She..."

Cole stared, horrified as Nina went through a litany of his mother's erratic behaviour. What concerned him the most was that it all made perfect sense for who his mother had been. She'd always done those types of things. Cole knew Nina was telling the truth.

"...The worst part came when she began threatening to kill herself," Nina said, her fingers picking nervously at a seam on the chair. "I wanted to end things with Frank again... because of her threats. It scared me that she might actually do it."

She clasped her hands to her chest, sniffling.

"I made a clean break with your mother," Frank explained, looking at Cole. "Angela and I didn't see each other except for the times you came to stay with me and Nina. I thought that it would be for the best..." His face crumpled. "...but I was wrong. And I'm sorry about that."

Cole's legs were wobbly, his hands around Ava. This was almost too much. He knew Nina's secret... and the source of her shame. Marta leaned forward, gesturing, open-handed, to Nina.

"Keep going," she prompted. "Share the rest. You've come this far."

"We'd been married almost two years when Angela decided to sell the house. The home that we have now... and move into town. She wanted to be closer to her friends. The house, as you know, is a bit out of the way."

Cole remembered that summer. The suburban neighbourhood they'd moved to, with its modern homes and convenient accessibility, rather than the too-big house on the water that always echoed with Hanna's ghost. Cole had loved the change of location. For the first time, he had been within walking distance of all of his friends. His social life had become so much better.

"The house had a lot of upkeep for one person, and Angela decided she wanted a new place to start over. When she listed the house," Nina said, looking over at Frank, "your father decided he wanted to get it back. It had been hers in the divorce, of course, but he wanted it now. He wanted the memories of Hanna, and the times there. The bedroom had never been changed..."

Cole nodded; he remembered his parents' mausoleum to Hanna. The untouched room, and the bed that still had one corner folded back, waiting for her return. He could remember how his mother had talked of moving away and starting fresh. She'd even brought in a pile of boxes, but they'd never gone further than the hallway.

"Frank offered to purchase the house back from her," Nina said anxiously. "Angela accepted, and the arrangements seemed fine at first. Hanna's room was left as it was, and your father hired movers to help Angela with the rest. We moved back out to the coast and you and your mother moved into town." She smiled tightly. "Everyone seemed to be happy with how it had all worked out, but there were consequences we hadn't expected..."

The hairs rose on Cole's arm. The story was nearing the horrible spiral, the dark part of his mother's life when everything went out of control.

"She started showing up at the house," Nina said, her voice reedy with strain. "Standing on the doorstep in the pouring rain, keys in hand, not sure how she'd gotten there. We had the locks changed, but... sometimes she got violent."

Cole's chest was being pinched in a vise as he sat, horrified by the story.

"We didn't know it then, but Angela had started drinking..." Nina's gaze darted over to Cole and away. "I think... I think that was part of it. Though it was depression too, and maybe some type of..." Nina winced. "... mental illness. It started to scare me, these episodes. Angela kept accusing me. There were some horrible, public moments when she called me a whore and a home wrecker, told people I'd stolen her husband. Then the late night phone calls started... the notes... the threats... broken windows..."

Cole tried to focus on the room, but his body was reacting in a panic: blood rushing in his ears, skin prickling with heat. He wanted to run. He wanted to get away from here, but Ava was sitting with him, sitting on him! All he could do was stay.

This was the secret no one talked about.

"One night, very late, she showed up... began pounding on the door." Nina's voice dropped. "Frank and I were at home. He was furious that she couldn't move on without him. The three of us were in the doorway, yelling. She tried to push into the house, and Frank stepped in the way. Angela said she'd changed her mind. Said she wanted things back the way they'd been. She… she wanted the house back… and her husband."

Cole's father winced.

"God!" Nina hissed. "None of it made any sense, but she was raging. She… she threatened to kill herself…" Nina took a heaving breath that sounded like a sob, her hand fluttering up to rest on her throat. "But she'd threatened that before… many times. Frank and I told her to leave or we were calling the police."

Cole felt as if he'd been punched. He couldn't breathe. One sentence echoed loudly in his mind: *'she'd threatened that before, many times…'*

This was the night she'd died.

"She left. Stormed off without a word. A day passed, and we figured things were fine. You would've called if something had happened, Cole. We knew that. And you didn't call, so we just assumed, you know, that she'd calmed down…" Nina's words tumbled out faster and faster. "You were supposed to come stay with us that weekend, but then we got a call from the police that… that Angela had killed herself."

Her words abruptly ended. Cole gulped. Frank was silent and unmoving, watching him. Father and son stared at one other warily, unspoken words and years of heartache exposed to the light.

"That's why you blamed me," Cole said, his voice hollow with the weight of the realization. "Because I wasn't there when she came home that night."

Ava was still struggling to keep up with the quicksilver shift of emotions. Her gaze swung from Cole to his father, grief leaving her mute.

"No, Cole!" Frank roared, surging forward, his whole body tensed as if waiting for a blow. "No! You were NEVER to blame for your mother's death!"

Frank was livid, his voice outraged and anguished. Ava recoiled, her shoulders bumping against Cole's chest. This was the part of his father's personality she'd been hoping to avoid. Frank's hands swung in wide circles, gesturing to Cole as he spoke. He was close to exploding.

"I said those things at the funeral because I was angry with you and with her! I just couldn't believe that she'd actually done it! I should have done something, warned someone! I didn't!"

Ava cringed. Marta watched him carefully, but she hadn't interrupted... not yet.

"I think about what I should have done every single day. But it can't be changed!"

Marta raised her hand – a visual cue – and Ava shifted closer to Cole while Frank continued to rage.

"Believe me, I know you weren't to blame," he roared, "I wish... I wish you had been there, Cole, but I wasn't either, and NEITHER of us can change that!"

Frank was still in control, barely, but it was making Ava uneasy. It reminded her a great deal of her mother: the unleashed temper. Her eyes slid over to Nina Thomas, and that's when she saw it. Nina's eyes were narrowed to slits, her hands in white-knuckled fists, her lipsticked mouth a blood-red slash across a white mask of a face.

She was seething with fury.

"God, I'm so sorry I said those things to you!" Frank cried. "So sorry for hitting you at the funeral. Son, I've never forgiven myself for that."

Ava blinked in shock, her chest tightening in reaction to Nina's emotions too. *'There's more?'* her mind shouted. She could see Nina changing. Could see the stoppered-up emotions welling up from somewhere deep inside. Chim's voice suddenly came to mind: *'What's her angle... what's she getting out of this...?'*

There was still no explanation ... no reason for Nina to open up this whole closet full of skeletons in the way that she had. Across from Ava, Nina's usually calm face contorted in fury as Frank continued to rant about his ex-wife.

"Angela made that choice!" Frank shouted. "She was sick, and she chose her own way out of it! I can't take the blame for that, Cole, and neither can you! "

"Frank..." Marta warned.

"Jesus Christ, Cole," Frank continued, voice breaking, "you were just a teenager! I should have done something! Something more, and I DIDN'T! I've never forgiven myself for her death! It was my fault! Mine!"

Ava watched, horrified, as Nina's fists rose. Gone was the speech position Ava knew so well. This woman was ready to attack. Everyone else was focused on Frank's release of pain, but Ava could see Nina's own frustrations flaring, emotions unchecked. Released.

"I KNEW how your mother was!" Frank howled, his hands shaking with tremors. "I'd LIVED with her moods for YEARS!"

"Stop it!" Nina screeched. "Just STOP IT!"

Everyone turned. For a moment, Frank's eyes darted to Nina, then Marta, then back to his son. He was as taken aback as everyone else. Nina was vibrating with long-suppressed anger.

"I am so GODDAMN TIRED of Angela Thomas!" she shrieked, face twisting into a sneer. "Do you know how many years she's been a third party to our marriage?! How often I've had to listen to this? For God's sake, Frank, she was the reason we went to counselling in the FIRST place!"

Ava glanced over to Dr. Langden, shocked to see her calmness. Not everyone in this room was surprised by the outburst.

'Marta knew...'

"Angela always used threats to control you," Nina snapped. "She KNEW how to control us ... and she might be dead and gone, but it has never EVER stopped!" Her chest heaved, voice shrill and bitter. "After Hanna died, you put the flag at half-mast, but you put it back up again the next summer!"

Ava felt Cole sit up straight in shock.

"When Angela died, you pulled the flag down again. Do you KNOW how angry that made me? That she gets your undying LOVE after everything she did!? That whenever things get really, really bad, it's HER grave you visit!"

"Nina, no," Frank muttered, face aghast.

"You have never EVER gotten over her death!" she taunted, arms crossing on her chest, fists under her armpits. "Do you have any idea what that's like for me? What it felt like to live in your dead wife's house? To see her pictures on the wall? To see you grieve for her year in and year out and never, EVER let go?!"

Frank's face was grey and sickly. He reached for her arm but she jerked angrily away.

"If I'd died in that car accident last fall, you would have NEVER have grieved me in the same way! You'd had moved on. Kept going… kept talking to Angela the way you do now when you think I'm not listening! She's never left us, Frank! You're still in love with her! You always have been!"

"It isn't the same, Nina," he gasped. "She was the mother of my children." He was bereft, his voice quiet. *Horrified.*

"It IS the same!" she cried. Her arms were no longer crossed, hands slashing the air to punctuate her words. "You sit in that den, night after night listening to that goddamn tape! Do you think I don't know that? Do you think I've never listened to it myself?!"

Twisting around, Ava saw that Cole's face was just as confused as she felt. She'd heard the tape, but all she remembered was Cole and Hanna. She looked back to Frank and then to Nina.

The answer was just out of reach. She could feel it there… waiting.

"The rain," Ava muttered. There was something else there. For a moment she could almost hear the voices of Cole and Hanna as little children. They were telling stories… suddenly – in much the same way as Oliver often did, she simply knew.

"It's the stories in the rain," Ava repeated, louder this time.

"You've heard it too," Nina answered, voice strangled with tears. She started to cry, her face crumpling like wet tissue paper as pain and frustration finally broke through the dam of her resolve. Around the room, all eyes were now on Ava.

"There's a recording that Frank listens to," she said, her voice nervous. "It's a video that Hanna had taken. One night when there was a storm. Hanna borrowed the camera from a neighbour to—"

"To film the lightning," Cole interjected.

Ava turned back to look at him; his face was full of awe, as if remembering the event for the first time in years. Ava smiled sadly.

"Hanna set up the camera in the den as the storm began and then she and Cole came in," Ava paused, squeezing his hand. "They sat down to wait, and they were telling stories…"

She turned back to the room, voice gaining volume. "The stories were about their life… about Angela… Hanna, in particular, talked about what a good mom she was… about how much she loved her mother."

She looked up to see Frank, his mask of anger torn away. He looked like a man who'd been flayed alive. When he spoke, his voice was grief-stricken and ravaged.

"We were happy once…" he gasped, before dropping his face down into his hands; the next words came out half-broken. "She was happy once. Hanna talked about it. She knew her mother had been happy."

Angela.

Everyone in the room had gone still, the revelations peeling back the layers of the years. There were ghosts here now. Too much pain to be managed all at once. It surprised Ava when Cole broke the silence.

"She wasn't."

Frank's face lifted from his hands. There were tears wetting his wrinkled cheeks.

"What…?"

Cole shook his head. Ava could see him warring with something. His body was tensed, but the set of his jaw steadied her. *'Cole's okay,'* her mind assured her.

"She wasn't happy," Cole said resignedly. "She was never happy, Dad. It just wasn't Mom's nature. She was depressed, but it wasn't because of you. It wasn't because of us... or even Hanna. She was always like that, as far back as I can remember."

Frank's eyebrows pulled together in pain and confusion.

"But you and Hanna... I've listened to what you said on the tape..." he stopped, glancing over at Nina sheepishly. He reached out for her hand, and this time she let him take it.

"It might be on the tape," Cole answered, "but it isn't true. It's what Hanna used to do: tell me stories to make me feel better. Those nights when you two would be fighting in your bedroom... or when you were gone and Mom was trying to cope on her own, and she just couldn't."

Cole's hands wrapped even tighter around Ava, pulling her against him. She fought down the urge to burrow her face against his neck. This story was too awful and raw.

"Hanna used to make up stories about our life," Cole explained. "She could always find a way to make me laugh... keep me going. In these stories, Mom was always happy, even though she never was." He laughed sadly. "It was all just a fairy tale."

Ava watched Cole's father. She saw his face break as the truth was finally revealed.

"Hanna made that up..." Frank murmured, the words barely a whisper. "Angela wasn't happy after all."

Ava relived a long-ago conversation with Frank:

"You hear it?" he'd asked her.

"No," she'd answered. "I don't..."

"Not as far as I can remember," Cole said.

Chapter 28: The Bottom of the Cliff

The session was over. Frank and Nina were still in Dr. Langden's office, talking about their own lives and issues now, leaving Ava and Cole on the outside. Ava felt like she'd just run a marathon; her whole body was weak. She couldn't imagine how Cole must be feeling right now... and he wasn't offering that information up willingly.

Instead, the two of them drove through the streets in heavy silence, the dismal day matching their emotional turmoil. Cole stared out the window; the clouds were a solid slate overhead, the greenish hue at the horizon promising rain. Ava glanced over at him once, and then again, waiting for the moment he'd break, anger replacing his pain. Part of her was too worried to consider that he might actually be able to cope with this information... to manage under the burden of it.

She was scared to hope.

The landscape opened up, the coast and the white-capped crashing waves appearing in the distance. Ava could see the large house; Nina's changes to the landscaping were underway. There was so much more to her knowledge of the place now. Dark secrets surrounded it. She could imagine Angela standing on the porch in the rain.

It made her sad.

Up ahead, a green sign marking a turnoff to the main highway appeared. The turnoff to the Thomas property was near. Ava lifted her foot off the gas, ready to turn onto the long road that led to the Thomas home.

"Can we just go back to the city instead?" Cole asked. "Go home?" His voice was rough from disuse. This was the first time he'd spoken since they'd left the office. He reached out for her hand on the wheel, squeezing her fingers so tightly it hurt.

"They'll be expecting us to stay," she answered. "If we leave, Cole – if we run – then we'll just have to deal with it all later. That won't make it any easier."

Cole nodded, eyes going back to the window. Ava frowned as she pulled the truck onto the driveway. She wanted to say yes to him, but she knew she couldn't. It was all out there now. This was where it became tricky. She was tired of the secrets. She wanted resolution for Frank and Nina, a little bit for herself, but most importantly, she wanted it for Cole.

Ava drove toward the house, hoping she'd made the right choice. There were logical reasons for staying, but a part of her wanted to get away from here, too. For a moment her father's voice came to mind: *The hard thing to do and the right thing to do are usually the same thing..."*

She pulled to a stop, turning off the truck and stepping out into the wind. The passenger door banged shut. Cole had his eyes on the ground as he buttoned his coat up against the cold. She hadn't gone more than three steps when she realized Cole wasn't heading for the house at all; he was walking in the direction of the beach. His rapid footsteps put an increasing distance between them as he strode past the front porch.

"Cole...?" she called out.

She wasn't actually sure he heard her over the blowing wind, but he stopped immediately. He just stood where he was, shoulders hunched, the dark ruffle of his hair the only movement.

And then he turned.

"Come with me," he shouted. His voice was a cry of pain.

Ava jogged to his side. His face was grieving and full of heartache, but he smiled when she reached him. *'That means something...'* He took her hand, kissing her knuckles, and then they headed down to the water together.

They walked for a long time without speaking. He knew he should probably try to talk it through – he could see Ava anxiously glancing at him – but he had too much going on in his head right now. Too many things to consider and balance. It felt like his entire world had been twisted around, turned upside down, leaving him struggling to find a foothold. Things he had assumed for almost a decade had changed, and he wasn't sure how he fit into it all.

They kept walking.

Cole headed up the beach, going the same direction they'd driven out the last time they were here. The route by foot was more direct, and soon they made it to the small, secluded cove where a wall of rock rose up on all sides. They took the rocky trail down to the beach, standing in the lee of the cliff. It was the place where he and Hanna had gone cliff diving. Cole's footsteps slowed as they neared; he and Ava stood together on the shore, listening to the roar of the waves. The power of the sea had been unleashed by the coming storm.

Ava glanced upward, her eyes on the rocks high above them.

"This was where you'd wait for her to jump," she said, eyes wide.

"Yeah."

"That's a hell of a long way up," she said. Her voice grew quiet. "And a hell of a long way down too..." She turned to stare at the bottom of the cliff. There was open water, but rocks breaking through it at intervals. Dangerous. "Shit, Cole," she muttered. "That scares me."

Cole turned, smirking.

"You don't like my badass past?"

She scowled.

"I don't like the idea..." she started to explain, but her throat closed off almost immediately. She closed her eyes, taking a slow breath. "I don't like the idea that a stupid choice as a kid could have changed... *this*."

She pressed against him, her arms wrapping around his waist, holding him close. Cole's expression shimmered, growing tired and sad.

"Hanna never cared, you know?" He glanced up at the cliff face. "Just figured she could do anything she wanted to. She never worried. Didn't occur to her."

The waves crashed against the beach, the rising wind whipping Ava's hair into her eyes. The blonde strands swirled and danced, blinding her. Cole reached out, tucking her hair behind her ears.

"Is this where you come when you go walking?" she asked.

"Yeah," he nodded, his eyes darting to the cliff. "I like this place... find it easy to think here."

Ava pulled herself tighter against him and Cole's arms wrapped around her shoulders, his chin coming to rest on the top of her head. Her voice was muffled against his coat.

"Why?"

His eyes moved back up again, and Ava lifted her chin. When his gaze came back to her, the silver depths were full of pain.

"She used to make me wait. I'd be out in the water there," he pointed to the churning surf, "just watching for her and hoping." Cole stroked her cheek with his thumb. "I guess I'm still waiting for her."

Ava nodded, remembering her father's words.

"Yeah. But the two of us are out there in the water together now." She tipped her head. "You're not alone anymore, Cole."

He smiled down at her, hands tightened against her back. Even though his face was still weary, Ava knew somehow that it would be okay, because now there was peace in his expression, too.

. . . .

They reached the stretch of beach leading up to the Thomas house just as heavy drops of rain began to fall. Cole pulled off his coat and he held it over both of their heads as they quickened their pace. It was a futile attempt. Within minutes, the sky had opened, soaking them through to the skin. The downpour scoured the beach, turning the sand to a slurry mud that grabbed at their shoes, leaving Cole and Ava laughing like children as they ran through the rain toward the house.

They came in the front door still giggling. The house was laced with the heady smell of supper, and it struck Ava that they were probably late. Nina popped her head around the corner from the kitchen. She looked tired and her eyes were red, but her face broke into a wide grin as she saw them.

"You're here," she said in amazement. She stepped up to the balustrade, leaning over and shouting upstairs. "Frank! Cole and Ava are back! C'mon down and eat!"

Nina came forward, hugging Ava first and then Cole. Ava watched, noticing the slight hesitation before Cole's hands settled down onto her back, and then the moment he pulled her close. Accepting.

Nina stepped back, smiling and making small talk about the weather. Then she sighed, turning back toward the empty staircase, a flicker of annoyance sharpening her face.

"Supper's on!" Nina called out again, voice louder. She turned back to Ava and Cole, shaking her head in exasperation. "I swear that man needs a hearing aid, but he's more stubborn than anyone else I know." Her eyes jumped to Cole, a smile curling up one side of her mouth. "Well, except maybe for his son," she teased.

He grinned before his attention drifted to the stairs.

"I can go get him if you want," he offered. "He in your room?"

Nina's face changed, growing wary. She reached out and touched Cole's arm.

"He's gone up to Hanna's room..." she paused. and Ava saw the surprise in Cole's face. "He's starting to put a few things away. Clothes for now, nothing else." Nina smiled. "But it's a start."

Cole swallowed hard, his eyes on the empty space at the top of the stairs.

"I'll go help."

Chapter 29: The Rented Room

Thomas awoke in the darkness, mind hazy with sleep. Around him, a faint blue light marked the borders of his limbs and the undersides of objects wrapped in sooty shadows. *'Payne's gray and indigo,'* his mind whispered, and he frowned in confusion. His torso was cast in shades of blue, the muscles highlighted with pale bands. This wasn't any place he recognized... *or was it?* A thrill of realization ran the length of his spine.

This was Ava's painting... the one of him in the nude.

He shifted, fabric brushing against bare skin, and details began to appear. He recognized his own heavily-muscled body, the sight of it reclining an echo of another image. He squinted, a long-ago conversation answering his unspoken question.

"Why am I blue?"

"Because it's night... and you're swimming in the dark... the only light is the moon that's just come through the storm clouds. It's just you and the water..."

He couldn't remember when they'd been talking about that, or why.

As the fog of sleep lifted, things pulled into focus. He saw, to his surprise, that he was in a room. *'Not water at all,'* his mind whispered. He was lying in an unfamiliar bed, moonlight coming through the mullioned panes of a bare window.

"It's just you there ... Nothing and no one else as far as you can see... You're free. It's a new beginning... like a sacrament..."

The ripples he could see under his hip and leg were the loose folds of threadbare covers, the shimmering patch near his shoulder a pool of light coming through the nearby glass. He recognized the shape of the quickly-fading image, but the story behind it had changed.

He tried to dredge up the memory.

'A painting...?'

He closed his eyes, trying to draw the dream forward, but the threads linking his thoughts were fragile. His lids fluttered open and he stared upward at the raftered roof, his eyes adjusting to the lack of light. For some reason, he knew that Ava would appreciate the interplay of moonlight and shadow. That, in turn, lifted the memory from the depths once more.

"It's your beginning," she whispered.

"There's no point to a beginning if you have to be alone..."

He couldn't remember when she'd said that to him.

Without warning, someone shifted next to him in the darkness, and Thomas jerked in surprise. Rolling onto his side, he caught sight of a woman's curving back and pale sheet of hair, blending into the pillow. Shrouded by mismatched blankets, Ava was stirring.

"Is it morning already, Thomas?" she mumbled.

He smiled as the memory rushed forward.

They'd married hours ago. Tomorrow they set off to the new world.

"Not yet, my love," he whispered. "The boats don't leave until dawn."

He wrapped his arm around her, pulling Ava into the hollow of his arms, their bodies blurring into the shadowy folds of the bed. She made a soft, dove-like sound as he dropped his mouth to hers. Ava kissed him with a fierceness which still surprised him, lips sliding against his in a heady dance. The night on the wharf had altered things between them... *and it had changed Thomas and Ava too.* There'd been months of uncertainty for

Thomas as he'd waited for her to decide, but they'd been burned away by a single moment in the rain.

For a brief moment, he remembered Ava in the weeks after her father's death, meek and subdued, her face colourless. She'd been bound by an obligation so strong Thomas had feared she'd chose someone else at her mother's insistence.

'Jon...' his mind hissed.

He pushed the thought away, refusing to entertain his fears. That night in the rain, he'd been desperate. He'd pulled her into his arms and kissed Ava, and that had changed it all.

This *here* was the result.

Ava was all the things he wanted; no other woman had ever been close to the connection he felt with her. He moved nearer, sharing his meagre heat as he lay alongside her in the narrow bed. The kiss deepened, while his hands explored the length of her, tugging the thin cotton of her chemise up to her hips, leaving him free to play. Ava sighed into his mouth, her body melting against him as sleep faded. He stroked her inner thighs, feeling her shiver under his caresses.

"Thomas..." she moaned. The sound of her voice left him gasping for air. He couldn't imagine life without Ava. Couldn't imagine *not* having this moment.

Leaving her lips, Thomas's mouth travelled the length of her neck and downward, tasting her flesh. Reaching her chest, he tugged at the ties of her chemise before taking one nipple in his mouth, then the other. Ava gasped, arching against the thin mattress, half sobbing with pent-up desire. Thomas revelled in the freedom their vows had bequeathed: to do the things he'd dreamed of doing so many times.

Thomas' fingers moved deeper, finding her ready for him. Ava's breath hitched with each brush of his fingers, one hand tightening on his shoulders, the other tight in his hair. Cautious of hurting Ava, Thomas eased himself atop her, awed by the flood of sensation which met him: her body, lithe and warm, wrapped around him. He slid forward, groaning at the perfection of their fit. A rising tide of passion began to build as they moved together in a familiar rhythm, a sensation he could almost *recognize* fluttering just beyond his awareness.

In minutes, Ava's movements grew unsteady, mewling gasps growing into cries. She put her mouth against his shoulder, muffling a sudden shout as her body stiffened and then relaxed. In that moment, Thomas, realized what the familiar sensation was...

Ava felt like coming home.

An image flickered to mind unexpectedly: *the two of them laying together on a couch, sheets billowing around them, the air sharp and cold. Behind them was a painting of Ava, fury marking her features...* With a groan, Thomas tumbled into the scattered euphoria of their connection, the memory lost. He shuddered to a stop, ecstasy dragging all other thoughts away. Ava's hands ran slowly over his head and shoulders, petting him the way his mother had when he'd been a little boy, and he smiled.

"Love you," he murmured against her neck. "Always, Ava... always."

Chapter 30: Triptych

Jon stood on the deck of the ship, the shouted prayers disappearing into the roaring voice of an enraged ocean. He *knew* the psalm, but he couldn't hear it. Still he clung to the meaning of its words.

"They cried to the Lord God in their distress; from their difficulties, He rescued them..."

A stone's throw from him, two sailors were lashing the sails, indifferent to his words.

"He calmed the Storm to a gentle breeze, and the rage of the sea was stilled..."

A wave, the height of a house rose on the starboard side and he grabbed hold of the rails, his voice rising.

"They were joyful that the Seas were calmed, and that He brought them to their peaceful destination..."

The wave slammed downward with a weight that drove the air from his lungs. Jon coughed and gasped, choked by seawater. When he opened his eyes again, there was only one sailor holding the ropes.

"Let these Sailors give thanks," Jon screamed, terror rising. *"Thanks to the Lord God for his Kindness!"*

The deck underneath him groaned, the mast snapping under the power of the wind. Jon's voice faded to nothing, eyes wide like a child. The ship lolled on its side, dark hands of water reaching out for him.

"We're lost..." he gasped.

Fear was an anchor in his chest, dragging him down.

: : : : : : : : : :

Hanna O'Mally walked along the sand, her bloodshot eyes squinting into the distance.

It was morning, the night's tempest spent. Debris cluttered the shore, the once-proud ships now broken down to kindling by God's wrath. Hanna lifted her hand, hastily crossing herself. She shouldn't think such things, but the force of the storm had left little doubt in her mind.

She was alive by the grace of God alone.

There was a man's boot a and a cask bobbing just off shore. She'd been walking since she'd awoken on the sand, her body bruised and battered, but still, impossibly, alive. There were other survivors too; a barber-surgeon from Dorset who was assisting the wounded, and her Ladyship, Hanna's employer, who'd shown herself surprisingly effective at doling out food and water. There was a Protestant preacher with a broken arm, a lean, unsmiling man, who sat, whey-faced, on the shore. He'd been staring out at the waves as she'd passed him, his shoulders hunched and sagging.

"Are you praying?" Hanna had asked him.

He'd shaken his head, not lifting his eyes. Hanna had turned, meaning to help others, but something about his grief-stricken face had stopped her. She turned back, shifting nervously. They didn't share a faith, and she wasn't sure what he'd say to the prayers of a so-called Papist.

"Would... would you like me to pray with you, sir?" she asked gently.

He'd lifted his gaze, the brokenness of his expression shocking her into silence.

"There's no point," he muttered, "My faith is gone... G-god has forsaken me." His face crumpled in despair.

On the beach, Hanna crossed herself again, steps quickening.

There were several sailors amongst the survivors. They'd located one of the small dories, upended but still seaworthy, a little ways off shore. They trawled up and down the coast, searching for the lost. For every person they pulled from the waves, another five were floating face-down in the water. Ahead of Hanna, a small outcrop of trees spread out toward the shore, the limbs dropping down toward the ocean. She could hear water running somewhere and she narrowed her gaze, trying to locate its source.

That's when she saw them.

Far in the distance, their bodies shadows of blue against the bright gold sand, were two figures. As she reached the trees, she could see that they were lying side by side on the beach.

"Hullo…?" she called. "D'you need some help there?"

: : : : : : : : : :

Kip lurched upright in bed, gasping. "Please, God, no!" he shouted, struggling against an unseen opponent. The sheets were tangled around his legs and he couldn't move, the nightmare still hanging just out of reach.

"Kip," Raya mumbled, her hand brushing his shoulder. "Wake up. You're dreaming."

He froze at the sound of her voice. He didn't feel like he was asleep, the panic a noose around his neck. He scrubbed a hand across his face, reorienting himself with his surroundings. Raya flicked on the lamp on the bedside table. The dark wood headboard was exactly as he remembered it, the ochre walls, the large mirror on one side… nothing had changed.

And yet it felt like something had.

"You were talking in your sleep," Raya said. "Praying, I think."

He turned in surprise.

"Praying?"

She shrugged.

"That's what it sounded like to me."

Kip struggled to recapture the dream, but it was already gone. Across from the bed, Ava's three panels hung on the wall. He'd had them since early Spring, but they were still untouched, her brushstrokes exactly as she'd left them. The truth was, Kip hadn't been able to bring himself to add to them. They meant something. The riddle behind the story of the painting felt closer than ever tonight.

"Kip...?" Raya prompted, touching his shoulder again.

When he didn't answer, she rolled toward him, leaning so that her naked breast curved against his arm.

"You okay?" she asked. "You seem pretty upset."

"Yeah... I'm fine. The dream was just... different," he uttered, his body starting to relax. "I'm okay now."

He settled down, turning toward her. In the dim light, her body was hazy. He ran a hand up her neck into her hair, pulling her into a kiss. She was warm and soft and his body jumped in reaction. The two of them had been together for the last year and a half – had been friends for years before that – but things had solidified in the last months. His free hand rose to cup her breast and she made a throaty growl, the kiss deepening. With a quick shift of her hips, she climbed atop him, rocking gently. Kip's hands slid to her narrow waist, holding her steady where she straddled him.

"Wait a minute," he muttered, dropping his eyes to her lithe form and then back up to her face. "I need to do something, first."

She sighed in exasperation, climbing off. Clambering out of the bed, Kip walked over to the far side of the bedroom and lifted each of the three panels, turning them around to face the wall.

Hidden.

When he turned back around, Raya's eyes glittered brightly despite the dim room. Kip knew that his refusal to put his own graffiti atop Ava's paintings had bothered her as much as his insistence on hanging the panels in their bedroom. Her eyes were wide and worried, not quite ready to ask, but curious. Kip gave a boyish grin.

"I showed the panels to Rick the last time he came by the studio," Kip said sheepishly. (He knew how Raya felt about his continued interest in the career of Ava Brooks.) Raya pulled the covers up over her breasts, annoyed.

"Oh really..." she said tartly, one thin eyebrow arching like a question mark.

Kip chuckled.

"He wants to buy them."

Raya's irritated expression flipped into surprise.

"Honestly?"

He nodded, walking back to the bed, and sitting down beside her.

"Yeah," he said quietly. "At the time I said no, wouldn't even give Rick her name..." Kip trailed his hand along the cotton sheet that obscured her skin, imagining the long legs underneath. His fingers traced words, leaving random love letters in invisible script atop her flesh. "Kept telling myself I didn't need the competition, seeing as Rick's the one doing my promotions for Asia."

Simpson rolled her eyes.

"You sound like me."

Kip leaned forward, brushing her lips in a light kiss.

"The art field's competitive," he said with a shrug. "Everyone knows that, Ry. I do know how to look out for myself."

His fingers trailed higher, reaching her hip and then her waist, continuing to leave ephemeral graffiti across her body. Raya shivered, goose-bumps rising where his hand had passed.

"And now...?" she asked, her eyes moving over to the reversed panels. Kip knew that Ava Brooks bothered her. He slid closer, his fingers reaching her ribs and from there to her arms.

"I've decided that I am going to sell them to Rick." Kip said with a shrug. "They bother me. I can't explain it, Raya... I just need to make..." he closed his eyes, the dream like a word hovering just out of reach, "a clean break."

He opened his eyes to find Raya watching him. Her expression was soft and tender.

"You sure about that?"

Kip grinned.

"I can handle a bit of competition. And Ava deserves some recognition. She's pretty damn good"

Next to him, Raya moved closer, the sheet falling past her nipples.

"Yeah," she said quietly, "she really is."

Kip's fingers reached her bare chest, his fingertips slowly tracing individual letters across her heart. Raya's eyes dropped down, watching the tag appear as if inked on her flesh. He laid his hand on her skin, holding it there until her eyes met his.

"I love you too," she whispered.

Chapter 31: Decisions

The last few weeks of University rippled by like old films, becoming more poignant for the fact that they were ending. There wouldn't be another semester after this, except for Cole. He'd been accepted into the university's graduate Curatorial program; he had a full scholarship once again and would start classes in September. Professor Wilkins had already assigned him a teaching assistantship for the Fall: an art history foundations class.

"Not ready for real life yet?" Marcus teased. "Don't want to grow up with the rest of us?"

The four of them sat in The Crown and Sceptre, feting the end of university. Chim had already started putting in regular shifts at the Amnesty International centre downtown. Mrs. Quan's office was working several human rights cases with Suzanne as an unofficial go-between, allowing them to work together.

"Not if I can help it," Cole answered, pulling Ava tight. "Besides, Ava's gonna let me be a kept man... I'm good with that."

The table of friends erupted in boisterous laughter. Cole and Ava had now unofficially moved in together. Cole would continue with grad school and she'd work on her pieces for the upcoming shows at the National Gallery. Ava still needed to talk to Oliver about living arrangements. (For weeks, she'd been weighing how to bring up the idea of splitting the rent and adding Cole into the mix.) Her father only lived there a few months a year; Ava was pretty sure they could work it out.

"It's a better deal for Cole," Ava said, elbowing him, "I've seen his place. He's definitely moving up in the world. I'm just losing half the bed."

Cole leaned in, smirking. Seconds later, his hands slid under her shirt.

"Oh I think you'll get some benefits too," he added. Behind the screen of the table, his fingers roved higher. Ava laughed and leaned closer as his mouth dropped to her neck.

Chim ordered another pitcher of beer and they spent an hour reminiscing about parties, and close calls with the police, and newfound adulthood. The evening slowly disappeared. Cole and Ava had gone out to his family's place the last three weekends in a row; Marta Langden had been working with them. Slow progress was being made. Hanna's room was now empty and several photographs of Angela had been removed from the walls. The house felt newer... younger somehow. It was a fresh start. Ava smiled to herself, remembering the first weekend they'd driven up to the house after the explosive revelations. Cole's head had twisted in shock.

The flag had no longer been at half-mast.

Classes had finished a week previously and the convocation ceremonies were still three days away. Nina's plan for a post-graduation party had come together, though it was now limited to a small dinner. Cole and Ava and Oliver, the Thomases, Marcus and Suzanne, and a few family friends would get together at the Thomas house next weekend. It was another step toward reconciliation. More progress.

"So what're your plans for tomorrow?" Suzanne asked. "Feel like coming down to the flea market with us? I'm gonna see if I can pick up a few things for my next sculpture."

Ava took comfort in the studio the three of them still shared. When they were all there painting, and Chim came up the stairs stinking of pot, carrying coffee and day-old muffins, she could almost pretend that they'd be there forever.

"Actually," Ava said happily, "Cole and I are running out to the airport, so we can't."

Marcus glanced up, grinning.

"Your dad's coming back!"

: : : : : : : : : :

Ava and Cole stood in the airport, their hands clasped together. She vibrated with energy, the excitement coming out in the steady bouncing of her legs. Cole glanced over at her, beaming.

"I love that you do that, you know?"

"Do what?"

He chuckled, imitating the slight side-to-side of her steps. She snorted.

"I do not do that!"

Cole pulled her closer, his mouth next to her ear.

"You do..."

She giggled.

"Do not."

Cole pulled her into his arms, kissing her hard. Ava's hands rested against the front of his shirt, lips parting.

"I want to see what you'd be like if I was the one coming home," Cole said with a lopsided grin.

Ava tightened her hands in the fabric of his shirt, pulling him closer.

"I wouldn't want you to leave at all."

: : : : : : : : : :

The three of them sat in the small diner downtown, a few blocks from Ava's studio. Oliver had one side of the booth, Ava and Cole the other, the remains of breakfast between them. They'd been chatting for an hour, reliving the last few months. Oliver was completely involved in the final production of his new album and the audio work that Pete's son had done for him. He was ecstatic about the cleanliness of the sound; the recordings had finally achieved the purity he always strove for.

Cole and Ava told him about school, and their plans for the summer. Ava had broached the subject of Cole sharing the apartment, and Oliver – after a healthy dose of teasing – had agreed. Ava's costs would drop, allowing her to focus solely on painting rather than having to get a summer job before the National Gallery show. Ava hoped that the sales of her artwork from that particular event would mean she wouldn't need a job other than painting after that, either. That's what she was focused on.

Real life.

Across the booth from her, Oliver launched into another story about the symphony's latest tour. He would be going back in a week, right after the Thomases' dinner. He laughed while Cole joked about his family.

"Everyone comes from a messed-up family, Cole," Oliver said with a wink. "I mean, not too many people would consider teacup reading and past lives their thing. You seem okay with it, though."

"Yeah, well," Cole said with a chuckle, "it grows on you."

There was more laughter and stories about the last months, especially Spring Break on Martinique and the turtle. Oliver winked again at Ava as she described it. It felt, Ava thought, like her father had never left.

Pete brought around the coffee pot, refilling their mugs, and there was a short lull while everyone drank. Ava's eyes were on her father. He was watching her and Cole. She saw his expression flicker – pain? fear? – and then it disappeared, covered with a patient smile. He cleared his throat, setting down his coffee mug, and leaning forward.

"So, uh... how did things with your mother turn out?"

Ava jumped at his words, the coffee mug clattering down and sloshing its contents across the tabletop. She resettled the cup, her palm flattening against the table as if trying to hold herself steady. She hadn't mentioned Shay's reappearance to her father... wasn't sure how to bring something like that.

"I... uh..." she stumbled. "She was in rehab, Dad, but she took off. She, um… she OD'd a few weeks ago."

Ava was aghast. Her father reached out, putting a comforting hand over hers.

"I figured. Sorry, Kiddo."

Ava's chest began aching, her breath coming in shallow gulps. Cole slid closer in the booth, his arm dropping over her shoulders.

"How...?" Ava squeezed out. She stared at her father, the skin of her arms rising in gooseflesh.

He smiled sadly. "I read your teacup."

Ava swallowed hard, her eyes swimming with tears.

"But you *didn't see her!*" she yelped. "I would have remembered that!"

He shook his head. He reached for his breast pocket but dropped his hand back down, a sure sign he wanted a cigarette, but was delaying getting one. Oliver cleared his throat.

"Yeah, I saw Shay in your cup... but I didn't tell you." He shrugged. "Didn't feel like it'd be fair."

The news left Ava reeling.

The world outside continued on. The day was just as bright – people going about their daily lives, cars driving by – but everything had changed for Ava.

"Why not?"

Cole gently squeezed her free hand under the table.

"If I'd said you were going to see your mom again," her father said. "And that it'd be good for you... but that she'd screw it up in the end..."

Ava couldn't follow his train of thought, her mind still jumping from one idea to another. *'He knew!'*

"If I'd done that," Oliver continued sorrowfully, "how would you have felt about it?"

"I dunno... I just... " her frown deepened, the *'what ifs'* suddenly real. "I guess I would have expected it, been a bit more prepared... known what to do..." Her voice trailed off.

"Exactly," he said wearily. "You would've felt obliged somehow. If I told you, you'd see her again... you'd feel like you had to. If I told you that she was in your cup and you didn't talk to her... then you'd expect that instead."

Her father sighed, drumming his fingers on the table. Ava looked over at Cole. He smiled, and she wondered if this was how he'd felt when all of his dark history was being revealed in front of her.

He squeezed her fingers again. *I. Love. You.*

"I needed you to make that decision for yourself, Ava." Oliver said. "It was the choice that was important, that it was yours. Sorry, Kiddo, I just didn't feel I could tell you without... affecting it."

That of course, made perfect sense.

"Thanks."

He winked, steepling his hands on the table.

"I knew it'd work out – I saw it – but you needed to make your own decision."

: : : : : : : : : :

The three of them – Cole, Ava and Oliver – sat together, talking in the dim apartment. It was past two in the morning, but Oliver, still on Greenwich mean time, was wide awake. At some point, the idea of a teacup reading had come up, and Cole was surprised when he'd found himself agreeing to have his read.

"Yeah," he said, grinning at Ava, "I'd like that, actually."

Oliver smothered a smile under his hand. He stood, going to the cupboard and laying them out on the table. They were the same three cups from before, with the curved bottom and the faded pattern of leaves. Oliver measured out one quarter teaspoon of Darjeeling, watching the dry leaves drop to the bottom, then pouring the boiling water on top. He settled in, waiting for them to steep.

This time, Cole enjoyed sitting and sipping the black tea, listening as Oliver and Ava talked about the multi-print project. She'd saved the last, tenth, zinc plate – plus one of the prints from it – for her father to keep, and he was planning on framing the plate itself, rather than the actual print. The variegated silver image was visible only through the play of light on its surface disappearing without it. Cole couldn't explain why, but it somehow made sense that Ava's father would want the print's source, rather than the print itself.

"The word intaglio is Italian, you know," Oliver explained. "It's from the verb *'intagliare'* which means to cut into... to scar..."

Cole leaned onto his elbows, listening to Ava's father talk. He seemed to have an anecdote for everything, as if his whole life had been categorized into a million little moments that appeared in story-form when they were needed. Oliver loved the idea of etching, the echoes of previous images sneaking through at random moments, never fully obscured. It was almost with disappointment that Cole realized that his tea was gone and the reading would begin.

Oliver turned on a jazz record in the living room before wandering outside to the fire escape for one last cigarette. Ava sat next to Cole, smirking.

"You don't have to do this, you know."

Cole slid closer.

"I'm not worried about it anymore," he said with a shrug. "Pretty sure I know all the worst parts about my life. Might be nice to get a foot up on some of the good things."

She grinned, leaned in to kiss him. A few minutes later, Oliver returned, sitting down and rolling up his sleeves.

"Let me hold your hands for a moment," Oliver said, reaching across the table to Cole. "Nothing weird," he said with a chuckle. "I just need to connect to you somehow. Right now I only know you through Ava. I need to be able to read you, not her."

Cole nodded, placing his hands against Oliver's palms. He wasn't sure if he was imagining it, but there was something there. It wasn't the same as when he'd shaken Ava's hand for the first time, but he could sense a faint buzz, a vibration. Ollie's fingers were warm, and he closed his eyes, brows pulled together in concentration.

Ten seconds passed, then twenty...

"Alright," Oliver said, suddenly releasing Cole's palms, and sitting up straight, "got it."

Cole waited uncertainly.

"Make a wish," Oliver said, gesturing to the upturned cup, "and turn it clockwise three times."

Cole closed his eyes. He knew what he wanted and though he was sure that he was close to getting it, he wouldn't mind having the assurance on this one. He turned the cup once, twice, a third time. He opened his eyes to find Ava and her father watching him.

"Are you ready?" Oliver asked, voice serious. "We don't have to do this if you don't want to."

Cole grinned, reaching for Ava's hand.

"Nah, I'm good. Let's get started."

Oliver nodded and picked up the cup, lifting it near his face, a knowing smile beginning to tug at his mouth. His eyes jumped from Cole to Ava and then back again. He cleared his throat. Cole could see him trying not to smile.

"You've got your wish," he said dryly.

Cole felt Ava's fingers tighten on his. She'd seen the reaction, too. For a moment, Oliver opened his mouth, seeming like he was going to say something about it, but then he shook his head and closed his mouth again. Instead, he held the cup in his palm and squinted into its base.

"Alright then, Cole, let's see what's going on here," he said, voice dropping. "Ah yes, okay now... well, the bottom of your cup is a bit muddy. Lots of things going on, things that aren't really clear. Hmmm..."

He gestured as he spoke, guiding Cole's attention to the leaves. Sure enough, Cole could make out the dark flotsam in the bottom, bits and pieces of broken leaves smeared together.

"Is that bad?" Cole asked. His fingers had tensed around Ava's but he forced them to relax.

Oliver chuckled, glancing back up at him.

"Well, I mean, that isn't good, but I'd say it's all going on right now... so you'll be able to answer the question for yourself. Is it that bad?" he asked, twisting Cole's words back around.

Cole blushed, not answering, and Oliver's attention moved back to the cup.

"Whatever is going on, it doesn't have to do with Ava. Don't worry about that. You two are good... I can see that too. So I'm guessing this is either school issues or other stuff."

Cole released his breath, repeating the words.

"It's other stuff. Stuff with my fa—"

Oliver stopped him with a raised palm.

"Don't help, alright?" he said with a chuckle. "Okay... so there is a time when things are muddy... messy... just really busy. That's all going on right about now – whatever it is – and it seems like it's all tied together somehow. I can't tell how, but it is..."

He caught Cole's eyes and gave him a sympathetic smile.

"It's gonna be fine," he said firmly. "Don't worry about it, Cole. You're already doing the work to fix it; it's underway. There's someone else there too – an older man, I think – maybe your dad? He's got a weight on his shoulders. See this? The image I'm getting is a really heavy pack. Too heavy for one person to carry."

Cole peered into the cup, and perhaps it was his imagination, but he almost thought he could see it.

"It's all of these things pressing down," Oliver continued. "You're helping him to get rid of them, helping him with the burden... the two of you working together." Oliver smiled. "It's a good thing."

Cole nodded, remembering the last few sessions with Marta and his father. They hadn't been fun, but he and Frank were changing the way they related to one another. Next to him, Ava smiled and Oliver's words resumed.

"... so after that, you've got a time when you're working closely with someone." He turned the cup around so that Cole could see down into the interior, pointing with the tip of his finger to a smear of leaves. "See this part here? It's a woman. Her hair's in a ponytail." He smirked at Ava for a moment, and then back to Cole. "She's standing next to you. You're busy for this next part of the cup, I'd say getting ready for school or planning something. All these different elements coming together, but she's right there beside you, helping you out... and... and..."

He abruptly frowned, his face dropping down almost to the rim. He was scowling. Cole's chest tightened in dismay. Oliver had definitely seen something. When he looked back up, his expression had changed; light humour gone. He glared at Ava.

"Were you going to tell me about the motorbike at some point?" he asked, voice sharp. The 'protective father' rather than 'easy-going dad.' Cole held in the urge to laugh at the resemblance to an outraged Chim.

"I, um... yeah, Dad, I was. I just hadn't had a chance," Ava stammered. "Sorry! I just know how you feel about bikes and I figured you'd worry about me."

"Damn right," her father muttered.

Oliver's lips pursed together in annoyance. The seconds ticked by in silence. Cole felt a nervous twinge.

"Well, you're both adults," Oliver finally said with a dismayed sigh. "God help me, kid, but I'm gonna go grey over this, you know."

Ava giggled and nodded to the forgotten cup in her father's hands.

"Cole's teacup, Dad."

He glanced back down.

"Yes, well... first thing," he said, glancing back up in exasperation, "is that I see both of you on motorcycles... and you're taking a trip up the coast, stopping at various places. It looks like you have a good time. You stop at a whole bunch of resorts and towns... I can see the two of you next to a wharf, lots of big ships beside you. Don't know where that is, but you'll know it when you see it." He smiled, the tension easing. "It'll be a good time… just the two of you together, enjoying yourself."

He twisted the cup closer, reading the leaves that stretched up the side toward the rim.

Time passing.

"There'll be some kind of event…" He chuckled. "I can see what looks like a hell of a lot of graffiti." He turned the cup to show them. "So I'd say this is Ava's show. There's someone there, Cole. Someone tall and kind of skinny, and you're going to go talk to this person... a guy, I'd guess. It's a good thing. Seems like things are going to settle because of it." He winked. "There's a dragon attached to that meeting."

"A dragon?" Cole asked.

Oliver nodded, lowering the cup to the table.

"Yeah... everything is images for me. Bits and pieces coming together in pictures." He grinned. "I see good fortune as dragons, and..." he turned the cup, pointing at a rippling shape along the edge, "and that thing there is definitely a dragon. Whoever this person is – this tall guy you talk to – it's a good thing for you. Some kind of resolution, and a change for the future..."

Cole frowned, wondering why he was convinced that this person was Kip Chambers. It bothered him; he wanted nothing to do with Kip.

"Anyhow, whatever it is... something is settled by that meeting, leaving you feeling better. And," Oliver said, nodding, "that all leads into some kind of event that happens a bit later. It'll be important for grad school, or maybe it's work…can't tell, but it's happening in a gallery. I think maybe you're curating a show for this person. That stretches up the side of your cup… important stuff, good fortune, money and opportunities, more dragons…"

Oliver smiled, leaning in.

"You and a woman are going on a trip somewhere," he said, his eyes moving from Ava to Cole, "This is the same woman with the motorbike, so let's just call her Ava, shall we?"

Next to Cole, Ava giggled again.

"So anyhow, you and Ava take a trip on a plane… looks like it's to Japan." He stopped for a moment, gesturing to a shape. "Yup, Japan, that's what it looks like to me… and the two of you are together… good things leading off from there." he said, eyes twinkling happily. "Just happy."

With a sigh, Oliver placed the cup on the table, running his hands through his hair.

"That's the end of the first cup. So tell me, do you want to go another year forward? You want to know more?"

Cole turned to Ava with a grin.

"Nah. I know all I need to know."

: : : : : : : : : :

Cole and Ava were in the living room, the jazz music still faint in the background. Oliver had given up on sleep and decided to go into the music studio instead, determined to get some composition done. He'd been working endlessly on his latest piece, and when he got into the flow of writing, he often lost track of time.

He laughed as he left.

"Be good kids," he said, lifting a hand in farewell.

Cole blushed, but Ava cackled.

"I always am, Ollie," she retorted.

Her father shook his head.

"I don't believe it, but I don't want to know, either."

Her laughter followed him into the hall as he locked the door behind him. Ava stepped toward Cole, throwing her arms over his neck.

"You and I are gonna make up for some wasted time," she said, kissing him.

Her mouth slanted across his, tongue pushing insistently forward to taste him; in seconds, they were tangled around one another. Cole broke the embrace with a groan, gesturing to the door.

"How long do we have?"

Ava grinned.

"Dunno... but I'm guessing a while."

"Well, let's stop wasting it then."

Before she could respond, he leaned down, putting one arm under her knees and the other behind her shoulders, picking her up and walking to the bedroom decisively. Ava laughed, squirming in his arms.

"Oh my god, you're not kidding about wasting time!" she shrieked as he moved her sideways through the doorway.

Cole glanced down, face serious.

"No, not at all," he said, "now stop wiggling, or I'll drop you."

She laughed even harder, and Cole dropped her roughly onto the bed, reaching down to help her out of her clothes. He threw his own in a pile at his feet and then reached over to slam the door. Ava was still giggling, her cheeks flushed with excitement.

"Just in case," Cole said, locking the door before stepping over to the bed.

: : : : : : : : : :

Cole woke in the dark.

Ava was asleep in his arms, but the silence had been broken by something. He heard the key in the lock of the apartment's front door, and then the steady tap of Oliver's feet walking upstairs from the foyer. He was whistling a repeated refrain as he headed to his bedroom.

Cole smiled, pulling Ava closer into the curve of his arms. Her shape pressed against his own, fitting together like two pieces of a whole. "Love you," she murmured, before going limp in his arms.

Cole closed his eyes, and followed her back into sleep.

Chapter 32: Hanna's Dream

Hanna crouched in the sand, staring down at them. The man cradled the woman in his arms, their eyes closed as if in sleep, the way two children might rest: like spoons. Her hand was tucked in his, his mouth pressed in a final kiss to the back of her neck.

Hanna reached up, wiping away unexpected tears. They were both dead.

Taking a shuddering breath, she hoisted herself to her feet, eyes taking in the rest of the destruction as she began to walk once more. In the distance, there were faint grey bands – rocky cliffs – rising out of the water. There was flotsam littering the sand, the winged figurehead of the ship rocking gently in the waves off shore.

Everything destroyed…

Hanna's eyes rose up the long stretch of beach, to the cliffs, and from there into the sky. Above her head, two birds wheeled lazy circles against a shimmering expanse of blue. She squinted, caught in the sight, her feet stumbling to a stop.

She turned back at the figures on the beach, throat aching. There was something about them that bothered her more than the others she'd seen, but what it was she couldn't say. She lingered uncertainly. The waves insistently lapped at her shoes, and with a resigned sigh, she began walking again.

There were other people who needed her.

Chapter 33: Déjà Vu

Ava stood in the vaulted main room of the National Gallery, a crowd of people including potential buyers and curators from across the country vying for her attention. Cole waited to the side, watching proudly as she mingled. Tonight she'd handed out a stream of portfolios, answering questions and gesturing to her work.   This show was the next big step, her foothold in the art world. Tonight changed things for her.

Cole had been thinking of Oliver's reading a lot lately, wondering how things would play out as this new part of Ava's life began. The movement into a professional career was a huge transition. Cole's job at the university, along with his own studies, kept him busy; he knew that Ava had worried about this show and its reviews.   If attendance tonight was any reflection, the career of Ava Brooks, graffiti artist, was about to launch in a big way.

The gallery was packed.

Oliver had already arrived; Cole had seen him duck outside to have a cigarette with Marcus a few minutes ago. Cole glanced over to the door again. It was his own family he was watching for. Frank and Nina would arrive soon, and he was surprisingly eager to see them. He and his father had continued their sessions over the course of the Spring and Summer. It hadn't been easy. Cole was amazed by the sheer amount of work there was in their communication, but he was far more settled than he ever had been with his father. They could talk. Nina and Ava had also grown closer, and the two women were developing their own connections and dynamic.

Ava was family. The thought filled his chest with happiness.

Cole had just turned back to watch Ava, talking to an elderly man wearing an obnoxious orange tie, when a familiar figure stepped into view.

It was Kip Chambers.

"Hey, Cole," he said warmly. "How're you doing, man?"

Cole tensed. He didn't like Kip, – never had – but he was here now, offering his hand. Cole reached out, shaking it quickly.

"Good... good. How 'bout you?" he asked tersely, glancing at the woman on Kip's arm.

It was Raya Simpson, though she'd changed since the last time he'd seen her in the police station. Cole struggled to pick out what it was... the process of finishing a stone sculpture popping, unexpectedly, to mind. It was like all of Raya's sharp edges had been rubbed away, leaving her looking softer than he remembered. Her hair curled around her face; her body more curvy. She smiled, offering her hand too, and Cole noticed that she was wearing a pair of bands on her left ring finger.

'Married,' his mind prompted. That might explain the change.

"We're doing great," she said happily, squeezing Cole's fingers before stepping back. "Kip and I wanted to talk to you for a second."

A sense of déjà vu rose in Cole. *'Oliver was right...'*

"I'm not sure if you've heard," Kip began. "But Ry' finished her documentary this summer. Editing is gonna be a few more months, but we had an idea we wanted to talk to you about."

He glanced at Raya and she picked up the story. They'd obviously talked about this more than once.

"Well, if the film just featured established artists," she said, gesturing to the room, "like Kip or Ava, then I'd use a well-known gallery to show the film and the graffiti. But in our case, a lot of the people are really young, some of them still in high school. There was one young woman, Moira... Mora..."

"Morag," Kip interjected.

"Right," Raya said with a smile. "Someone like Morag should get exposure, but given her age, we thought that perhaps the university gallery would be a better venue."

Cole's mind was starting to react with a series of ideas. He and the two other interns were curating the university gallery, and this kind of show would be perfect for his thesis and project. It was exactly the kind of real modern artwork Cole always argued about with Wilkins. The kind of artwork that changed the world and made a difference to people's attitudes.

Art that mattered.

Cole's gaze went back to Kip.

"So when Raya brought it up to me, I immediately thought of you." He grinned boyishly. "I just figured since you and Ava are together, you probably have a better sense of how to set up a show that really captures this art form. It wouldn't be pre-packaged or warped by preconceived notions. It'd be real."

Cole found himself nodding, adrenaline pulsing through him. This was exactly what he wanted to do as a curator.

"Yeah, Kip," Cole said, smiling genuinely now. "I'd definitely be interested in something like that."

Chambers nodded, clapping his hand on Cole's shoulder, then stepping back to Raya. Kip had a matching ring on his left hand, Cole realized in surprise.

"Well," Kip said, glancing at his wife, "should we get going?"

Cole hesitated.

"You don't want to say hi to Ava?" He could see she was deep in serious conversation with the man with the orange tie. "I could go get her if you wanted," Cole offered. It felt weird even saying it, but he felt like he ought to ask.

"No, no… don't interrupt her," Raya said, "I'm not feeling great tonight. Evenings are a bit rough for me."

Kip dropped his voice conspiratorially.

"First trimester's a bitch. Besides…" Kip added as Ava shook hands with the man in the orange tie, "I think Ava's just about to steal my agent."

Cole glanced to Simpson in shock as she rolled her eyes.

"Kip's agent for Asia. I'm still his North American agent, or at least for the next six months or so."

Kip pressed a kiss to her temple before turning back to Cole.

"We figured we'd just pass on our congrats through you," he said with a grin, "and I'll contact you in a week or so about the university show. There are several really amazing graffiti artists in Ry's film – Morag in particular. You'll like what they've created."

Cole's heart was thudding in excitement. He needed to talk to Ava… now!

"Good man, I'll look forward to your call."

"Alright," Chambers said, "We should run."

Cole shook their hands again before they left the gallery, arms linked.

Dragons.

: : : : : : : : : :

Oliver and Frank stood in front of one of Ava's paintings, making awkward small talk. The show had been a resounding success; now, hours later, it was slowing down. The Sergeant Major cleared his throat, glancing over at the man beside him.

"So you're just back in town for the show then?"

Oliver nodded, his eyes on Cole and Ava. They stood with Chim and Suzanne, grinning and laughing together as if nothing else in the world existed.

"Yeah, I'm in the city until Tuesday, then back on the road," Oliver answered. "I'll catch back up with the symphony in Copenhagen. Not to worry though, I'll be back next summer." He looked over at Frank, waggling his eyebrows. "Had to twist some arms to get that into my contract the last second but I did it... things are in the air then."

Frank Thomas shifted uncomfortably. It was the vague sort of reference to knowing things that made him uneasy. It wasn't the first time it had come up with Oliver Brooks, and he was still not sure he believed in it no matter what Cole said.

"Something's going on next summer?" Frank asked guardedly.

Oliver winked.

"Nothing for sure yet..." he answered, his eyes drifting back to Ava and Cole. She leaned into him, Cole's arm looped around her waist, their motions somehow in sync even as they talked. "Just a sense I've got."

Frank nodded.

"Well, then, I'll make sure Nina and I plan to be around. The house and the grounds are beautiful that time of year." He coughed nervously. "Lots of room for... uh... outdoor events and such. I'll make sure we don't plan a vacation away."

Oliver chuckled, reaching out and squeezing his shoulder.

"Might be a good idea."

: : : : : : : : : :

The gallery was nearly empty except for a few final patrons and the curatorial staff. Ava stood at one side of the room, barefoot, her shoes held in one hand. Cole was beside her.

"Richard Ashton," Ava said, grinning. "Kip sold him the panels I did."

"The ones from the collaboration?" he asked.

She nodded.

"Kip apparently just couldn't bring himself to paint over them," she explained, "so he showed them to Rick, and he got really excited about my work."

Cole grinned, kissing her gently before pulling back.

"The guy in the orange tie?" he asked. "I remember him from that first opening. The one Kip had earlier this year. He was on the phone, talking in Mandarin the whole time."

Ava giggled.

"Yeah. He's Kip's agent in Asia. He wants to set up a couple shows for me next year." She grinned, one hand sliding up the front of his shirt, grabbing hold of his tie and pulling him in. "So what do you think? You feel like taking a trip to Japan with me sometime?"

"Drop everything and just go?" Cole said with a laugh.

Ava shrugged.

"That's the plan."

Cole reached out, brushing a stray hair back from her face.

"Wherever you are is where I need to be."

18464985R10152

Made in the USA
Lexington, KY
06 November 2012